First Night

Carol Sabik-Jaffe

For my family...

Thank you to my amazing husband, Dan, and my children, Michael and Shaina for their endless support and encouragement.

You believed I'd do it before I did!

Contents

Chapter 1

"Always take a moment to compose yourself. Take a breath and pause so you don't look like a complete mess. You don't have to rush. An extra minute or two isn't going to matter in the grand scheme of things, Maria. Remember to make an entrance. And, by the way, it doesn't hurt to put on a little lipstick either."

Maria couldn't get her mother's voice out of her head as she waited. She had missed the express elevator that would take her directly to the fiftieth floor. Instead of waiting for the next one to arrive, she awkwardly pushed through the first doors to slide open. She juggled a Starbucks Iced Caramel Macchiato in one hand and a large portfolio in the other. The oversized purse draped on her right shoulder caused her to slouch unevenly, making her arrival look as far from graceful or unruffled as possible. The Rum Raisin-colored lipstick she had remembered to apply was not going to make up for her disheveled appearance today.

Score another one for Mom. This is me making some kind of entrance and, as usual, I'm as far from composed as possible.

Antonetta Vigliano, her mother, had spent most of her life freely handing out bits of unsolicited guidance to anyone and everyone as if she had memorized a *Bible of Rules* set forth by god-knows-who, or Saint somebody. Maria was convinced she had made up most of her rules and they were really only created for, and directed at, her daughters to keep them in line. Despite her mother's quips looping through her brain at inconvenient times, most days Maria paid no attention to Antonetta's practical life advice because she simply didn't have time for composure, or to give a thought about making an actual entrance.

The elevator car Maria rode in crept along, pausing intermittently to gather solemn-faced souls that entered and looked at their feet; cranky people working on this holiday. It seemed strange to Maria. *Why haven't they left to prepare for the big ball drop?* But here she was at work on New Year's Eve too.

The last recession had hit the agency world hard and most businesses had made large cuts to their advertising budgets. Even though most mainstream media and expert talking heads hyped economic recovery, no one was fully restored to pre-crash robust. Most agencies played it safe, thankful they still had client rosters. Always apprehensive that they were on the verge of being fired by their clients or having business poached by other agencies, the staff did what they had to do to keep their accounts and jobs. Life, and weekly status meetings, were focused on clicks, the never-ending battle for Google rankings, platforms, web traffic, and viewer engagement. The staff ate Search Engine Optimization stats for break-fast, anxious they were skating on thin ice. Maria was sure she wouldn't have a job through spring and didn't want to push her luck.

As the elevator doors slid open, Maria spot-ted her boss, Hal Tobias, exiting one of the express elevators across the lobby. Hal, a tall silver-haired man who looked much younger than his seventy-two years, looked at Maria and pointed to his eyes with two fingers and then at her and mouthed, "I'm watch-ing you."

"Your mother's on line two," shot in her direc-tion as she stepped into the expanse that was Rotelle, Herbert, Tobias and Associates, aka R.H.T. and Associ-ates. Her assistant, Lyndon, waved a phone in the air and frowned at her.

"Ohhhhhhhhh. Tell her that I'm in a meeting. Please?"

"I did, when she called at 8:57. And 9:53. And 11:42. Didn't you see my texts? Take it please, please, please. The trees will thank you," Lyndon whined as he ripped sheets off of a message pad and shoved them in her direction. "Pretty please? This is pathetic me begging. Talk to her before she gives me another re-cipe to try."

Lyndon knelt, his steepled fingers pressed to-gether holding the papers. He pushed them towards her again. "Pul-leeze. If I don't make the dish, I can't pass the quiz when she calls. Maria, I've gained ten pounds in the last year. This cannot go onnnnnn. I'm getting love handles," he whined as he crept forward.

"You are not," Maria shot back.

"I am. And you know how Darius hates love handles. He pinched them yesterday. Ewwwwwwwwww. For the sake of my love life, and my wardrobe please take your mother's call." In a last-ditch sympathy play, he fell on the reception area sofa. Shoving one hand still clutching the papers up to the ceiling, he whimpered, "Pu-leeezze." When Maria didn't react, he hopped up from the sofa and took his place at his desk.

"God, you are such a drama queen," she teased.

Lyndon scrunched his nose, flicked away imaginary sweat from his brow, shrugged, and said, "And don't you ever forget that, sweetie."

Maria loved him for his over-the-top reactions and carefree attitude. She felt on edge all the time, afraid to really express herself to anyone. *I mean who really wants to know what I think anyway* was always in the back of her overactive mind and surfaced at inconvenient times. Lyndon, king of word vomit with no filter, was her opposite and could be counted on to blurt out whatever flitted through his brain at all times. She secretly wished that she could be more like him, but was way too worried about her words being judged and used against her.

"Stellar meeting again?" he asked as he reached for the ringing phone, and said, "R. H. T. and Associates. How may I direct your call?" He nodded in her direction. Maria frowned and shook her head no. "I'm sorry. She's in a meeting. May I take a message?" he said and scribbled something as he hung up.

"Hal announced out loud to the clients in the middle of the pitch that I'm his latest handpicked on-her-way-up hot-shot of Madison Avenue. His rising star. According to him, I'm the girl who's going places."

Lyndon's eyes narrowed thoughtfully, "Ugh. He really needs a new script."

"Hey, this girl-going-places is only one of the latest young fools in a long line of young fools desperate to take on as much work as possible for recognition and advancement. Now, most of all, also the one trying hard not to get fired."

"Okay, GGP, call the printer after the holiday, okay? He wants a sign-off on that proof," Lyndon added and snickered at her.

Maria glanced at her reflection in one of the colorful over-sized pieces of contemporary art that hung on the perimeter of the office. She knew she shouldn't care about how she looked, but she did. Her blue topaz eyes looked a little bloodshot and just short of weepy and her usually styled and blown-out hair wasn't reacting well with the combo of snow flurries and a too hot interior. The hair that began the day sleek and straightened was now a frizzy mass of brown waves circling her flushed and shiny olive skin. She wrinkled her nose and pushed her hair back as she sized up her overheated and slightly damp face.

"Do you want to blot, sweetie?" Lyndon teased as he lifted a box of tissues.

"Am I sweaty? I look sweaty, don't I?"

"Ohhhh, a little moist, maybe..." he whispered

as he tossed the box towards her.

"I hate that word."

He gave her a thumbs-up as she batted the box in the air several times, trying not to spill her coffee as the carton landed on the floor.

Maria retrieved the box, yanked out three tissues, and tossed it back to Lyndon. She glanced at her reflection again, blotted her face, shoved the tissues into her coat pocket, and said, "Thank you," with an exaggerated sigh tacked on. "Girl going nowhere," she whispered, convinced her reflection said the opposite of "girl going places." She was certain she still looked like the shy girl from South Philadelphia, not sure why she was in New York in this office faking it daily, positive that everyone saw right through her.

"That's much better, sweetie," Lyndon said as the phone rang again. Maria rolled her eyes as he reached for the phone and whined, "Oh my god, it's a holiday. What is happening today?"

"I'm not here," Maria blurted.

"R.H.T. and Associates. Hold, please," he chirped into the phone. "It's your mother. Again," he hissed through gritted teeth.

If Maria's turbo-charged helicopter mom had her way, she would still be safely ensconced somewhere in South Philadelphia, preferably within a stone's throw of the immaculate brick row house on Dickinson Street that she had grown up in. Even Center City, twenty-five blocks north of her Bella Vista neighborhood, would have been considered too far for Antonetta. To this day, her entire family, except Maria, lived within blocks of one another. Aunt Sylvia and her daughters, Maria's cousins, and best friends, Ava and Bambi, lived right next door.

College in New York was one thing, staying in New York was a knife straight through her overly dramatic mother's heart. At least this was what Antonetta had told everyone within a fifteen-block radius when Maria took the job with R.H.T. and Associates two years ago. Maria had applied everywhere, and anywhere, like everyone else she went to school with. Most people were glad to be offered an unpaid internship or a part-time gig to have a foot in the door. Maria admitted then even she was surprised when she was offered the job. Both relieved and conflicted, she grabbed the opportunity, convinced separation would eventually be accepted by her mother. It wasn't.

Lyndon's phone rang again. "R. H. T. and Associates. How may I direct your call? Hold please." Lyndon's eyes shot open wide, "She's on line three, too. How does she do that? You need to take this call. Now. Ri, please."

Maria, again balancing a coffee in one hand and a portfolio in the other, pushed her office door open with her hip and entered. The latest campaign for Cee-Cee Berg's newest cosmetic line circled the space. Stunning models with glowing faces and perfect eyes and lips taunted her. She took a long hard breath in, dropped the portfolio, and sat down at her desk.

Her sketchbook was propped next to the phone, open to a page of flashy feather and sequined costumes. Reminiscent of vintage Liberace, the glitzy get-ups were her latest designs for the family's team, The Bella Vista Brawlers' performance in this year's Mummer's Parade—Philadelphia's New Year's Day event and the oldest folk festival and number one holiday parade in the country, according to *USA Today* readers. String Bands and Comic and Fancy Brigades competing in ornate costumes marching and performing elaborately choreographed dances along Broad Street for large crowds in this day-long spectacle.

The Vigliano family tradition was a day away. Generations of her family had made this same trek strutting and playing in these bands for almost as long as the parade had been held. This was an event not to be messed with. Ever.

Maria reached for the phone, but stopped, sure that in her mother's mind there was some imaginary emergency needing immediate attention. Stalling, and trying to steel herself for what was to come, she picked up a green marker and absentmindedly colored the large fan of ostrich and peacock feathers that made up the circular plume that would frame each of the performers.

Maria had scribbled drawings for the band ever since she could hold a crayon in her chubby little-kid hands. After successfully lobbying for a deluxe art set full of paint, markers, and colored pencils one Christmas long ago, her designs took off and her talents evolved into her being the band's design team. Unfortunately, the team was her alone and was now more than she wanted on top of her day job responsibilities. But, try as she might, she couldn't explain that to her mother.

She took a deep breath, picked up the office phone and punched the blinking button, and said, "Hi, Mom."

"Maria. Maria. Maria. Where have you been? I've been calling all morning. Office and cell. You had me worried sick. I thought you were dead."

"Not dead, Mom. Meetings. I had meetings. All morning. I turned my phone off," she said.

"Your father said to leave you alone. But you know how I worry."

"Meetings, Mom. Not axe murderers. Mom, I have a huge deadline. What's wrong?"

"I know you're busy, honey. You're a very important person in New York, and all. I just told Stella Morrone that very thing yesterday when I picked up the almond paste at Esposito's so I could make my Pignoli cookies for the New Year's Party."

Maria moved the marker over the drawing, quickly laying in color in fat, fast strokes, as her mother spoke. Her hand picked up speed as her mother's words accelerated. "Mom," she prompted.

"What?"

"Mom, please. I don't have a lot of time."

"Okay. I know you're busy. You're coming, right?"

"Uh, I don't know. I, we…We've got a huge presentation the day after New Year's. It's a three-million-dollar account. My job is on the line."

"But, the parade."

The burden of this account and the precarious state of Maria's job was lost on her mother. Antonetta didn't understand her living in what equated to a closet, or her need to be away from the family, away from her, or the need for her to succeed at this career of hers. Nothing stood in Antonetta Vigliano's way when she wanted Maria present for a family event. And nothing, not business or a cosmetic account, could be used as an excuse when the holidays were involved, and most especially not on New Year's Day for the parade. Even though the event was an important part of her family history, and hers, this year New Year's and all that came with it was the last thing Maria needed right now. "Ugh..."

"Wooahhh. Wait... three million for lipstick? That's a bit much, huh? Think she'll have any pinks I'll like this year? Can you get samples?"

"Mooooooommmm. Focus, please. I've got to go."

"Well, we don't want you to lose your job or anything."

"Mom! I'm hanging up now."

"Wait," she pleaded again, "Your father needs you home. The costumes. They're just not right, Ri. Something's off."

Maria rested her head on the desktop and closed her eyes. Most days Maria could tune her mother out, but today her exasperated tone exhausted her. Whenever she called her Ri, Maria felt her mother's grasp tighten. It was as if her roots had somehow extended all the way up I-95, through the Lincoln Tunnel, across the city, into the building and were now wrapped around her ankles. It was almost as if at that very moment, she felt them constrict.

"Mom," she interrupted, "The costumes were fine a week ago when I saw them last. Uncle Iggy and the guys followed my designs. They did a fine job this year."

"You looked at them so fast. You were in such a rush to get the train back to the city that you didn't even stay for dessert. And I made you Pizzelles. Aunt Sylvia's still mad you left the piece of brownie cheesecake she wrapped for you. I haven't heard the end of that yet, either. You work too hard. What about P. T. O? Vacation days? Anybody get those anymore? It's the holidays," flowed out in what seemed like one long whine.

"Mom."

"They followed your sketches, honey, but something's missing. I don't think they're even going to place this year."

Not placing would be a first and might just knock the Earth out of orbit. "Oh, c'mon, the Brawlers have NEVER, ever not placed in the parade." Maria knew that was a fact. Everyone in South Philly knew that. "Ma, you know that it's not just the costumes that count. I'll see what I can do."

"That can't happen. Not placing. You know how your father gets if they don't win something. It's..."

"Tradition. I know. But they've never *not*

placed. Even when Nonna..."

"Phhhtttt. Don't even say it. Disaster that was a dis-as-ter."

"I'll do my best. But I'm not promising," Maria promised.

"Okay, wonderful." she sighed. "I'll tell him. You know how much this parade means to your father. He works so hard all year long."

"My best, Mom. I'll do my best. Maybe you should wait to tell him. No promises. Okay? I really have to go. I'm late for a meeting," Maria lied.

Chapter 2

Hunter was fast asleep on the sofa when his assistant, Laurel, pushed the office door open and entered. "Mr. Reed, your father is on line one," she said as she shook his arm, "Mr. Reed. Hunter!" Hunter jumped as he awoke, sat up, and rubbed his eyes. Confused as to his whereabouts, he blinked and stared at the kind face framed by grey blond hair, not recognizing Laurel as he tried to focus.

"Your father, Hunter. Line one," she said as she spun, headed to the door and shot over her shoulder, "And another package came. I think it's from your mother. I put it with the others."

Hunter had spent more than a few nights lately in the mostly deserted building, after deciding there was really no point in wasting time going home to an empty apartment when there was work to be done. Somehow being jolted awake left him feeling like he'd been caught slacking. He glanced at his cell phone to see it was only 7:45 and that he had six missed calls from *Dad*. Great. Hunter could almost feel the judgment pouring through the line as he picked up the office phone and moved to his desk. Stretching and sitting up straight in the chair, he ran a hand through his tousled hair, cleared his throat and said, "Morning, Dad," trying to sound as awake and upbeat as possible.

"Just getting in?"

"Dad. No. Here for hours. Yes. Up to my ears in work. You know how it is. I'm trying to get ahead before everyone returns after the holiday."

"Time management, son. Time management." Hunter stifled a groan as his father continued, "Did the gifts arrive? Tiff shipped them two weeks ago."

"Yes. Thank Tiffany for me." He glanced at the small, once cheerful, now dried-out Christmas tree, its fallen needles scattered on the windowsill around the foil wrapped pot. Several gifts, ornately wrapped, sat next to the tree. "Yes. Just what I wanted. Perfect."

"She spent a lot of time selecting them, son. Send her a note, or at least a text. I shouldn't—"

"Will do, Dad."

"I shouldn't have to tell you."

"Got it, Dad. I'm on it."

Hunter's father, a three-time Congressman from suburban Philadelphia, was the epitome of a straight arrow. Valley Forge Military Academy. West Point. Army. Politics. Straight path. No deviations. He was conflicted when Hunter went to PENN. Most parents would have been thrilled, but he insisted it was too close to home and had a long list of reasons that Hunter should broaden his horizons. Staying at PENN for law school didn't sit well either. If not West Point, then Harvard or, if necessary, Yale were the only appropriate choices in his father's mind. Hunter's path to Washington was finally something his father couldn't find fault with, the one exception being Hunter had done it himself, without his father's guidance or interference.

His father's weekly calls were always a combination of inquisition and lecture and today he wasted no time. "Have you given any thought to your next steps? I want to discuss a few things with you before —"

True to form. Next steps? The question threw Hunter. Not wanting to dive into this subject at this hour and without caffeine, he interrupted, "Next steps? Sorry, Dad I have a meeting with the Senator in ten. You know how it is. Can we talk when you're in town? Or in Aspen? I'm going to try to schedule time off for your Spring Break trip. We can discuss in depth then. Okay? Say hello to everyone. And give the twins a hug for me. I've really got to run." Hunter hung up before his father could get another word in, leaned back, and stared up at the ceiling. *Next steps? Really?* Ending a call before his father had a chance to sermonize about his career trajectory somehow always felt like a small victory. Today was no different.

Hunter sipped his third coffee and aggressively red-lined an already heavily marked-up press release as Olympia, a short, round woman with a smooth round face, entered his office pushing a cleaning cart. She gently hummed a holiday tune interrupting his reading. He glanced in her direction. Her soft features and friendly face reminded him of someone, his prep school guidance counselor perhaps, he thought, though he wasn't sure. He couldn't place her, but there was something that made her seem somehow familiar. He thought she had started working in his building in late October or maybe November. Again, details eluded him. He hesitated, thinking he should remember. It's not like he was totally oblivious, just busy. She hadn't made a regular habit of chatting him up. He was sure they had only ever exchanged an occasional *Hello* or *Good Evening.*

Olympia nodded and grinned as she swept the dried pine needles into a dustpan, rearranging the gifts and Christmas cards under the little tree as she worked. "Your sister's beautiful," she said as she studied a photo card of a stunning blonde in a sexy Mrs. Claus outfit surrounded by two handsome, shirtless young Santas.

"Mother," he said as he typed and added in a matter-of-fact tone, "Mother. My mother, the Cougar."

Next to his mother's greeting card was another with a photo of a statuesque blonde next to a salt and pepper haired man–his father, holding a toddler girl with eight-year-old twin boys, bookending the shot. The card was signed: Merry Christmas. Love – Dad, Tiffany, Reid, Greer and Madison. "Father. Trophy wife number four. Family number two," he said, diverting the next awkward and expected comment.

Olympia knitted her brows and muttered, "Lovely."

Hunter forced a faint smile.

His father had moved on when Hunter turned

nine. His mother, the place holder in the early years, was the one that dutifully waited through Valley Forge, West Point, and the family's numerous Army moves. Hunter's birth and childhood were to keep her busy and quiet for a time. Too young to wallow, she smartened up when he left and forged her own color- ful path embracing her waning youth. She embraced a lot of things... Alex, Nunzio, Chipper, Henry, and a few other names that Hunter had tried hard to erase from his memory bank.

Olympia silently studied the photos. Hunter, raising an eyebrow, nodded and said nothing more as she left.

"Go home, Mr. Reed." Hunter looked up to see Olympia glide into his office again. She emptied the trash can next to his desk. Having completely lost track of time, he glanced at the computer's clock and was surprised to see it was now 4:00 p.m. "Everyone is long gone preparing to count down to the New Year. You don't get extra credit in the Senate if you stay and work through every holiday," she chided. "You put in your time on Thanksgiving *and* Christmas."

"Funny, very funny," he answered, not sure how she knew about his schedule.

"It's not like law school, you know. People do take breaks. There's nothing to prove here when the other suits are gone, young man. Go home. Better yet, don't you have some fabulous party to go to? Hand- some young man like you ought to be wearing a fancy tuxedo and be strutting down K Street with a pretty date going to that Ball everyone's dying to get into. In fact, I hear that the President and the First Lady might even make an appearance before the night is over."

"Not in the mood this year," he said as he shot her a look that he hoped would end the chatter. "Opinions to research," he said as he turned back to his desk shuffling papers to suggest that she move along.

She didn't bite. Her eyes locked on him. "I think they should have their own opinions if you ask me," she offered.

Out of the corner of his eye, he watched, and blurted, "Speeches to write." His words sounded sharp; the reply terse.

"Uh-huh, like I said," she shot back as she dusted the tables in the room. She added a "Tsk. Tsk," for effect, or maybe to annoy him. He squinted, tried to focus, and typed something on his computer doing his best to ignore her. Olympia was not deterred and continued, "You should get in the mood, Mr. Reed. No sense letting life pass you by. You're only young once. You ought to get out there." She put one hand up and the other arm out as if holding a dance partner, swayed, and sang, "At last... My lonely days are over..."

Hunter frowned. "Okay, Olympia, I get it. I get it. Before you do the whole Beyonce thing, I'm out of here in ten. Satisfied?" he said, too tired to argue.

"If you tell me you're going to go and put on a tuxedo and get in the game, then yes, young man, I'm satisfied. If not, I've got whole other lectures I can send your way. And, so you know, I am not afraid to use 'em." She winked as she turned and pushed her cleaning cart through the door. "Me, I need the time and a half. You? The night is young, Mr. Reed. The night is young. Go. Before you're not. Atttttttt lastttt-tttt," she sang loudly as she left.

Thoughts scattered and the song now stuck in his head, Hunter was beyond distracted. He powered down his computer, grabbed his coat, and left the office.

Pennsylvania Avenue was deserted but for a stray jogger or two. He headed into the Metro alone, took the escalator down toward the tracks, and waited for the train. He impatiently tapped his foot and glanced at his phone. The screen read: Four missed calls. Joe. He punched the screen with a thumb.

A voice bellowed, "Dude. It's Joey. Where are you? You can't still be working, can you? Man don't those senators ever take time off. No bill is going to get passed on New Year's Eve. You've got to meet us. Philly. Tonight. Everyone's going to be here. Seriously, bro. Get on the next train." A screeching *Beep* interrupted.

Hunter thumbed his phone again.

"So, we haven't seen you in two years. Get on the next train. NOW. We're all meeting in University City at the old TKE house. Come on, dude. You've got to come. Then we're going to party at the Ballroom. Come on, man. You've got to be here—" *Beep.*

Hunter shook his head and grinned.

"Dude. That's seriously short message time. What kind of plan do you have? Is this what government employees get nowadays? Call me back. You don't want to miss this. You've got to come back to Philly. Do it." Joey sang, "Re-united, 'cuz it feels so good..." He sounded drunk and off-key. "We'll get Pat's Steaks after. Okay, Geno's if we have to, just to get you back up here. Call me." *Beep.*

Hunter couldn't help but chuckle as he tapped again on the phone screen.

"Dude. You suck. Get a better phone. I've texted you the deets."

Hunter shook his head as the train pulled up and screeched to a stop. *I do miss those guys.* But, going back? It felt—well, backwards. He entered the train, plopped down in a seat in a deserted and quiet car, sighed, rubbed his eyes, and tried to get comfortable.

Chapter 3

"Always have a Plan B, Maria. Do you have a Plan B? You never know what a day will bring. Life is funny like that. Things change. Be flexible. You should always be flexible. Go with the flow." Maria knew that sometimes her mother sounded a little woo-woo and her "do as I say, not as I do" was exhausting. Despite what she preached, she never went with the flow.

The call with her mother had zapped any energy or enthusiasm Maria had left for this day. She'd spun her chair toward the windows. Snow was falling outside of the room length floor-to-ceiling glass making her view look like a magical snow globe. Madison Avenue below was quieter than usual and almost peaceful. *If only I could channel a bit of the serenity.* Everyone said the holidays were magic in New York. This was her second. She didn't understand it. It was crowded everywhere. Streets, shops, restaurants were full of people pushing, shoving, trying to experience a classic New York holiday as they fought for a glimpse of the window decorations in the Manhattan flagship stores like Macy's, Bergdorf's, and Tiffany's.

It occurred to Maria that a walk around the block in the snow to clear her head before it was too late might help her mood until Lyndon chirped, "Cee-Cee Berg's on three. She wants to do drinks. Today."

"Oh. My. God. Today?" Maria groaned as she reached for the phone and took another deep breath before sing-songing, "This is Maria. Hello, Cee-Cee. What can I do for you?"

A shrill, "Hold please for Ms. Berg," followed. She should have expected that Cee-Cee's assistant, Sherman, would be on the line and not her. Why would she call directly? She was Cee-Cee Berg and Maria was a lowly Junior Creative Exec who jumped when she said jump, making sure to also think, How high, Cee-Cee? How high?

A full two minutes and thirty seconds passed before she heard, "Darling...drinks? Tonight? At eight. No, make that seven. Buddakan. I'll need time to get dressed before the party at Le Circ. I'll send a car. We need to discuss changes. Six. Make it six o'clock." Cee-Cee groaned and added, "Wait. Maybe five would be safer. Five. Be there at five."

"No problem," escaped Maria's mouth before she could think of a way to get out of this meeting, "See you at five o'clock."

Buddakan? Downtown? Great. Today? Now?

The sound of dead air on the other end of the phone was a perfect way to end Maria's already ridiculous day. She had somehow spent the morning promising Hal and a major client the sun, moon, and stars, and a complete last-minute consumer campaign, including social media concepts that was somehow supposed to launch pre-Super Bowl. Cee-Cee's demand zapped the rest of her already depleted enthusiasm. "In an hour? At five? Is she crazy? I'll need time to dress before the party at Le Circ," she snarked aloud.

Lyndon popped his head in the doorway, "Really?"

"Not me, Cee-Cee," she sneered, "I hate New Year's Eve. All that effort to watch some stupid ball drop. Geez, it's just another night."

"No date again, honey?"

She flicked a legal pad across the room and just missed Lyndon's head as he ducked out of the way. "Isn't it time for you to go re-apply product?" she said.

"Ahhhh, it isn't droopy all ready, is it? Lyndon squealed.

"Yeah. Droopy. Definitely droopy."

Lyndon popped his head back through the doorway and said, "Really?" He gently patted the tips of his blond spikes standing straight up on his head.

"Any more product and you'll poke somebody's eye out," she snapped.

"If only. You don't have to be mean, Maria," he said and rolled his eyes at her.

She hadn't intended to be mean, "I'm sorry. Oh, who cares. I'll be on the Acela anyway. I'm sure there are feathers to glue or sequins to sew," she whined.

"Poor little Cinderella."

"Ugh, New Year's Eve is such a night for amateurs."

"Any real New Yorker leaves, you know. All those out-of-town crazies come in wearing adult diapers because you can't even leave to pee once you're in the pen. Ewww. Why? *Just* to do the Times Square nonsense and catch a glimpse of Ryan Seacrest or the newest boy band *or* American Idol they've brought in for the circus."

"Wow. That's a little harsh even for you," she snapped. "Are *you* leaving?"

"Maybe next year, honey," Lyndon spit back over his shoulder, unfazed as he made a face and slid back to his desk. "That is, if you lobby for a cost-of-living bump for me," he added.

"No problem," she said and sighed.

"I heard that. Boy's got to eat," he yelled from his desk. "And...you can't sleep with those Addy awards, you know."

She and her team had somehow managed to win three in her first year. Unheard of, Hal Tobias had said at the award dinner that night, as he beamed at her. She was officially crowned one of *Hal's Gals* and given a private office the next day.

"All work and no play makes Maria..."

"A dull girl, I know."

"I was going to go with horny," Lyndon fired back not missing a beat.

"Taking that on the road?"

"Yeah, opening at the Comedy Club tonight. Be there."

"Really?" Maria laughed and snorted as she wondered if he was serious this time.

"Heard that," he shouted back. "Just remember, hot shot, Holly's probably skiing in Sun Valley before her star-studded mountain top party tonight." Lyndon chuckled and sang, "Have a holly, jolly Christmas. It's the best time of the year. I don't know if there'll be snow. But I'll have a cup of cheer...

"That is so last week."

"What would Holly do? Have a holly jolly Chri —"

"Stop, just stop," Maria said and laughed. "I've told you. I am not following in Holly's path," Maria shot back in his direction.

"Hey, I have an idea! Let's pregame. Blow off the meeting with Cee-Cee. She probably won't show anyway. Let's go. Say good riddance to this year! C'mon, you have the corporate card. It'll be fun."

Maria had inherited Lyndon from the previous R. H. T. hotshot, Holly Day, whose job and office space she had taken over. She giggled with Lyndon one day at Happy Hour that Holly Day sounded a lot like a stripper's name, but Lyndon revealed that Holly had sworn to him that her first name was given to her by her older sister because she was born on Christmas day and her last name was because she was part of the *DAY* clan. Her grandmother was a fourth cousin, twice removed, to Doris. She thought Lyndon was going to lose it that night when she squinted and asked, "Who?" Her obvious lack of a Hollywood history database brain was incomprehensible to him. "Oh, come on. Doris Day, God rest her soul," was all he could manage to say between yucks.

Her bigger office was amazing, but when Lyndon first shared Holly's story she vowed that she had a plan that was all hers. Her career just wasn't going to be a pit stop to another life. She had things to accomplish even if she didn't always feel like Hal's rising star.

"Blazing my own trails—" she added not sure he was still listening to her.

Lyndon slid his chair back to Maria's office door, peeked in, and whispered, "It's probably going to be a huge Holly-Jolly birthday bash. What do you think hubby number three is getting her this year?"

Maria shooed him away and glanced around the room taking it all in—the space, the art, the view, Cee-Cee's million-dollar campaign as she listened to Lyndon whispering in the background making his plans for the evening.

In addition to the promotion and larger office, she counted Lyndon as a job bonus. After two years he was a friend—her only real friend in New York. She remembered back to her first week and their first Happy Hour when he had shared, "It's Lyndon with a 'Y' because my mother wanted to *suggest* pedigree."

Maria had giggled nonstop and between laughs said, "Please, I'm going to pee my panties."

"Very unbecoming, darling. And so un-New York, the panties, that is, and who admits that?" When she snorted at him, he giggled and continued, "Luckily, she didn't add Baines to it. That would have been so over the top. Lyndon Jansen is bad enough."

"O. M. G. You're so totally making that up," she

said.

"Honey, stop. Really. Stop." She couldn't stop laughing, no matter what he said. "You are the most darling thing, but don't ever think I'm crossing back over for you my sweet little innocent. Really. Now. STOP. And. You don't tell *anyone*. Swear?" She giggled again and nodded as he continued, "I was conceived in Linden, New Jersey. She just didn't want anyone to make the connection. You know?"

She covered her mouth with her hand, and tried hard not to spit her drink in his face.

"So, me either, the connection, that is! We moved to South Orange when I was four months old and stayed until I was six. At least then she came to her senses and brought me to Brooklyn. Lyndon with a "Y" from Brooklyn. Somehowwww... I pulled off the *Summer at the Cape* branding when I went to RISD! My mother...she had her own way of keeping track of things. You know what I mean? Guess what my sister's name is?" He didn't give her a chance to speak, adding, "Ro-selle," with a wave of his hand and a guffaw.

At that, she spit her drink across the table and squealed, "Park?"

Lyndon lost it. He was drunk. She was drunk.

They were friends.

It wasn't long before she heard Lyndon's sing-song, "Ma-ri-aaaah, Hal wants to see you before your meeting with Cee-Cee. Have a holly, jolly—"

"Great." She groaned and thought that she might never get out of this building as she shuffled past a giggling Lyndon and the now empty cubicles. She hurried down the quiet hallway and knocked on Hal's open office door. The office was a dimly lit, staged, vintage facade, a quaint remnant of the Mad Men era. The overhead lights illuminated an in-office bar next to a stunning collection of black and white Man Ray photographs. Maria often studied the one titled *Glass Tears* as she wondered about the significance of the subject to him. Hal was hunched over his desk packing up for the day, oblivious. "Hal? You wanted to see me?"

"Oh, Maria, good. A moment, please. Your meeting with Cee-Cee..." He paused and stared at the ceiling for what she thought was a beat too long, the vacant expression on his face something she hadn't seen before. His look startled her and she was convinced that this was it. She was getting fired.

Hal noticed her reaction, smiled, "Yes. Cee-Cee. You know what to do."

"Uh. Yes, of course."

"That's my girl. That is all. I'm late. So, so late. My better half has plans to drive out to the Hamptons before midnight. Ha. We're not going to make it if I don't get going," he said with a flick of his hand to dismiss her.

Maria tried hard not to cringe, or roll her eyes, as she spun and trudged back to her office.

"You better get going," Lyndon shouted from his desk. "Don't want to be late for Cee-Cee." Maria grabbed her coat and bag and shuffled toward the elevator. "Happy Neeeewww Year, Ri-Ri!" She watched

Lyndon giggle, blow her a kiss, and wave in her direction as she entered the empty elevator.

As the elevator doors started to close, a blur of black designer clothing blew past screeching, "Lynnie! Baby. I'm back." Maria watched a speechless Lyndon be enveloped in someone's arms and his eyes open wide as if he'd seen a ghost.

Chapter 4

For the first time in a long time, Hunter was happy to leave the office. Olympia's prodding had brought up so many mixed feelings for him that it had made his head pound. He was grateful to be in a quiet car alone with his thoughts and not feeling like he had to explain or justify his life. The train buzzed across D.C. One after another, familiar stops came and went until the Conductor announced, "Union Station, next stop. Next stop, Union Station."

Maybe Olympia is right. I've got nothing else going on shot through his mind as he stood up. *Why not?* Perhaps it was time to do something impulsive and out of character. He was beginning to feel really old when in fact he hadn't yet turned thirty.

Hunter bought a ticket for the next Acela train heading north to Philadelphia and looked at his watch. It was 6:00 p.m. He glanced around at the quiet and mostly vacant station grateful to see Anthony's Tuxedo store across the concourse still open.

"Well, as I live and breathe," Abe called out from across the empty store as Hunter entered. "How are you, stranger?" Hunter extended a hand as Abe rushed toward him. Abe shook his hand excitedly, patted Hunter's shoulder, and looked him over head to toe, "Good to see you, young man. You're looking good."

Anthony's Tuxedos was the first shop Hunter had spotted when he arrived in Washington. Hunter was not fully prepared to dress as a professional in the Capital so he made Anthony's his first stop. Abe, a tall thin man with dark soulful eyes, was the first person he had encountered in the city. He bought three new designer suits and a half dozen white cotton pinpoint shirts and neckties to go with them that day, two years ago. Hunter returned as he needed to update and fill in anything, socks, boxers, shoes—anything. Abe took care of him and usually put things aside ahead of time. Truthfully, Hunter had come to rely on him. Abe would call him once in a while if too much time had passed. He somehow knew before Hunter did when he needed new clothes, or life lectures.

"You've got to make a presentation," Abe had instructed then. "I'll take good care of you. Don't worry. You're like the son I never knew I wanted. Six girls. Aye-yi-yi," Abe joked as he laid out assorted shirts and ties. Abe was a kind man. Hunter looked forward to stopping in and having someone advise him without judgment or expecting something in return. He had come to count on their chats. What Abe didn't know was that he was really like a father to him, more than his own.

"I've got something for you," Abe said excitedly. In minutes, Abe had fitted Hunter with the last black Ralph Lauren tuxedo in the shop. "I thought you might be coming in. I put it aside in case you needed one. Lots of parties this year I hear," Abe said and winked. "Oh wait. Take these too." Abe picked up a box containing a pair of horseshoe-shaped cufflinks. "My wife ordered a bunch. They're yours, a gift. Maybe they'll bring you some luck," he chuckled as he waved his hand over them as if ceremoniously bestowing them.

Hunter squinted at the gold jewelry. They weren't really his style, not that he had a style, or a reason for a style. His uniform was those suits, shirts, and simple ties that Abe had set him up with and casual jeans and tee shirts for the few times he wasn't planted in the office. Hunter knew when to let Abe have his way and laughed as he slipped the links through the button holes and snapped them in place. "Luck. Hmmm. Can't hurt, huh?" he said as Abe handed him the suit bag with his clothes. "Thank you, Abe."

"You're going to miss that train of yours. Hurry, sign here," Abe said. As Hunter signed, he added, "I want a report when you get back, you hear?"

"Just a bunch of old frat brothers getting together. Really."

"Yeah," Abe laughed. "Report, you hear. Nothing official in writing or nothing. Just give me the highlights. Got a girl up there?"

"Nah, no girl right now. But no problem, Abe, no problem. I'll be sure to report in. It'll be the first thing I do when I get back."

"Don't forget, my Luanne's still available. She's

the third one from the left," Abe winked and pointed over his shoulder at the family photograph hanging behind the register. "She's a senior now over at AU. International Relations major. Smart as a whip, that one, and beautiful."

Hunter was sure that he must have made a face that said "no" because Abe stopped talking. Abe had been trying to hook him up with Luanne for as long as he knew him. Hunter had told him multiple times that it wasn't as if he wasn't interested, he was just busy. "Abe, I still don't have time in my life for a relationship," Hunter said apologetically. He didn't want to explain that he spent his days and nights at the office most weeks and working through weekends was always in play. Hunter was focused on only one thing, his career, and was committed to remaining that way for a few more years.

"Eh, can't blame me for trying. Now, go. You're going to miss your train." Hunter nodded and waved as he turned to leave the store. "And, yeah, I know. No relationships for now. One of these days, Hunter Reed, one of these days!" Abe yelled as Hunter headed to the stairs and the train.

Hunter found his track and waited to board. After a few minutes, he was settled into a seat watching the winter bare Mid-Atlantic landscape flicker like an old black and white movie as the train slid along heading north, the bleak countryside only fully illuminated at station stops. This impromptu reunion was far from how he expected to spend the night, but after Joey's last message he realized he really did miss the guys. Joey, and this group at Penn, were the closest thing he'd had to a family.

When his parents went their separate ways, he had opted to go away to boarding school. It was a bold decision to make at nine years old, but Hunter was sure that he didn't want to pick sides without a sibling to weather the storm. He wanted to be neutral and far, far, away from home. He had chosen John Adams Boys Academy in New Hampshire, because it was several states away. He had read about the school in a Sunday *New York Times* article his father had discarded on the breakfast table one day. The article had suggested that attending an Eastern Prep school was a calling and it was a sure way into Penn or one of the other Ivies. Hunter decided on the spot that morning that he had to go, convinced it was his only way out. Even at nine, he was sure it would be an excellent education and he used that in his argument when he sat his parents down and pleaded his case with colorful hand lettered posters as visual aids.

"Wilmington. Wilmington, next," bellowed a conductor from beyond shaking Hunter from his thoughts.

Hunter had spent a lot of time on these trains traveling up and down the East Coast between home, school, and now, D.C. The familiar sing-song reminders of station stops was forever etched in his brain and somehow comforting at the same time.

School was what he did. And, he did it well. But, that's all he did, first at John Adams, then at Penn, and Penn Law. He considered it his job. Now in Washington, working for a freshman senator from New Hampshire, it was all work, all of the time. It all seemed so thought out, so well planned, so on track. It was, but it wasn't lost on him that it was also dull, boring, and a little lonely.

The train unexpectedly seemed to slow and then groaned to a stop. A conductor announced, "We're going to be waiting for a few minutes, folks. There's a problem up ahead."

Annoyed people grumbled in the background.

Hunter's phone buzzed. He picked it up, and tapped his thumb on the screen, but before he could speak, "Man, you had better be at 30th Street station, dude," bellowed from the phone. "You should be at this party. I don't know how they found us. But, man, they are in the house. When are you getting here?" Joey yelled.

Hunter was sure Joey was exaggerating. It was a really quiet party if he wasn't, which was okay with him too. He wondered if maybe things had changed over time with all of them too. "Uh, we had a slight delay outside of Wilmington. I should be there in about forty minutes or so. I'll get a cab to the house."

"Slight delay? Dude. Did a Senator have another train wait for him or something?"

"Maybe, but somebody did say it might be a body on the tracks or something. It's New Year's Eve, you know."

"Wow, dude. That's dark. Damn. Everyone is here. Goose, Frankie, and Elmo. You've got to get here."

"Elmo too?"

"Yeah, Elmo too."

A grin spread across Hunter's chiseled face, "Wow. He came all the way from Seattle?"

"Yeah. It's been too long since we were all under one roof. Really, when you get here the house'll be complete and we'll par-tay! Like old times."

"Like old times." Hunter leaned back in his seat, his grin gone as he stared at the ceiling and wondered if it could ever really be like old times. It struck him that six years since their graduation was a *long* time. It was hard to go back. "Did Frankie bring Rumor?"

"Nope. Married *and* divorced already."

"Geez. Are you kidding? Did you go to the wedding?"

Joey laughed, "*True* love happened fast. They eloped. And, like the last time, nobody was invited."

"Kids?"

"No. Frankie's shooting blanks. At least that's what he says!"

"Well, no collateral damage is good, I guess," Hunter added as he recalled his own childhood experience of weathering the attacks and counter-attacks between parents. "But, that's a lot of paper-work."

"Hunter, you won't believe it, but the place is exactly like we left it. That gross chair you salvaged and dragged home from South Street is still here," Joey said and snorted.

"No. Oh come on."

"Oh, yes. And, all of the children have gone

home to mommy and daddy," Joey continued. "Well, there is one exchange student here and he's wasted already. My guess is he'll be passed out by ten thirty. He's playing beer pong with Goose," Joey yelled over what sounded like cheering in the background.

Heads turned to Hunter as people sitting nearby could hear Joey and the yelling clearly. An older woman, seated across the aisle, leaned in and listened.

"With Goose? Oh no. Poor kid. Somebody really should have warned him," Hunter laughed.

The woman moved in closer and cooed, "Oh, sounds like fun."

Hunter glanced up as she slid to the edge of her seat. She wore a clingy silver polyester gown that hung below a soiled black puffy coat. Her long grey-blonde Botticelli curls poked out in several directions from under a red Phillies baseball cap.

The woman pulled at her black socks that had rolled into the tops of her Nike sneakers and said, "Fun." When Hunter didn't respond, she grinned wide and grabbed her Whole Foods *I Used to be a Plastic Bottle* bag and dug through its contents.

Hunter forced a smile and twisted away from her towards the window. He saw his reflection in the window and he realized that his grin looked more like a grimace. He wondered how he was ever going to work on his people skills if he never left the office. He knew he had to do better if he expected to have any chance of a political career.

Hunter squeezed his eyes shut. He remembered

following his father around to community events before his parents split. He and Mom would attend every one of his speaking engagements. She would stand tall and proud, wave at the crowds, and lovingly gaze at his father. Hunter, however, wriggled in the tight jackets and pulled at the little bow ties she insisted he wear, and refused to look at anyone. Even as a young boy, he resented being used as a prop. He'd watch his father smile, lean in and listen to every person's story as if he truly cared about them. Hunter knew the truth. He knew he didn't care. He knew that he cared only about himself and used others when it benefitted him. He never listened to Hunter's stories because he had nothing that could further his agenda. Hunter was simply holding him back.

"Okay, Joe. I can't make the train go any faster. They're probably scraping the guy off the tracks now. I'm sure we'll be moving soon. Save me a six-pack," Hunter said.

"You got it," Joe laughed as he hung up.

"Me too, Joe," the woman snapped.

This time Hunter turned, made eye contact with the woman, and forced a wide grin at her thinking this was probably as good a time as any to practice.

She pushed a bag of candy at him and said, "Twizzler?"

Chapter 5

"Always get to your appointments early, but not too early," was among Antonetta's self-inflicted life requirements and a habit that Maria had also incorporated not only in her day-to-day, but also in her handling of this particular client even if it usually made her rush, breaking one of her mother's other rules.

She always arrived a few minutes early, prepared for anything.

Or, so she hoped.

Maria marched into Buddakan and positioned herself at a "Cee-Cee approved" table, near the bar and close to the enormous gold Buddha statue so that they could be seen by whomever was in the restaurant. She glanced at her phone. *Fifteen minutes early.* "Phew," she exclaimed and shifted in her chair.

She surveyed the crowd. *Oh, you all think this is so New York. Philly had this particular dining experience first, and soon after, Atlantic City too.* It was almost like opening a play on the road to work out the kinks before bringing it to Broadway. Except this concept had been perfected on Chestnut Street in Old City, Philadelphia, before its New York debut. Maria knew she was being judgie, but Philly was Philly, and as a Philly girl, she was loyal.

Five o'clock arrived and she noticed two older, desperate looking men sitting at the bar watching her. One of them stood and slithered over. She tried to project her *"I am not going to give a crap about what is going to come out of your mouth, so go away"* look.

It didn't work.

"Your date seems to have stood you up. Care to join us?" Maria shook her head no and sipped her drink hoping he would disappear. "C'mon. Let us buy you a drink. Champagne? It's…"

"No, thank you."

"It's New Year's. C'mon."

"I'm waiting for a client," she said.

"Ohhhh," he said and nodded.

Wait. What? No. Oh, seriously? Fabulous. What am I being mistaken for? Woo-hoo! Happy New Year to me.

She looked down at her outfit. Really? She was wearing a simple black dress, a statement necklace, and boots. Okay, the boots were killer with a four-inch heel to give her a little height. But, really? What vibe am I giving off? She made a mental note to invest in a new wardrobe once the after-Christmas sales started.

She watched as the guy shrugged and slinked back to the bar. He lobbed, "Bitch," over his shoulder in her direction so his buddy and most of the bar could hear.

Maria's cheeks blazed. *Why do I care? He's old and creepy.* She blinked hard, took a deep breath, and was ready to bolt to the door as she heard footsteps stop next to her.

"Good. You're here." When she opened her eyes, she was relieved to see Cee-Cee's assistant, Sherman, standing next to her holding a small envelope. She glanced over to the bar at the guy and saw his bleached too-white grin flash as he lifted his drink in her direction, smiled, and winked.

"Have you been here long? Sorry. She just told me to come over here, like ten minutes ago," Sherman said.

"No. Noooooo. Not long at all."

It had already been a long day. Furious thoughts raged... *Yes, thank you, Cee-Cee. You're the only one with a life. Not. The. Rest. Of. Us. Peons. I don't have a life. I bet Sherman doesn't either. So, what does it matter to you when you or your assistant arrives? Huh? Huh? I, for one, have nothing to do anyway except to get on a train to Philly to deal with a crazy parade catastrophe back at home. But, then again, that can wait. My father and his buddies will be working all night around the clock, and now, so will I.*

So much for being prepared for anything.

"I thought I was meeting Cee-Cee," was all she could manage to spit out.

Sherman shook his head "no" and shrugged. "I got here as fast as—" Sherman stopped mid-sentence as a perky waitress approached with two glasses of champagne and deposited them before they could stop her.

"From the Manager. Happy New Year," she

chirped.

He waited until she walked away. Once it was safe, continued as if he was revealing a state secret that could not be overheard, whispering, "She said the color of the headline needs to be changed. It'll clash with her dress or something when she presents to the Board of Directors. She said that she wants to pop more than the ad. I figured you'd know what that meant."

Sherman paused and stared at Maria's blank look.

Words escaped her.

Maria wondered if she was projecting what she'd overheard one of the partners call as her resting bitch face. She was stunned at the passive aggressive control Cee-Cee was leveling at her at this hour on a holiday when she couldn't do anything about this change.

"Uh, yeah, well, here's a swatch. I think she said it's from the dress. Don't lose it. She wants it back with alternatives. A.S.A.P," he continued. Not waiting for a response, he spun, blasted away, and left the restaurant.

Maria glanced at her phone. It read 5:20. "Great. Just great." No missed calls. She thought she should be grateful she had no calls to return as she slipped the phone back into the oversized red Louis Vuitton bag she'd been given as compensation for her first unpaid internship. The bag cost more than the two NYU credits her parents had begrudgingly paid for that enabled her the privilege of spending the summer doing coffee runs. She would never admit that to her mother. She told her it was a knock-off that she had bought off of a street vendor in Central Park for twenty dollars.

Maria stared at the sliver of fabric, then at the champagne. She chugged the bubbly trying hard not to choke. A six-minute meeting on New Year's Eve to change a color in an ad so Cee-Cee would pop. She couldn't believe it. This was ridiculous even for Cee-Cee.

"Wait," she uncharacteristically ordered as the waitress reached for Sherman's untouched glass. Maria grabbed it and chugged it too, then stood.

On her way to the door, the hostess stopped her and pointed at the manager near the bar as a waitress handed her a glittered wine bag. "Compliments of the house. For you and Ms. Berg. Please take it with you. Happy New Year."

"Why not? Thank him for me, please," Maria said to her. She waved toward the bar hoping that the manager was watching and thought to herself, just what I need…an overpriced bottle of Cristal. She glanced back and watched as the guy from earlier waved back and blew her a kiss.

Her night was off to an outstanding start.

A blast of cold air hit Maria's face hard as she made her way out of the door and stepped onto the sidewalk glancing up and down Ninth Avenue. Relieved, she saw Cee-Cee's Town Car still waiting. Johnny, the driver, dutifully opened the car door and she slid into the back seat glad to be safely inside.

Johnny had delivered her to Cee-Cee's offices, or a specified "hot spot," or returned her home after being summoned for a face-to-face with his boss more than a few times in the last two years. Johnny was nonplussed by Cee-Cee's demands and took everything she threw at him in stride. Maria was sure he thought her to be a complete weakling.

She felt uncomfortable being served by hard-working men like Johnny. He reminded her of her father and uncles, men who did whatever was necessary to provide for their families. She always tried to thank him or chat with him about whatever current event she could manage. Although, at first, he did seem really surprised that she'd ask him anything.

Johnny and Maria found a friendly patter that worked for them after a few trips. She'd learned all about Juliette and his two girls. If Antonetta Vigliano had taught her daughters anything it was how to make small talk with people. Unfortunately for Maria, lately her mother's chats with strangers were mostly in quest of men for her to date. Anyone's single brother, nephew, or son was fair game. Maria often found wounded and available lonely hearts much like the UPS delivery guy on Christmas Eve waiting at the dining room table, collected by her ever-hopeful mother as potential boyfriends.

"Uptown, Ms. Vigliano?" Johnny asked. "I can probably swing wide up The West Side Highway. I have to warn you, traffic's a bear tonight. Cops got streets closed all over the place for the big show. It's amazing we got downtown when we did."

Heading uptown was all she wanted. She had a nice bottle of Chardonnay in the fridge, a line-up of movies in her queue on Netflix, and a pile of frequently watched DVDs waiting. She knew she could start with *The Holiday* and work her way through a rom-com or two, or binge-watch a series until she was asleep, or the night was over, and the confetti was in a landfill somewhere in New Jersey.

Instead, she said, "No. Thanks, Johnny. Can you take me to Penn Station? Please? I'm taking the Acela home to Philadelphia."

"Oh, Miss. That's not going to be possible, I'm afraid. Not tonight. Not if you have to get to Philly before midnight?"

"That was the plan."

"Oh, Miss, that's not a good idea," he said.

"There's a bottle of Cristal in it for you. I'll bet Juliette would love this." She felt bad as the words slipped out of her mouth knowing Johnny would never be incentivized by a bottle of champagne.

"I don't touch the stuff. Guaranteed headache for me in the a.m. I'm sure Juliette would like it. But even Cristal isn't going to get us through this traffic tonight, Miss."

Maria felt her stomach fall. She felt really awful having offered the bottle. Her cheeks blazed, and she stammered, "Oh sorry. Maybe try Sixth Avenue. Let's just go as far as we can, and then if I have to, I'll jump out, and walk fast."

"Okay. If you say so. I'll do my best. I could drive you home," he offered as he glanced at her in the review mirror.

"No, Johnny. That would be ridiculous. You should be home with Juliette."

Johnny opened his mouth to argue until Maria raised her hand and shook her head to stop him. He drove as far as Twenty Fifth Street where traffic gridlocked. She dug around in her tote and pulled out a worn pair of sneakers. She shoved her feet inside, laced them up, folded up her boots, tossed them into the bag as he double parked. Maria looked at the bottle, sure that Cee-Cee had left far worse things in the car and said, "I don't want to carry this all the way home, Johnny. I'm really sorry." Johnny just nodded as she handed him the bottle and he quickly maneuvered to let her out of the car.

"I'm good from here. Thank you," she said as she quickly slid out.

"You sure, Miss? I don't have a good feeling. There's lots of crazies on the street tonight."

"I'll be fine," she said as she showed him her key chain with a small can of mace attached. "From my mother."

"Your mother's a smart cookie."

"So, they say." Maria glanced at her cell phone. It was 6:10. She had twenty-five minutes to jog the last blocks. "The train doesn't leave until 7:05. It'll probably be a little late anyway. Always is on holidays. Give my regards to Juliette. And, Happy New Year, Johnny."

"Same to you, Miss," Johnny said and tipped his hat. She waved and started to jog. The streets were jammed side to side with people heading to Times Square. Most wore *Happy New Year* party hats and glittery tiaras and were already blowing horns and spinning noise makers as they moved. Maria pushed her way through the crowd as best she could, bobbing and weaving, and getting knocked left and right while trying to run and clutch her tote bag.

She pushed her way into Penn Station as waves of people were pushing the opposite way and plowed down the steps toward the concourse at exactly 7:00. She shoved a credit card into the express ticket machine and tapped her foot as the paper spit out of the slot. She searched the board to find the track and scooted down the steps just as the announcer screamed, "Train 2173 Acela Express to Philadelphia, Penn Station, ALL ABOARD."

She jumped inside as the doors started to close and the train crept forward, maneuvering past the odd reverse reveler or two towards an empty row in first class and settled into a seat.

"R. H. T. can spring for the extra bucks for your ride. It's the least they could do after Cee-Cee scheduled a meeting tonight," Lyndon had announced when he booked the ticket online and upgraded her to first class earlier this afternoon.

She sucked a deep breath in and sunk into the seat. Thank God for Lyndon, she thought. After a moment or two, the train was moving fast. She dug around in her bag for a travel pillow and leaned against the window. She closed her eyes for what seemed like a second or two and started to doze.

The announcer's gravelly voice interrupted her serenity to report, "Ladies and Gentleman, there will be a short stop-over in Newark. There's seems to be some activity on the tracks further south. We're going to wait it out for just a little while before we continue on to Philadelphia. I've been advised that it shouldn't be long. You will be in Philly long before the clock strikes twelve. No worries."

Moans and groans began as someone shouted, "Are you friggin' kidding me?"

A chorus of complaints followed. A large woman yelled, "Give me a break."

Another yelled, "Can you believe this?"

Several more groans and "This sucks!" were heard throughout the train.

Chapter 6

After the woman's third, "You got a girl in Philly, Hunter?" he moved to the front of the car and sat across from a snoring barrel-chested man wearing a bright orange Philadelphia Flyers jacket, spread across three seats. *At least he won't talk.* Hunter thumbed through *The Washington Post* again and he glanced at the man. *Yup. Really stellar peopling skills right now. Just great.*

"Ladies and Gent...we'll be..." the conductor's voice cracked and was drowned out by loud static, making the rest of the announcement incomprehensible as the train lurched forward and moved.

The man across the aisle woke up in mid-fall as the train picked up speed. He landed hard on the floor, blinked, and looked up at Hunter and chuckled, and said, "Dude!" Hunter sighed and watched the man crawl back into his seat.

Hunter reached for his laptop and powered up. A Facetime chime caught his attention. Joey's face filled the computer screen as he opened the program. "Tick-tock, bro. Where are you?" Elmo's head popped into frame, his curly red hair blocking Joey's face.

"H, only you could turn an Acela ride into a

slow boat," Elmo chided.

"Good to see you too, Elmo. I'll be there soon."

The scruffy man stood, rubbed his protruding belly and leaned in to look at the computer. "Yeah. Soon. Or I want my money back," he said. On the computer screen, Elmo and Joey's eyes popped open wide as they moved back and out of frame, laughing hysterically.

Goose, all nose, neck, and tiny head, slid into view on the screen. "Hunter?" he asked as Hunter pushed the scruffy guy away. "Oh, okay, cool. I thought I was really messed up. Dude, Amtrak says ETA in fifteen or so."

"Excellent. Save me a beer. And wake Frankie up before I get there."

Goose turned around and looked at Frankie snoring in a beat-up recliner and said, "Copy that, H. Will do."

When Hunter had met Joey in his freshman year Comp class, a thought occurred that maybe he *could* manage to have some fun too. So, he allowed himself one night a week to hang out with the Joey and the TKE guys. Joey was from a different world, and smart. The no-work-required kind of smart. He was on a full ride at Penn and took nothing seriously. "Life's too short, my man," he'd always say as he smacked Hunter on the head whenever he tried to persuade him to stop studying and go out. "Don't count on your tomorrows." Joey had always insisted.

Hunter suspected Joey acted that way because he had lost his father when he was twelve. They had that in common, sort of. Hunter had counted his always withdrawn and absentee father the same as Joe's dead one. In his mind, gone was gone.

Hunter hadn't seen Joey in two years and he really did kind of miss him and the group.

The scruffy man counted on his fingers, "E. F. G. H...J." He looked at Hunter, grinned wide and said, "You boys need an 'I' and I'm an I. Ingram. I'm an I. My name is Ingram. Dudes. I'm an I." Hunter stared at his computer screen and watched as the guys lost it, guffawing and falling on the floor until he snapped his computer shut. "Hunter, man, I'm an I," Ingram said excitedly shifting foot to foot.

Lyndon didn't give her a chance to say a word. Maria could only shake her head as she heard the words, "Are you dead?"

The question didn't take her by surprise except for the fact that the words came out of Lyndon's mouth and not her mother's. *Now what?* ping-ponged in her head as she anticipated the why of his question. She inhaled and thought about how to answer. Was I dead? Dead, in what sense? Dead because I'm swimming hard against life just barely hanging-on-dead, she thought. Or dead because I'm alone and lonely in New York City at the most wonderful time of the year again? For once she really wanted to come up with a snappy answer and fire it back at him, but instead, she answered annoyed, "No, I'm not dead. I'm just stuck in Newark."

"Isn't that the same thing?"

"My train is delayed in New Jersey."

"How novel."

"Well, we're waiting out an event on the south bound tracks somewhere near Wilmington, Delaware, I think. They said the entire East Coast is stalled, or some nonsense."

When the conductor had advised that it might be a while until they moved, much to the dismay of the few travelers seated around her, and after a bawdy chorus of complaints echoed through the car, she got off of the train in search of much needed caffeine. She had been bolting up the steps to get a Starbucks when her phone rang.

Lyndon rapid fired at her, "How did your mother get my number?"

"Uhhhh... She probably lifted it when I wasn't looking last week," she admitted.

Maria wasn't sure why the term "helicopter" parent had become such a trendy label other than it being necessary fodder for pop psychologists and morning television teams to chew on and a convenient keyword for internet searches in the last few years—mothers in her family had been mastering helicoptering moves for generations. In fact, she thought her mother had perfected the helicoptering that generations before her had crafted. If she had a way to be by Maria's side twenty-four/seven, she would have done it. She had kept track of and catalogued every one of her children's moves since birth. She wasn't going to stop now.

It would not have been unusual or beneath her

to take Maria's phone while she wasn't looking so that she could have a record of her contacts. "You live and work in New York City," she would have said if confronted, as if that fact had eluded her. "For peace of mind, Maria, just in case. What if I needed to find you in an emergency? What would I do? Who would I call?" she'd undoubtedly explain to justify her anxiety and over protectiveness, a trait that she had inherited from her mother who had probably inherited it from her mother, even though in those days, a trip across the ocean was quite different than Maria's two-hour Amtrak trip.

"I was home in South Philly for two days over Christmas," Maria explained. She had arrived on Christmas Eve, breaking one of Antonetta' rules and traveling on a holiday *and* not staying until the day after Christmas to dodge the volume of people returning home that day. "She probably grabbed my phone when I wasn't aware. I had to sleep at some point," she justified. "She's done this once before when I was in college. I'm surprised it's taken her two full years to get your number."

"Are you serious? You know better, Maria. Don't let her near your phone."

Someone running past her yelled, "Douche."

"What?" Lyndon asked.

"Watch it, loser."

Maria leaned against a wall, watching and waiting for a fight to break out between two goons dressed in tuxedos. "Not you. That's just some guy pushing another dude that budged in line for coffee. We're desperate."

"Get out of there, now before I have to lie to your mother for real."

"As soon as the Amtrak gods say so. Something's on the track. And I really needed caffeine," she whined.

"Ohhhhh. It's New Year's Eve. All those lonely hearts."

"Stop. It's probably a branch or something."

"Yeah. Something."

"You're so maudlin," she said.

"Who me? Maud...I looooove her."

"Lyn, you're drunk. Stop."

Lyndon giggled like a tween girl. "I am? Okay. I am. I'll stop, if YOU CALL YOUR MOTHER. I can't take the stress. She thinks you're dead again."

As she listened, she thought she heard laughter. If she didn't know better, she would have guessed there was a party going on at the other end. "Are you having a party? You can't stand having people in your space," she asked.

The Announcer started to chant, "Two. One. Seven. Three. Now boarding on Track Three."

"You didn't invite me?" she said.

"You would never have come."

"I might have," she insisted, even though she knew he was right. Putting herself in the middle of social events with groups of people that she didn't know stressed her out, even if they were Lyndon's besties. She hated being in those situations and feeling like she was being interviewed.

"Call your mother."

"When she calls back, and, she will, tell her that I'm not dead. I'm only in Newark," she said realizing that she sounded completely ridiculous. "Service is really, really spotty on the…"

"Wait. Before you hang up, I've got to tell you someth—" was all she heard as she hung up and ran back toward the train.

"ALL ABOARD," bellowed over the loud speakers as people scrambled to board, pushing and shoving down the steps. Maria joined them, running toward the train juggling her coffee, pushing into the car, and plopping back into a seat.

And then, they waited.

Maria glanced at her phone. The numbers 6:30 beamed back at her, taunting. "Great, just great," she said aloud to no one. *At this rate I might get to Philly tomorrow. I should have just stayed in the office. Why do I always have to listen to my mother?* She rocked her head back and forth, her neck cracked with each turn. She took a deep breath and waited. And waited. She closed her eyes and decided that it was really time for this day, this year to be over.

The train didn't pull out of Newark until 7:15.

"Plenty of time, H. Plenty of time, man," Ingram said with a toothy grin as Hunter glanced at his watch. It was 9:10. There was time enough to jump in a cab and get to University City, find the guys and hit the New Year's Eve party that Joey wanted to go to. Hunter grabbed his stuff and stood sandwiched between the groggy barrel-chested Ingram and the woman in the Phillies cap. They waited with the fidgety line of other anxious travelers to exit the train as it squealed and jerked to a stop, and then slowly inched their way out of the car onto the platform.

Hunter headed toward the door to upstairs and pulled it open, turned slightly and gestured to the woman to go first. "Such a gentleman, Hunter. I'm impressed," she said as she stepped on the escalator and headed up. He waited for a moment to put some space between them. She turned and mouthed, "*Call me*" while gesturing with her thumb and pinky as if holding a phone. After she was sufficiently far enough away, he took the steps two-by-two and entered the concourse.

Hunter watched as an attractive woman approached Ingram, kissed his cheek, grabbed his arm, and guided him toward a door. Before she could push him outside, Ingram turned to Hunter and yelled, "H, remember, I'm an 'I'. And, you guys need one. I'm available. Look me up. Twenty first and Locust. The corner. Ya' can't miss it," he said and then added, "It's the one with the red door. Remember. The red one." Hunter nodded as the woman pulled Ingram away.

Hunter took a step forward and glanced around. Grand Art Deco chandeliers hung over the mostly empty grand Thirtieth Street Station. An odd assortment of people dotted the cavernous room, a few were dressed elegantly for the occasion, some dressed as if it was any old day, some meandered around, an older couple sat on a bench holding hands, and a few others stood in lines. Hunter spotted the twenty-ninth street doors where he knew there would be taxis waiting outside and glanced at his watch, which read 9:15. He readjusted the shoulder strap of his bag and rushed toward the door.

Chapter 7

"Don't travel on the actual day of a holiday, any holiday, Maria. It's too crowded and not worth the hassle. Traffic is always ridiculous."

Well, she had done it. Maria had broken one of Antonetta's BIGGEST cardinal rules of life, because her mother was adamant that Maria be at home with the family. Maria should have reminded her mother of her own rule and stayed in New York.

Why is she always right?

It had taken almost three hours to get to Philly. She could have driven there and back in that amount of time...well okay, maybe not. Even on a good day you can never tell what waits on the Jersey turnpike. Maria didn't own a car or have a current driver's license, Uber's surge charges were too expensive on holidays, and as she had debated with Lyndon numerous times, car shares seemed too much trouble when Amtrak was almost a direct connect between her homes. Her little extravagance, the Acela, usually chopped off travel time. It should have only taken about an hour, tops. They had finally admitted there had been track trouble, and now at this point, she was rushing, breaking yet another rule.

Determined, she pushed her way past the odd reverse reveler or two and jogged up the steps in Thirtieth Street Station toward the taxi stand adjusting her bag and her coffee, not paying attention to her surroundings. She thought the station would be empty. It should have been empty, everyone in place for the night's festivities. Everyone with plans. Everyone except her. Right?

Wrong.

She was four paces away from the steps when she plowed into him.

Him.

Oh, my god.

Her bag flew off of her shoulder and skidded across the floor. Her coffee swirled in the cup. She wasn't even sure why she was still holding it. It was cold before the train passed Elizabeth, New Jersey. His *Washington Post* fluttered to the ground. She took her next step and her foot landed on the paper sending her sliding across the polished stone floor.

Noooo.

Her arms flailed back-and-forth; her body jerked. This was not a graceful slide, if there is one. And, then she felt herself begin to fall, panic roared, and her throat tightened as she braced herself for the landing, until...

She heard, "Whoa," as his arms reached out and caught her. A hearty laugh drowned out the holiday instrumental music softly playing in the background.

Humiliated, she felt her face flush as her stomach knotted and her thoughts raced about what had awkwardly played out. *Seriously? How was this happening? Am I living some kind of real-life "meet cute?"* If only this experience had been a rom-com saved on her DVR in her apartment so that she could freeze frame and rewind to watch again and *not* her life.

That did not happen, did it?

The *Post's* headline, *President and First Lady expected to attend numerous First Night Balls* taunted her from the newspaper's front-page inches away from her foot. Another reveler pushed past, hit the newspaper, and did a Three Stooges-like slip-and-slide and bumped into them. This time, she fell hard and landed right on her slightly plump butt, the same butt she had been meaning to work off by now with a series of daily squats at the gym that she didn't actually have time to use.

Her heart sank and she felt her cheeks blaze and heard, "Oh geez, I'm so sorry."

She looked up and blinked. She was face to face with one of the most amazing images she'd seen since her days of gluing photos of male models torn out of magazines to her long-abandoned vision board looking down at her and smiling.

Great! Just my luck.

His eyes crinkled at the corners as he smiled. Twinkly blue eyes. Dimpled cheeks. Golden brown hair tousled with perfect mini-spikes, and attractive. Not just attractive, but movie star handsome.

She felt something she'd never felt before as she looked up at him. The jolt was something she'd only read about in all of those magazines she had studied over the years and never thought was real. She decided at that moment that she was wrong. Really wrong.

He offered his hand and grinned. She took it, managed a faint smile as she struggled to stand, planting one of her sneakers squarely on the photo of the exquisite White House Christmas tree, and slipped again. This time, her coffee cup went flying. The lid popped off first and the coffee showered his shirt. Somehow his *Washington Post* was in her hand. As he bent over to help her stand up again, instinct took over. She wiped his shirt with the paper, mopping up coffee and smearing a rainbow of ink from the glittering tree photo across his crisp white tuxedo shirt.

Oh. My. God.

He was dressed in a classic tuxedo. Perfect. Exquisite. Beautiful.

He looked at the shirt, then up at her, smiled again and said, "My fault. I wasn't watching where I was going. I was checking the time," as he tried to brush the coffee and the ink off of the front of his shirt. "So sorry. I'm rushing. Always rushing. Sorry."

His fault? The man was clearly a god, she thought, and I am such a loser.

"It's late," she said.

"Yeah, it is late."

She did her best to gather all of his newspaper. "Yup, late," she said, her voice a little too loud as she handed him the wet rumpled pages. "I'm sorry. Really so, so sorry."

"It's okay. I've read it. Four times. Long ride. No good news."

"Me too. Long ride. From?"

"Washington. You?"

"New York. Lawyer?" She blinked and shook her head astonished that her brain was refusing to engage. Somehow, she'd lost the use of the English language and was managing to only mouth two or three words at a time. She felt her cheeks flush red again and her eyes opened wide. *Lawyer? Why did I assume lawyer?*

"Don't hold it against me," he said as his eyes revealed a mischievous glint and he handed over her bag and looked her over head to toe.

Maria glanced at her feet and tugged at the back of her coat trying to adjust her clothes without looking obvious. She spotted her knee squeezing through the ripped tights and glanced at her clunky sneakers realizing that she looked ridiculous and out of place on New Year's Eve even in the train station. Her lips turned into a slight frown as she assessed this particularly shining moment of hers.

"I was getting a cab," he said and nodded toward the doors and motioned with his arm. As they took a step, she thought, hmmm a gentleman. So unusual today. The doors opened automatically to a line of waiting taxis. "After you, Happy New Year," he said and smiled again.

"Happy New Year," she said back. "South Philly. Tenth and Dickinson," she mumbled as she opened the cab door and tossed her bags in. She glanced over her shoulder as another car pulled up. She smiled a crooked grin in his direction as he moved toward the next taxi.

She wasn't sure why, but she strained to hear where he was going. She thought she heard him say, "University City. Thirty-fourth and..."

She couldn't make out the rest as she slid into the car and pulled the door shut. She cringed as she listened for at least the four thousandth time this season to the bouncy upbeat words, *It's the most wonderful time of the year...*blaring from the Cab's radio. As the car pulled away from the station, she glanced out of the rear window and watched as his cab made a hard-right turn. "Take Spring Garden, please," she ordered.

It had been a long day and couldn't possibly get any worse, she thought as she leaned back into the seat and stared out of the window. At this point, she'd really had enough and only wanted to get home, climb into her childhood bed, and get ready for the next morning's events.

As it was every year, New Year's Day was going to be a very long day.

Chapter 8

Hunter looked down at his shirt again, shook his head, and rewound the prior few minutes.

He saw her out of the corner of his eye bounding up the stairs at track twelve, jogging as fast as she could across the concourse toward an exit. She was juggling coffee and a bag, and heading right towards him. With no time to react, they collided.

His reflexes had taken over as she started to fall. He dropped the suit bag and briefcase. They landed with a thump as his copy of *The Washington Post* fluttered to the ground. Somehow, he caught her in his arms before she hit the marble floor. Her eyes were squeezed shut as she braced herself for impact.

"Oh geez. I'm so sorry," she stammered as her eyes fluttered open and she tried to stand.

"My fault. I wasn't watching where I was going. I was checking the time," Hunter said as he helped her up. They performed what felt like a *Three Stooges* routine, slipping, sliding, and apologizing. As her cold coffee hit his shirt, he glanced at the wet splotch, smiled and said, "I am really sorry. I was rushing. Always rushing. Sorry. It's okay. My fault."

She hurriedly scooped up some of the wet

newspaper and tried to wipe up the cold coffee, the damp paper creating a rainbow of colors across the front of the crisp white shirt. Her blue eyes glittered as she looked up horrified.

He saw that she was adorable even as she stood in front of him flustered, her hair falling over one eye, staring at the mess.

"It's late," she said.

"Yeah, it is late."

She stooped to gather up the rest of the scattered paper. "Sorry. I'm so, so sorry," she stuttered as she tried to fold and rearrange the newsprint and hand it to him. "I wasn't paying attention."

"It's okay. I've read it. Four times. Long ride. No good news."

"Me too. Long ride. From?"

"Washington. You?" he said as he retrieved her bag and handed it to her.

"New York. Lawyer?" she asked.

Hmmm. Not sure why she assumed that.

Hunter had felt something that he hadn't felt in a very long time as they exchanged what he thought might be a heartfelt look. It was only a moment, but images and thoughts swirled. And, those eyes. "No problem," was all he could say.

He took her in again. *Wow.*

Even after falling she looked amazing in her dusted-up overcoat and a simple black dress and sneakers—not pretentious like most of the women he crossed paths with in D.C. who always seemed to be attempting to level up in both their dating lives and careers.

"I was getting a cab."

"Me too," he said, nodding toward the doors and motioning with an outstretched hand for her to go first, "After you." This time he smiled and meant it.

She stepped outside toward a taxi, turned to look over her shoulder, hesitated for a brief moment, smiled, and waved.

His crumpled newspaper and bag in one hand, he grinned, nodded, and waved back with the other, and said, "Happy New Year," as he stood motionless on the curb.

"Happy New Year," she'd purred as she opened the cab door and tossed her things inside. "South Philly. Tenth and Dickinson," she instructed as she got into the car and it sped away.

"University City. Thirty-fourth Street," Hunter said as he got into the next car. "Damn." *Had I really let her walk away?*

"Something wrong?" the Cabbie asked.

"No. No. It's late, that's all."

He looked ahead and thought he saw her turn around as the cars sped out of the station and onto Market Street.

I'm such an idiot. I really do have to get out more. If Joe had been here, he would have bought the girl a drink, gotten all the pertinents, Facebook friended her, and paid for her cab. Hunter thought back to times they were in bars in Center City. Joey would have a list of new possibles within minutes, while he would just spend time talking to the bartender about how bad the Phillies were playing and who they should have traded.

My social skills blow.

Within minutes, the cab pulled up to the familiar TKE house on Thirty-Fourth Street. Hunter peeled off a ten-dollar bill and said, "Keep it," to the cabbie who stared incredulously at the bill as he got out.

"Yeah, Happy New Year, Bud," the cabbie shot at him.

Hunter looked at him, handed him an additional five, and thought, we only drove four blocks as the car sped away. Hunter shook his head. He could hear music blaring as he walked down the overgrown path and up the massive stone steps. He pulled hard on the old familiar oak doors and stepped inside.

A sad-looking dried-out half-decorated Christmas tree stood in one corner. Christmas lights rung the room, taped to the ceiling and every available surface. A dozen or so fuzzy red stockings were hung on the banister trailing up the steps to the second floor; each with a name written in glitter on the top. The room was full of early-undergraduate discard furniture; a keg sat on ice in the corner of the room opposite the tree.

Hunter scanned the room. All of the gang was there, dressed in tuxedos, waiting. Joey and Frankie were hunched over in front of a computer watching Classic Baseball and cheering on the Phillies in the 2008 World Series. True blue fans, this rerun was somehow still exciting. Hunter watched them scream and high-five as a ball sailed over the outfield fence. Goose and Elmo were jamming and jumping in the air rock-star-like with toy video game instruments in another corner in front of a TV. Not one of them heard the door creak open, or noticed Hunter standing there.

Hunter laughed out loud and said, "Don't all get up at once."

"Lookie-lookie who's here, Mister Washington D.C., himself," Joey yelled.

"Dude," Elmo said as he bounded across the room and slapped Hunter's back.

"Senator," Frankie chided.

"Not yet Frankie, not yet," he said. They swarmed him, fist-bumped, hugged, and smacked each other around. "It's good to see you maniacs," was all he could manage to get out.

"We missed you too," Goose said.

"Somebody, get the man a beer," Joey yelled as he punched a fist in the air.

Goose was the first to spring into action. He jumped across the room, yanked on the tap and filled up a red plastic cup. "Here you go, Hunter."

He took the cup, raised it to the group, and drank. "Man, it's good to see you all. Really good." Hunter was more than a little surprised that it felt this good to be back.

He looked around the room again. "What do you know! It does all look the same. You all look old, but this—"

The group exploded into laughter and clinked

cups.

Chapter 9

"Holidays matter, Maria. They punctuate the year."
Holidays and the family were life. And life and holidays
according to her mother were to be held at home and were
not negotiable. She knew that this rule was paramount
to Antonetta and the generations that came before her. It
was their glue.

Maria tried hard to erase the last few mortify-
ing minutes from her memory, positive that she was
scarred forever, but grateful she wouldn't ever have
to see the man again to be humiliated all over. She
sighed as the cab maneuvered through South Philly
and stopped in front of her parents' house.

"Hey. Yo, watch it, babe," the driver barked as
the taxi door slipped from Maria's hand and slammed
shut.

"Sor-ry," Maria sing-songed as the car sped
away. "Welcome home to me," she muttered.

Maria stood on the curb taking it all in. Glittering Christmas lights canopied the narrow street from
side to side, end-to-end, lighting up the whole block.
Almost every rowhouse still overflowed with holiday decorations. Bright bows, sleighs full of wrapped

gifts, and scene after scene of jolly Santas dotted the homes. Neighbors were popping in and out of each other's homes, drinks in hand in anticipation of midnight. Saxophones and banjoes could be heard in the background, a joyful cacophony of sound readying for the morning's show. Normally, this familiar scene cheered her, but today after this ride home her stomach was a tight ball of knots and the festivity only irritated her. *Was it that big of a deal not to have anyone to kiss at midnight?*

"Ri. You're here. Your mother thought you were dead," Ava said.

Punctuation, here I come.

She spun around to see her cousins, Ava and Bambi, bursting out of her parents' front door, running down the steps to the sidewalk. They were dressed to kill in sexy evening dresses, slinky stilettos, and Pashmina wraps.

Ava and Bambi. Woo-hoo girls extraordinaire, the kind of girls that no matter what appeared to be having the time of their lives, and truth be told, they usually were. Tall, blonde, beautiful—the all-in and ready-for-adventure kind of girls. They were the complete opposite of Maria's petite, introverted brunette self. How could we possibly share any DNA, she had wondered back in middle school biology class when they were typing their blood and tracing their family trees.

"She and Ma are doing a novena for you in the dining room with Grandma's beads," Bambi added.

"Nobody's seen those beads in like thirty years,

Ri. And, on a holiday. Nice going," Ava chimed in.

"I'm not dead. I was just stuck in Newark this time," Maria shot back.

"There's a difference?" Ava asked as she adjusted the girls that were spilling over the top of the low-cut cocktail dress she wore. An ample C-cup, she used what she had when she could, she had announced more times than Maria could count. It looked like she was planning on using them tonight.

"Wait. What? Did you talk to Lyndon?" Maria asked.

"Huh? Who?" Bambi squinted at her, fixed the lock of hair that was lying across Maria's face and tugged at her black overcoat so that it hung correctly on her body. She glanced at Maria's ripped tights, sneakers and black dress, shook her head and asked, "What happened to you? Did you get mugged?"

Ava didn't miss a beat, and added, "And, who died? You're dressed for a funeral. And, sneakers, really?" Ava glanced at Bambi who was now tugging on her thong adjusting it. They both shook their heads at her like judgmental bobble-head dolls.

"Really, Ri?" Bambi said just in case she had missed their disapproval.

Maria looked down at her mess. Her coat looked like she had been dragged across the floor at Thirtieth Street Station. The whole right side of her body felt out of whack, so weighed down by the oversized tote bag that her right hand felt like it almost touched her ankle. Her knee was pink and squishing through the ripped tights. She felt tears sneaking up on her. As her eyes welled…

"Let's go," Bambi said and grabbed one of Maria's hands. Ava looped an arm through Maria's other arm and together they dragged her inside.

The three women tiptoed up the stairs pausing only for a second to glance through the banister at Antonetta and Sylvia at the dining room table, oblivious to them, nibbling cookies and thumbing rosaries between sips of coffee.

Ava covered her mouth to stifle a giggle and they bolted into Maria's childhood bedroom. The space seemed locked in a time capsule—posters of boy bands, memorabilia, and awards ringed the space. Maria took it all in, pivoted and stood in front of the full-length mirror hanging on the closet door. She stared at her reflection and the horror of her appearance. "Oh noooo," she said as she peeled her coat off and flopped on the bed, secretly glad to be home. "Was I really out in public looking like this?" The memory of Mr. Perfect flooded back. She covered her eyes with her hands and blurted, "CRAP!"

"Get up. You're going to the ball with us," Ava demanded.

"What? No way."

"Oh, come on, Ri. You need to get out. It's New Year's Eve," Bambi added.

"And there are costumes to fix. Feathers to glue. You know the routine," she said.

"Give me a break, Cinderella. They've been strutting up Broad Street since forever. I'm pretty sure your father, and ours, and all of the Bella Bums can handle their costumes and find their way. They always do," Ava shot back and waved dismissively.

"Even with Grandpop's debacle of 1974, they came in second," Bambi interrupted.

They exchanged looks and burst into giggles.

"Only because Nonna Mary broke into Shriver's Hardware and stole gold spray paint for the shoes," Maria added as they tried to catch their breath.

"Who forgot to pick up the paint?" Ava asked.

Bambi and Maria turned and stared at her and both said, "UNCLE BRUNO."

"Nonna always did have a way with simple B & E. Our very own South Philly queen of smash and grab," Bambi added as she looked up at the ceiling.

"How'd she make bail?" Ava asked.

Ava was two years younger than Bambi, and even though Maria was sure that she had memorized the details just as they all had as kids, she always wanted them to review the story for her. It was their version of a once-a-year recitation of *The Great Vigliano Family Fairy Tale*. The story sometimes grew with crazy details, depending on who told it as all good stories do. These days nobody was really sure of the veracity of some of the specifics.

"Oh, young one, it was rumored that Father Franco anted up—one of his last duties before Monsignor reassigned him to Scranton," Maria recited.

Bambi jumped in, "Nobody would ever say for sure," she said and winked. "But I've got to say, nothing stops them. We didn't have dinner that year 'til someone got her outta..." she paused to mime air-quotes, "...the joint, a*fter* the parade! I really think that they just let her sit there and wait."

They lost it, laughing until they were grabbing their sides, bending over or flopping onto the bed. It was what they all did when anyone talked about, or thought of, Nonna sitting behind bars in Police Headquarters, or the Roundhouse as it was called in Philly. The building was aptly named for its Brutalist style design. The smooth round fortress-like concrete building with no ninety-degree corners hadn't ever hosted the likes of their Nonna. The family was all sure of that. The Sergeant on duty that night told Uncle Bruno she screamed at everyone the whole time while she paced nonstop. Detainees begged to be moved away from her. Uncle Bruno always said she yelled the whole way home that if her prized meatballs were ruined there was going to be hell to pay. They were fine and everyone was off the hook.

"And they still somehow came in second that year. You know, Ri, it is okay for you to have some fun once in a while. All work and no play," Bambi added as she rolled her eyes.

"Make Maria a fat, dumpy, lonely, old maid," Ava added just in case Maria had missed the dig.

That stung. She lobbed back, "Nice. What decade do you live in?"

"I'm just saying." Ava paused to adjust the girls again and smooth her hair. "Don't seem like you've got much going on in the romance department. You're here *all* the time. Why'd you leave?"

"You should get out," Bambi added.

"I get out."

"Not just back to South Philly. You got to get *out*. Live a little. Party. Maybe get a guy," Ava continued.

A guy. The cousins were never lacking in the guy department. It was really something she just didn't excel at even though she tried to meet new people. "I don't need a guy to be fulfilled. I'm fine," she said, not sure why she was trying to justify her current situation to them.

Ava frowned and said, "Fine?"

"Ri, you trying to tell us something?" Bambi fired at her. "I won't judge."

"What? No. No. I date."

Ava asked, "Yeah. When was your last? Not enough men in New York City these days, I hear." Without taking a breath, she continued, "And, Sal, across the street, who's still there, by the way, and now with some girl from Lower Merion—he don't count! You never actually went anywhere. Sitting on the stoop isn't a proper date."

Maria had to agree with her as she thought about Sal. "Lower Merion? Really? I thought I saw him on Christmas Eve. Bringing a tree home with someone." From eighth to eleventh grade, Sal and Maria spent every summer evening sitting on the Vigliano stoop, talking. Well, she did most of the talking. He mostly listened, that was until he met Virginia from Northern Liberties and Maria got dumped.

"I mean…Lower Merion?" she said and pulled at her tights and rubbed her sore knee.

"And don't even try to count that Carny dude you fell for in eleventh grade," Bambi said interrupting the memory.

"Right. I met Stefan. I never even really liked Sal. He was just geographically convenient for me back then. And if you recall, my mother had a maternal GPS from the day I was born. I couldn't have even wandered off the block without her knowing it and freaking out. It was like I was chipped."

"But, seriously, Ri, Stefan?" Ava said.

"Yeah, seriously? Give me your wallet," Bambi insisted as she bolted for Maria's purse.

"No. I said no, Bambi. Don't." Maria tried to swat the bag away, but before she could reach it, Bambi tossed it to Ava who grabbed it, dug inside and pulled out a wallet. She slid something out and handed it to Bambi.

"I knew it," Bambi squealed.

"Stop. Give me that," Maria barked as she felt her cheeks warm.

Ava continued to pull things out of the wallet, "You've still got the photos and the ride tickets?"

"Geez, Ri. He was a Carny," Bambi said.

"Yeah, but he was cute. A cute Carny," Maria insisted, feeling silly for justifying her long ago crush and mortified by this particular challenge from her cousins.

Ava and Bambi laughed as Maria grabbed for her stuff. "You rode the ferris wheel seventeen times that last night of Saint Peter's Carnival," Ava said.

"Ahhhhh. To be with Stefan," Bambi said and

added, "You were so adorable."

Maria sat on the bed and stared at the photos. Her young face and the exotic Stephan taunted her from the photo strip. That night, that boy, seemed like a million years ago and also like yesterday all at the same time. For some reason it still hurt, even now. She collapsed backwards onto the bed, stared at the ceiling, and whispered, "Ugh. My life sucks."

Maria watched Ava pull out an armload of dresses from the closet. She knew that there simply was no fighting with them. She would have to give in and try them on one-by-one.

Ava handed her a dress. It was *very* senior prom. They giggled hysterically and shook their heads "no." Bambi grabbed it and threw it on the bed.

The next was a bridesmaid's dress, never expected to be worn again and duly picked so that none of the attendants would outshine the bride. Maria slipped the dress on and remembered the day clearly. It was her high school best friend Emily's wedding in the summer of her college sophomore year. Emily had dropped out of college to marry her boyfriend before he shipped out to Iraq. Maria had been paired up with a groomsman named Dugger, who couldn't keep his hands off of her the entire day. She couldn't wait to rip the dress off at the end of the night.

Ava stuck her fingers into her mouth. Maria yanked it over her head and tossed it aside as Ava helped her slip on the next one—a bright yellow number with puffy sleeves and a high neck. She groaned and shook her head, looked at her cousins who were also shaking their heads. Ava helped her pull that one off too, and tossed it onto the pile on the floor as Maria retreated into the walk-in closet.

"Why were they even still in your closet? Good-will? The trash?" Ava said as Maria exited the closet wearing a very red, very slinky dress open almost to the navel with a back that was missing. Her cousins studied the dress and shrugged. "Hmmm, maybe. You will get attention," Ava finally said.

"I did when I wore it," Bambi giggled. Maria shot her a look. "Uh, I borrowed it. What? It still had the tags on it. You were never going to wear it. Why'd you buy it?"

"I was talked into it by an aggressive sales lady at that store on Walnut Street that you like." The woman had craftily played on Maria's combined self-doubt and poise and convinced her that she could pull it off. "It was for that Atlantic City trip. The one I had to miss because of work." Bambi scrunched up her mouth and nodded. "I left it in the closet for a someday. Clearly, someday never came."

The one and only time she met Ava and Bambi at the casinos she was stunned by the sight of elderly people sucking on cigarettes and feeding coins into the slot machines. The scene was about as far away from the crowds depicted in the glamorous ads they were familiar with. Ah, yes, the power of advertising, she thought at the time, feeling somewhat complicit even then in her early days as a young professional knowing she was partially responsible for manipulating reality. She was glad she hadn't bothered with that dress.

Maria headed deeper into the closet pushing rows of clothing out of the way until she found a vintage Bonwit Teller Department Store garment bag. The grey flannel fabric looked aged, but still elegant. She gently lifted the hanger off the rack, walked out of the closet, and gently placed the bag on the bed.

Bambi gasped.

"Wow," Ava chirped, "Is it...?"

Bambi and Maria nodded as Ava's eyes opened wide.

"It is," Maria whispered.

Maria applied some of Cee-Cee's best-selling Retro Red lipstick, smoothed her hair with a flat iron, leaned into the mirror, and brushed a bit of powder onto her cheeks. She entered the bedroom from her tiny bathroom and stood next to the bed in front of Ava and Bambi. They stared at her wide-eyed and speechless.

"What?" Maria asked, not sure if their silence was a good or bad sign. Her cousins were never without a comment or three, or four.

Maria pivoted to face the full-length mirror. The flat iron had calmed and straightened her frizzy hair into waves of layered curls. And, the dress—the dress was beautiful. The stunning vintage gown fit her perfectly, hugging all of the right places. The satin top had aged to a color somewhere between royal and ice blue and the scalloped neckline and off the shoulder sleeves showed enough, but not too much of her décolletage. The fitted waist was dotted with subtle beading that shimmered in the light. Yards and yards of layered blue tulle and lace made up the tea-length skirt.

Bambi handed her a sparkling crystal necklace. Ava handed her a pair of strappy stilettos covered with tiny silver and gold seed beads. She put them on, faced the mirror again, and couldn't believe the reflection staring back at her. She felt like she was channeling Grace Kelly or Audrey Hepburn.

"Wow," Ava said. "Now that would've made Nonna Mary really proud, Ri."

Maria smiled at the thought of their beloved firecracker of a grandmother being pleased that one of them would wear her treasured dress.

"Wait," Bambi added as she tossed a mini hair spray bottle and disposable toothbrushes into an evening bag and handed it to her. "You never know." Maria touched up her lipstick and put the tube and her phone into the bag. "Good. Now, let's roll," Bambi ordered.

They tiptoed down the stairs, peeking through the banister at Antonetta and Sylvia. Sylvia was pacing with a phone to her ear and chewing on a fingernail as Antonetta followed two steps behind. "Okay. Uh-huh. Yes, Officer. I understand. Right. Forty-eight hours." Maria's mother, in true Antonetta Vigliano form, blessed herself like she did whenever she was worried or didn't want to jinx anyone. "I'll tell her. Yes. Thank you," Sylvia said, as she hung up and turned toward her sister. Antonetta burst into tears as the grandfather clock chimed ominously in the background.

"Oh my God, it's ten o'clock. She's dead. I know it. She should have been here by now. Lyndon said she should have been on the train by seven. It doesn't take three hours. An hour tops. She takes the Acela. Always the Acela. An hour, that's all," Antonetta said as she covered her face with her hands and sunk into a chair.

Bambi and Ava's quietly giggled.

Sylvia turned her head slightly and spotted them. She squinted, but didn't react to the women kneeling on the steps, peeking through the banister like little children.

They were busted.

Antonetta dropped her hands and looked up at her sister. Sylvia's eyes opened wide and darted left toward the steps. Antonetta followed her sister's gaze, and shrieked, "Oh my god. Thank you, Lord. She's alive. My baby. She's alive. It's a New Year's miracle." She flew across the room and up the steps, grabbed Maria, and squeezed her tight. "Don't ever do that to me again."

"Mom."

"I thought we lost you."

"Mom."

"My hair is totally white under this Miss Clairol number 5. Maria, what the hell?"

"Mom. I can't…"

"What?"

"Breathe, Mom. I can't breathe," she said.

Antonetta abruptly let go of her and said,

"Breathe. Okay. Good. Breathe. C'mon. Breathe. That's it, baby. Breathe. You breathing?" Maria nodded. "Yes? Good. Cuz now, I'm gonna kill you. Where've you been? I was beside myself. When did you get here?"

"Uh, just a couple of minutes ago."

"Just a couple of minutes ago? A couple of minutes. I'm dying here and she's upstairs, a couple minutes."

Sylvia interrupted, "Antonetta. The important thing is that she's all right." She shot a look at Maria and asked, "You're all right, right?"

"She's fine. We're taking her to the party. To the ball," Ava interrupted.

Antonetta spun toward Ava and demanded, "What? Where?"

"The First Night celebration at the Broad Street Ballroom," Bambi blurted.

"Because everyone who's anyone is going to be there. Give her a break, Aunt Toni," Ava added.

"You know about this?" Antonetta fired at her sister who shrugged in response.

Most of the time Sylvia ignored her sister's over-the-top reactions and nodded, knowing a verbal reply would be ignored, learning long ago it was the easiest way to handle Antonetta. Sylvia had loosened her grip on Ava and Bambi years ago because as she had informed her sister, she couldn't control them and they had to grow up at some point. This detail seemed lost on Antonetta. Nobody knew why she acted this way with Maria and her sisters. They had hypothesized it had something to do with the one time she got separated from Nonna Mary in E.J. Korvettes Department Store. Antonetta had been playing inside of a circular clothes rack and Nonna had walked away searching for a new dress. Antonetta swore she had never felt panic like that when she realized that she was all alone and expecting she'd never see her mother again. Nonna Mary had, of course, screamed her name and she only had to run to the sound of her mother's voice.

Sylvia took a few defensive steps away from Antonetta without confirming or denying knowledge of her daughter's plans.

"We'll have her home early. By dawn at least," Ava teased.

"Dawn? What? Who stays out 'til dawn? What kind of girl stays out 'til dawn?" Antonetta demanded.

Ava and Bambi groaned. "She'll be back in plenty of time to re-glue feathers, sew sequins, even spray paint those gold shoes. No worries," Bambi promised.

"Geez, Aunt Toni. She's not a kid," Ava said.

"Mom. Really?"

"Let her go. She's fine. She's safe. Maybe she'll meet someone. You never know," Sylvia said.

"Mom. Stop. I'm an adult," Maria said. "And, by the way, how did you get Lyndon's number?"

Antonetta shook her head, threw her hands in the air, ignored the question said, "It's not bad enough your sisters went to that place on Chestnut. What's it called? Lucky Strike?"

"They're bowling, Antonetta. Bowling. Do I have to remind you what we got away with?"

Antonetta shot her sister a look that said *really?* and said, "Shhhh. I'm really getting too old for this."

Maria opened her mouth, readying for a fight as her cousins grabbed her arms, tossed her a Pashmina wrap, and pushed her towards the door.

"Ri. You look nice. Nonna would have been pleased," Antonetta conceded as they quickly moved outside.

Ava hit the street first, waved, and whistled for a taxi. They linked arms, exchanged glances and giggled as a car slid up and they got in. "Center City. The Ballroom on Broad. Hurry," Ava ordered. Bambi slammed the door. The driver looked in the rearview, scowled, and drove past groups of partiers and skidded around the corner onto Broad Street. "Is this as fast as you can go?" Ava asked.

Maria glanced at the clock on the dash. It read 10:10. The driver floored the gas pedal and the cab streaked forward for about half of a block until they heard a loud thump, thump, thump.

Maria turned, looked out of the window and asked, "What's that noise?"

"Do we have a flat?" Bambi shrieked.

"Oh. My. God. We have a flat," Ava said.

"Oh, come on. A flat tire? Really?" Bambi said.

"Of course, we have a flat. I'm batting a thousand today. Why would I ever think that this or anything would work out? It's a sign. The universe is telling me that I should just go to the clubhouse right now and plug in the glue guns." *What was I trying to do? Have fun? Me? My original plan of non-stop rom-coms back in my apartment was looking better and better.* "I should have stood stayed in New York."

The driver stomped on the brakes and the car screeched to a stop in the center of Broad Street. He mumbled something, popped the trunk open, and got out. The women followed and stood near the curb shuffling their feet and shivering. The driver slammed the car door hard, stomped to the back of the car, and cursed in a language that Maria couldn't place as Ava adjusted the girls and Bambi tugged at her thong.

Maria wrapped her Pashmina tighter and looked up and down Broad Street for another cab.

There wasn't another car in sight.

Chapter 10

Maybe Joey had texted, Tweeted, or Facebook messaged, but Hunter was genuinely surprised that by his second beer the subdued house went from a rock star wannabe battle with Phillies background noise to a full wall-to-wall blowout. Hunter wasn't ever sure how Joey had ever managed it. This party looked exactly like the kind he had perfected in their undergraduate days. Joey and Hunter stood off to one side taking it all in. "Man. It's like old times," Joey said and nodded.

A young guy blasted by them and ran out of the door screaming, "Happy New Year!"

"Some things never change," Hunter said.

"I'm really glad you made it, dude. It's been too long," Joey said as he smacked Hunter's back.

A shirtless Goose, dressed in only a large diaper fashioned out of what looked like a white blanket pinned at his hips, slid down the banister and landed feet first on the floor. He ran toward them with a young woman in pursuit, his head bobbing back and forth like the bird he was knick-named for. "Woo-hoo! This year is going to rock. I am telling you boys now, that it is going to be sweet. Sweeeet. I can feel it," he screeched and winked as he ran past with the girl trailing after him. "Best year ever!" he added as he turned back to them.

Joey glanced at his Patek Phillippe watch, announced, "Ten. Ten," and pulled a stack of tickets out of his breast pocket and fanned them for affect. "It's getting late. We should get going," he said to Hunter and then yelled, "ELMO. Frankie. GOOOOOOOSE. Now. Gentlemen, It's time. We are out-a-here."

Goose stopped dead in his tracks, the woman laid a long, wet, sloppy kiss on him, and said, "Happy New Year, Baby." Goose grabbed a tuxedo jacket and a top hat off of the floor, put them on, and yelled, "Let's go," as the woman mouthed, "*I Love You*."

Elmo, Frankie, Joey, and Hunter watched Goose slip flip-flops onto his bare feet. "You want to rethink the shoes, dude?" Hunter asked.

"Some things should never change," Joey said.

"And they never do," Frankie said. They had stopped arguing with Goose years ago. They knew better. He grew up near Lake George, New York. Philly weather, even in December, felt like springtime to him. They shook their heads in unison.

Goose looked down at his feet, shrugged, and said, "What? I'm cool, man. What's a little frostbite? You southern boys are such babies."

Joey motioned to the door and the group charged out of the house, down the steps to the street where a teenage boy leaned against the side of a car. Joey patted him on the back, looped the car once, inspecting, and then handed him a fifty-dollar bill.

"Fine job, my man. Fine job," Joey said.

"Any time, Joe," the kid shot back.

"That's Mister Mariano to you," Joey said as the kid skipped off. Joey held up a key and hit a remote. Headlights flashed on. A convertible top popped up, slid back, and off.

The four men just stood there and stared at Joey's gleaming silver and blue Rolls Royce.

"Holy crap," Elmo said.

Frankie whistled, and said, "Noooooooo. C'mon! A Phantom?"

"Whoa, dude, game design must pay well," Goose said between laughs.

Hunter could only stand there taking it all in, shaking his head. "Really?" was about all he could manage to say.

"You gotta believe," Joey said and shrugged.

Joey had announced during their freshman year that he was going to own a Rolls one day. He had repeated it many times over the years always adding, *You gotta believe, Hunter. You got to believe*, mimicking the beloved Phillies pitcher, Tug McGraw, who had coined the phrase decades earlier as a New York Met. It was the one phrase Joey remembered his father saying to him before he died, telling him that his grandfather had said it over and over during that 1973 baseball season making it *the family* mantra. It had become Joey's personal mantra repeated incessantly to all of them. They had teased him mercilessly about it for four years trying to get him to stop. Hunter had mostly tuned him out during those years. Clearly,

Joey *had* believed and they were the ones that hadn't taken him seriously.

Joey popped open the trunk, motioned for Hunter to throw his stuff in, opened the door on the passenger side, and said, "Get in."

They all followed Joe's directions and got into the car. Joey hopped into the driver's seat, started the engine and drove toward Market Street and City Hall.

Elmo found several bottles of champagne Joey had stashed in the back seat and popped one open and passed it around. Goose hung over the side of the car and yelled at passersby, "Can I borrow some Grey, freakin', Poupon? Anyone? C'mon. All I want is some DI-freak-in-JON mustard. We've earned it." Elmo pulled Goose back into the car as they passed a Philly police cruiser. "Okay, dude, okay. He's earned it," Goose said.

Hunter shook his head as his father's *have you given any thought to your next steps* ran through his mind. He didn't need to get stopped, arrested, or fined for an open container or silly antics only to have it pop up to haunt at an undetermined later date, and used as ammo by his father in one of his judgmental critiques.

Goose was oblivious and added, "What? I just saw it on freakin' YouTube. This rich guy in this bad-ass Rolls wants to borrow..." Hunter chuckled as Goose continued, "Hey, who knew Joey got like, Royal. Is anyone else hungry?"

"Dude," Joey said and pointed at a Philly Soft Pretzel box loaded with piles of soft pretzels and bottles of yellow mustard between him and Hunter.

"Sweet. Where'd they come from?" Goose asked as he grabbed a pretzel. "Pass me the Grey Poupon, please."

Frankie took a bottle of mustard and squirted the bright yellow goo at Goose's face and said, "Yo, Goose. Let it go. It's yellow or nothing. Where are you from, anyway?"

"Upstate, why?" Goose answered oblivious as everyone cracked up. "What?" he said as he looked at Hunter and Frankie.

"Never mind, dude. Just respect the car, man. Joey played a lot of Grand Theft Auto to be proficient enough to write code and design those games that waste so many young minds," Hunter said as he grabbed the mustard away from Frankie.

"Ha, wasted young minds," Goose laughed. "Been there. Done that."

Hunter and Joey exchanged looks. Joey glanced in the rearview mirror at the group and grinned wide at them, his reunion successfully begun.

Chapter 11

If she said it once, she said it a thousand times. "Think ahead, Maria, think ahead. Be prepared. Be prepared."

This was an important part of Antonetta's life motto. Maria knew she stole this one right from the Girl Scouts who were not only expected to be prepared, but were also expected to know how to do a job, even in an emergency.

She didn't think ahead, not for this. She couldn't. This wasn't her plan. She wasn't prepared. She hadn't prepped for any of this, especially not this emergency. She thought she wouldn't even have ever been in this emergency situation if she had just stayed in New York like she wanted. And furthermore, even if she was driving, she was sure that her plan would have been to call Triple-A. Because, isn't that what people who owned cars did?

Maria groaned, inhaled deeply, and shivered as she watched their frustrated cabbie struggle to change the flat tire. Ava paced next to her as Bambi stared at the back of the guy's head. Maria sensed that she was moments away from taking the tire iron out of his hands and either whacking him with it or changing the tire herself, an act she had perfected in auto shop at St. Anthony's High School. Bambi had bested every guy in the class for the fastest time and was voted by the class to be: *The Girl Most Likely to Own a Garage.* The yearbook photo of her dressed in overalls and slapping a tire iron in her hand was a little Mafioso-like and a St. Tony's classic. It was also hot. Every guy in the school wanted to date her and every girl knew not to mess with "The Bam." Bambi knew when to use this talent to her advantage.

Maria was surprised she was showing this much restraint in the moment. Maybe it was the dress. Maybe it was the night.

The cabbie loosened the last lug nut, yanked the tire off of the car and dumped it on the pavement. He muttered something again that Maria couldn't make out as he popped the trunk, opened the spare tire well, and yelled, "Damn."

This they understood.

Bambi looked into the trunk, spun toward the man, and said through gritted teeth, "You aren't serious. No spare?"

Ava and Maria leaned in to look for themselves as if they could have missed the wheel.

"This is ridiculous. Aren't there any other cabs?" Ava asked.

"Can you call your dispatcher?" Maria added.

The guy shook his head and said, "Even if I did, everyone's down by the river. For fireworks. There's nothing happening down here. Nothing."

"Oh, you can say that again," Ava said and stamped her feet.

"We are so late. We're not going to get there in time," Bambi added.

"In time for what?" Maria asked.

"Midnight," Bambi screeched. "Did you forget? What is the point of getting to the ball after midnight, Cinderella?" she added with a groan tacked on.

"I haven't forgotten," Maria whispered. As soon as she had heard the words, Maria remembered not only the where and why, but also the importance of their destination. Somehow, she felt responsible.

Her woo-hoo cousins lived for the moment—just like girls who had never worried about anything, or wasted any time considering a Plan-B. Maria, on the other hand, had a bucket list crafted as a twelve-year-old with several tracks of things she could do depending on various life factors, all planned and schemed by her. She felt somewhat triumphant because she had at least checked off "Move out of Parents' House" and "Start a Career." They, up until this point, had perfected their go-with-the-flow approach to life, until tonight. This current blip was just not something they would have ever considered, so Maria was very sure that no contingency was in place or even considered.

"Can't we call a car service? Or get an Uber?" Maria asked. As their giggling subsided, she added, "Lyft?"

"Oh my god, Ri. We are not paying surge prices," Ava barked.

"Whoa. Where do you think you are?" Bambi teased as she and Ava lost it again.

Ava, true to her go-with-the-flow form, stuck out her thumb and looked for a passing car, any passing car. Maria smacked her hand. "You have lived with your mother for too long. What do you want us to do, walk?" Ava fired at her.

Unable to come up with a better answer, Maria did just that. She started walking. Ava and Bambi soon followed close behind.

They walked a block or so north until Bambi stopped and whined, "My feet hurt."

Ava didn't miss a beat, "Well, these stilettos were made for other things. NONE of which include walking twenty blocks in them." Maria ignored them and kept going knowing that like toddlers, if ignored long enough, they would soon follow, which they did, taking teensy steps at a time.

"It's not far," Maria said pointing to the Billy Penn Statue on top of City Hall, "Look, Willie's getting closer."

"You have been away a long time," Ava teased. "It's too far."

"No Willie is going to get close to any of us at this point tonight," Bambi grumbled.

They put their heads down and focused on trudging up Broad Street. They had advanced about a block or two and were huddled together on the corner catching their breath for a moment when a car full of screaming, celebrating teenagers blew by shooting strands of fluorescent Silly String in their direction.

Maria jumped behind a car and looked down at her beautiful dress and screamed, "Damn it. Stupid. This is vintage, you morons."

She brushed the brightly colored spaghetti-like strands of goo off of the delicate tulle dress, stamped her feet, looked around, and said, "Really? Really?"

She was home.

Ava and Bambi laughed loudly.

"She's back!" Bambi blurted out as both she and Ava lost it giggling. Doubled over and trying to catch their breath, they were close to tears as Maria stomped around spinning back and forth searching for another car and a way out of this mess.

"Oh. Oh," she said and pointed down the street at an approaching taxi. The three women jumped up and down and waved their arms frantically. The car slowed down as it approached, then sped up, and blew right past them.

"What the—" Maria asked as she spun around.

"Anyone have any idea what time it is?" Ava asked.

Maria pulled her phone out of her clutch, "Ten twenty."

Ava rolled her eyes, "Great, just great. All I wanted was to party a little. Maybe, meet some cute guy. Get lucky. And here I am with the Kardashian sisters stuck on friggin' South Broad Street freezing my butt off," she whined.

Bambi looked up and pointed, "Wait. Look."

Just ahead was a huge neon sign in the shape of a cowboy boot jutting out from the second floor of a brick building. The giant time-worn and weathered metal foot glittered and blinked at them—The Boot and Saddle Bar. Dancing. Country & Western Music.

"Oh, no. Don't even. Not again," Ava stammered as she stood up straight and dug in her stilettos.

"What could it hurt? Maybe Uncle Bruno's in there. He'll give us a ride to the party. C'mon," Bambi insisted as she bee-lined to the entrance.

Ava and Maria had no choice but to hurry to catch her as she opened the door. A cover band squealing a Sugarland song blasted from inside. They entered the dimly lit bar and stood motionless at the door taking the scene in. They entered, taking one tiny step after another. Their stilettos making tiny tick, tick, tick sounds on the worn wooden floors blending and mixing with the background twang of the sad country song.

The scent of spicy barbeque hit Maria's nose first as her eyes adjusted to the dim light. She thought back to her cold coffee, the only thing she'd eaten since breakfast, and realized she had long passed hungry hours ago.

Maria looked around at the pressed tin walls and warm wooden tables crowded with giddy people. The space was dotted with the greatest collection of western stuff found east of the Rio Grande. The stuffed jackalopes, bovine skulls, wagon wheels, lassos, and sepia-colored photographs were overwhelming. Something like Dorothy waking up in Oz, she suddenly felt like she was lost somewhere in Texas, but strangely plunked on South Broad Street, Philadelphia. To top it off, the room seemed stuck in some kind of strange Eighties time warp.

The crowd was inexplicably dressed in southwestern garb: jeans, cowboy boots, and hats. More than a few cowgirl skirts swished and swayed as couples two-stepped around the dance floor. A mechanical bull spun and bucked up and down in the background.

As Maria swallowed down the urge to yell, *Let's get out of here*, over the music a hearty, "Yeeeee-haaaa!" ripped through the air. The three women froze in their tracks. One by one they turned as if on cue to see Uncle Bruno riding the bull, hard, waving a cowboy hat side to side above his head.

The crowd chanted, "Brun-no. Bru-no. Bru-no. Bru-no." Each syllable seemed to bounce off of the tin ceiling reverberating around the room.

A handsome cowboy in tight jeans and a red v-neck tee sauntered over toward them.

"Do you remember the last time?" Ava asked. The three women shuddered. Maria grabbed their hands and pulled them close thinking that she might somehow be able to create an invisible wall of strength.

"Hey, little ladies," the cowboy said as he flashed a smile and tipped his hat.

Maria watched Bambi hesitate for a split second and then as expected, like a moth to a flame... Bambi flung her hair, licked her lips, titled her head and squinted in his direction, then topped it off by batting her eyes at him as she took a step forward.

The cowboy tipped his hat, grinned ear-to-ear,

leaned in, and whispered something in Bambi's ear. She smiled, took two steps forward toward the dance floor, hitched up her tight dress and before they knew it, she was two-stepping around the room with him. Maria tried to grab her by the arm on her first lap, but missed. On her second lap around the room with The Marlboro man, he twirled her away from them. On the third, Maria had had it. She grabbed Bambi by the arm and dragged her out of the circle as several other cowboys started to make their way in their direction.

"What?" she asked Maria.

"No. No. No, you don't," Maria said to her as she tugged on both Ava and Bambi's hands, and towed them to the door and away from the round-up oozing toward them. "Let's go," she ordered, still pulling on them until they were all safely back outside on the sidewalk, *together.*

"Okay, you two. We've come this far. I'm not going to get sidetracked at The Boot. No more go-with-the-flow. No. We have a ball to get to and we are going to get to the ball NOW," Maria ordered, determined they would all get to the ballroom together. She marched forward about a block still holding on to both of their hands, knowing that Bambi had a really soft spot for guys with southern drawls in tight jeans and could, and would, bolt in reverse at any moment.

Maria sped up, walking as fast as she could toward a subway entrance and made her way down the steps with them beside her. As they hit the bottom of the steps and made their way toward a ticket booth, she turned, thrust her hand out, and said, "Septa pass?

Tokens?"

Nothing. Nada. Ava and Bambi's faces read nothing but deer in the headlights looks.

"Credit card? Money? Who's got money?" Maria asked. Her cousins stood there shaking their heads no. "Who leaves the house without any money? You think hairspray and toothbrushes, but no cash," Maria asked as a wave of exasperation moved through her.

"Uh, who has cash? It's debit cards and Venmo only. You have any?" Bambi asked.

Touché. Maria could only shake her head, *"No"* too.

"Oh wait. I have a debit card," Ava offered.

"Great," Maria said. "Perfect. C'mon."

They click-clacked across the concrete floor to the ticket booth in the deserted station digging through their handbags as they moved. This maneuver had been perfected and performed since they were teenagers sneaking out on Friday nights. One by one, each fell in line. Maria pulled a can of pepper spray out and aimed it as if ready to fire. Bambi took off a stiletto and pointed the heel in the air. Ava whipped her head back and forth like always, checking for perps as they had always enthusiastically referred to them back then, and pulled out a taser. Maria shot her a look as if she was nuts. She thought as if this ritual of theirs wasn't wacked enough, this current new element in their arsenal somehow made this act even crazier. Maria couldn't help herself and spit out, "Really? A taser?"

"I upgraded. You have a problem with that?"

Ava yelled as she got to the machine first. "Anybody can use pepper spray. That's so last century."

"And you fit it in your clutch?"

"It's a mini. Can't be too careful, Ri," Ava deadpanned.

Maybe they did have a Plan-B. Bambi and Maria didn't miss a beat. They took their places, turned around, and assumed their *Charlie's Angels* pose they had practiced many, many times.

"Nobody gets past the wall," Bambi whispered.

"Damn," Ava squealed. She moved aside and they saw the OUT OF ORDER sign taped to the front of the machine.

"Great. A token? One token will do," Maria squealed knowing how ridiculous and desperate she sounded.

"Screw it. C'mon," Bambi said as she slipped her shoe back on, hiked up her dress, and straddled the turnstile.

"Ah, perfect timing," a portly Septa Cop yelled in their direction as he quietly strolled up behind them. He whacked his nightstick on the side of the ticket booth. No turnstile jumping for them. Nope. Not that they could have jump if they tried. He folded his arms and ordered, "Don't even, Barbie. Trains ain't running tonight. There's a sizzle on Bainbridge. It's going to be a while."

Ava mouthed, "Ouch."

They grimaced as Bambi inched off of and away from the metal barrier. She looked at them and then turned, about to speak when the Septa Cop said, matter-of-factly, "I suggest that you three find other means of transportation," as he looked them over head to toe. "Uh-huh. Transportation. Something other than the back of my Cruiser. Now, get outta' here before I have to write this up." As they inched away, he added, "And, Maria, say hello to your mother for me."

Maria nodded at him suddenly feeling like a twelve-year-old in big trouble.

The streets have eyes, her mother had always said. This city, the fifth largest in the country, was just one big small town most of the time—especially when it came to Antonetta who had always made it her business to know everyone's business.

They headed back to the stairs. "What is it with train tracks and holidays?" Maria wondered aloud as they slowly headed upstairs, dejected, their night slowly slipping away.

Broad Street was now deserted. They stood on the corner and looked around. Nothing. No cars. No people. The clock was ticking dangerously close to midnight.

"We need a plan," Bambi said and sighed. "Anyone?"

They exchanged looks, understanding they had nothing.

Maria took a step forward moving closer to Morrison Street determined to make it the last ten or so blocks to the Ballroom as a group of people exited a tiny corner storefront—The Better World Asian Mennonite Church. Her scattered thoughts were interrupted as she watched the crowd slowly line up to board several white vans.

"Ooh. Ooh. C'mon," she sputtered, not wanting to waste time to fully explain her "eureka" moment to them, or wait for a group vote. Ava and Bambi looked at Maria like she had lost it, but followed her anyway. "Excuse me, Sir. Sir?" she said to a young Asian man wearing a flat brimmed hat and dressed in a long black coat and simple black boots.

He looked her up and down and whistled slowly through his teeth.

"Sir?" she asked, trying to end the gawking.

"Oh, Mama," he said as he made a strange clicking noise with his tongue. "Baby, you're hot. So hot."

Ava opened her clutch and put a hand on the taser as Maria took half a step backwards. Maria paused and held her ground. They were desperate. She was desperate. It was getting really, really, late and she was hoping that she hadn't put this dress on for nothing. She knew she could handle this. She leaned in close, looked him in the eye, and pursed her lips. She heard Ava say, "Oh no. Here we go."

"Easy, dude. My cousins and I just need a ride," she said.

"I'll bet you do, baby. Giddyup," he said as he motioned thrusting.

Ewwwww.

An older Asian woman dressed in simple Mennonite garb and a bonnet approached. Together, they watched him pretend to grind away. The older woman stamped her foot, grabbed his arm, and shook him, shouting something in a language that Maria again did not understand. She waved her hands as if to shoo the young man away as he shuffled away. She turned and bowed her head in their direction. "So sorry," she whispered.

"I'm so confused," Ava whispered as Bambi elbowed her.

"Oh, it's okay. Happens all the time, Ma'am." Bambi said as she genuflected and then awkwardly curtsied in front of the woman, "A ride. We just need a ride. Up Broad Street. To the ballroom. We're late for a, uh, engagement. The party. Would you be so kind as to help us?"

"Sorry. No," the woman snapped.

Ava adds, "Just a little ride? Our cab broke down. We're kind of stuck."

The woman pointed across the street and said, "Subway."

"We're out of money," Ava continued.

The woman raised an eyebrow and cocked her head at them.

"And, it's not running. A sizzle," Bambi added.

The woman grimaced as a second woman, also dressed in simple clothing, approached and whispered something in the first woman's ear.

Maria, Ava, and Bambi waited motionless afraid to interrupt.

The second woman bowed, and the first woman gestured to the last van and said, "It is God's will. Please join us."

Surprised and more than a little relieved,

Maria, Ava, and Bambi exchanged glances, and tried hard not to react, afraid that the women might change her mind. Maria bowed her head. Ava and Bambi followed her lead as they joined the somber line waiting to board.

"Ri, if we wind up in a cult, I'm never forgiving you," Ava whispered.

The young guy moved into the line directly behind them and clicked his tongue at them as they got into the van.

Maria looked at her cousins who were doing their best not to burst into another round of giggles and tried to justify this situation to herself. *I'd never, ever do this, but desperate times... It's really only a few blocks, okay, well, maybe ten blocks. We can't possibly walk that far and still make it to the ball before midnight.* "This will have to do for now. Besides, do either of you have a better idea?" Maria said between gritted teeth. Maria opened her eyes wide at Bambi who snorted a laugh and shrugged.

The driver looked over his shoulder to watch as everyone buckled up. They were squeezed into seats surrounded by praying people with bowed heads, all except for the young man who sat directly behind Maria. He reached out with one finger and stroked her bare shoulder and said, "Nice."

Maria spun, a little possessed and more Exorcist-like than normal, and glared at him wide eyed, smacked his hand, and ordered, "Praaaaaaaay." The man jumped back, bowed his head for a split second, then looked up at her and grinned. Maria spit out,

"Don't even," as he mimicked a kiss.

Ava elbowed Bambi and whispered, "She's back."

Bambi giggled and said, "Really back." as Maria reached over and put her hand over her mouth to try to stop the laughter. Bambi only giggled louder. Ava snorted and lost it, laughing out loud while Maria bit her lip as she fought back snickers of her own.

Chapter 12

Heads turned as Joey maneuvered the car through heavy traffic around City Hall, down Broad Street and towards the Ballroom. A few gawkers pointed. A homeless man on the corner of Walnut Street applauded before he threw something in the direction of the car. "Ah, yes, The City of Brotherly Love. We're home, boys, home," Joey said, and beamed.

A city with a reputation as a tough, but fiercely loyal town, Philadelphians could be counted on to express their unsolicited opinions freely, loudly and often, to anyone and everyone, Hunter thought fondly. This was the place he had some of the best times of his life and made these friends. He missed this, all of this.

Goose waved at people, pointed at Joe, and yelled, "He's the man. The man. I'm telling you. *THE* man." More than a few gestures were thrown in their direction as they traveled. Joey remained calm as he drove, enjoying the attention. Like a parade's Grand Marshall, he smiled, nodded, and waved at the crowd as they took in the car. Elmo, Frankie, and Hunter could only laugh and shake their heads as Joey ate it all up, the good and the bad.

Minus the very expensive ride, this felt a lot like old times to Hunter. He hadn't done anything fun or this close to frivolous in what felt like a very, very long time.

Hunter knew that his father wasn't the only critic to worry about. It felt odd not to be looking over his shoulder worrying about who might see him, or report something off the record to the Senator, and cost him his job. In Washington, he was always on guard and hyper aware of his perceived public image as was most everyone else. Folks seemed to have a carefully crafted agenda and public persona, something he too had quickly opted in on. He was cautious about putting himself in situations that might be interpreted as unsavory or worse yet, could be saved for a time down the road and dredged up to be used against him later. He had witnessed more than a few political careers combust with an oppo-dump.

Cruising around town in a Rolls convertible would not have been on his D.C. to-do list. There were too many chances of a photo winding up on Facebook or used as a meme, or becoming a video on YouTube, or finding its way to his father and Hunter having to justify his behavior. Hunter glanced at Joey who looked back at him, nodded in silent agreement, and offered a palm in the air. Hunter raised his hand and they high-fived as paparazzi snapped photos of the car.

This time Hunter wasn't concerned. His was just a face in the crowd here, not recognizable in

Philadelphia. He didn't want to give a single thought to any of the potential ramifications of Joey's plan or how it might affect him or his future, if and when, at a later date his destiny might include someone doing a deep dive to curate, and catalog his every life move to use against him. Hunter stared at the excited crowd and felt secure in the fact that he didn't matter to anyone here. Nobody knew him here or cared about tagging his face to cash in on a photo-op. And, he had earned this night. He hadn't had any time off in months.

They were stopped on Broad Street in a long line of cars waiting to park at the Ballroom. Goose jumped out and in his usual buoyant and lighthearted way shooed people away from the car, with a smooth, "Duuude. Please. Look, but don't touch the ride." An occasional, "Pretty? Huh, pretty?" was thrown at a passing woman or two. Goose followed the predictable rejections with a "Call me? Maybe?" as they hurried away.

After what seemed like hours, Joey finally made the turn into the circular driveway and inched along amongst the parade of other expensive cars toward the valets. Hunter glanced at his watch; it was already almost 11:00.

A crush of people waited in the long line in front of the grand building. Couples paused for event photographers, posing as if it was a red-carpet event as they moved along. Hunter watched groups of pretty people eager to be seen, surveying the crowd looking as if ready to trade up to the prettier and more connected people. Groups of singles preened, flirted, and looked for other availables. Hunter took it all in as more than a few men and women, with desperation streaked across their faces scanned the crowd. Social climbing wannabes always oozed anxiety as they tried to catch the attention of a more connected person to glom onto. This crowd was quickly approaching D.C. levels of six-degrees, but without the politics.

Joey closed the convertible top and tossed the key to a valet as he got out of the car. "Can you keep it out front for me?" Joey asked as he slipped the man some cash. The man nodded and handed Joey a ticket. Hunter, Elmo, and Frankie hopped out of the car. The group stood together in a line, shoulder to shoulder. Joey slapped Hunter on the back as they both took in the frenzy and the grandeur and said, "Wow. This is something, huh?"

"Yup. It's something all right, Joe," Hunter said and chuckled.

Elmo motioned with his hands to the group and yelled," C'mon!"

They had frequented many events near the Art Museum on the Parkway and on the waterfront as undergrads, but this was different. Hunter wondered if it was just his perspective a few years removed. They moved into the waiting line and looked up at the winding staircase and the massive multi-columned limestone building decked out for the night's festivities. Glittering white lights wrapped the entrance, the columns, the trees, and most surfaces, making them sparkle. This was a party.

Several horse-drawn carriages were parked at the curb opposite the line of luxury cars, the horses hanging their heads, occasionally stamping a hoof impatiently as another carriage drove up and parked. A driver dressed in formal tails and a top hat assisted a young couple as they exited the buggy and headed to the steps. A paparazzo snapped photos of them and then trained the camera at the other guests as they exited Mercedes, Audis, BMWs, and Jaguars and hurried to join the line that snaked behind red velvet ropes to the party.

The party staff worked the excited crowd snapping, "Here you go," as they handed out masks and New Year's Hats. Local reporters stationed at the curb fishing for interviews were treated like celebrities. Eager people posed for selfies and offered enthusiastic sound bites for the evening's broadcast.

Hunter watched as numerous guys blew past, photobombed the news crew, interrupting and yelling, "HAPPY NEW YEAR," as they mugged for the cameras. The unfazed reporters shoved microphones in faces and asked, "What are your resolutions for the new year?"

One after another, people fired back...

"Exercise more."

"Lose weight."

"Travel more."

"Anyone want to eat?" Goose asked and pointed across the street, "There's a Mickey D's. I could go for a Big Mac."

Joey yanked on Goose's tuxedo lapels and said, "Focus, dude. Focus." This was Joe's night, Joe's plan. His posse was finally together once again, and McDonalds was not on the itinerary...yet.

"Focusing," Goose said, trying hard to pay attention to the surroundings as Joey and Hunter pointed him toward the line. One of the event girls handed Goose a mask. He looked it over; put it on, grinned wide, and leaned in close. The girl smiled politely and moved away.

A white van labeled "The Better World Asian Mennonite Church" pulled up to the end of the Ballroom driveway looking very out of place amongst the upscale rides of most of the attendees. Hunter spotted the vehicle out of the corner of his eye. His head swerved. In his D.C.-always aware mind he bookmarked it *unusual* as something shot through him, causing him to mentally catalogue the info, just in case. Call it instinct, but he knew that these days at an event this large a detail might need to be remembered.

Hunter vaulted the make, model, and color of the van in his mind as he watched a man hop out. Dressed in a long black overcoat and a wide brimmed black hat the out-of-place man looked up at the glitter and excess, opened the vehicle's side door quickly and stood aside as two elegantly dressed young women pushed their way out and landed awkwardly on the curb. One adjusted the top of her dress, pushed up her breasts as the other one pulled at her backside wiggling as she tugged. Hunter breathed a sigh of relief, and smiled.

Joey turned toward the activity, nudged Hunter and said, C'mon, dude. Let's go."

As the group inched forward, Hunter glanced back to see another stunning woman, exquisitely dressed, poke her head out of the van and size up the situation. A man reached for her hand and helped her out and onto the sidewalk. She let go of his hand and smoothed out the skirt of her dress and glanced around at the crowd.

Chapter 13

"Gratitude, Maria! It helps to pay attention to the things in your life that you're grateful for instead of focusing on only the negative. It multiplies the good stuff. You'll see."

Antonetta was the reigning Law of Attraction Maven of Dickinson Street even though Maria was sure she didn't really have a single clue about manifestation, intentional creation, or using her powers to attract anything. "Pfffttt," was all Maria ever heard from her mother in response to her early vision boards.

The Ballroom was only ten blocks away. Granted their feet wouldn't have held up in their stilettos and Maria was grateful for the lift, but the ride, with their odd stalker and his quiet gaggle of saintly praying congregants was one for the books.

This wasn't Johnny.

This wasn't a town car.

This was a church van.

And, this was weird.

The driver had driven very slowly, hunched over the steering wheel, hands gripping at ten and two, eyes staring straight ahead as if he was afraid to move along Broad Street. Maria thought this bizarre even for her, even with her large and odd collection of extremely awkward life experiences forever burned into her memory. She glanced over her shoulder at the mix of people and tried not to let her imagination loose wondering which of her negative thoughts had diverted this experience to her, putting this night squarely into the very peculiar territory.

The bowed heads in the van prayed inaudibly for the entire ride, whispering and mouthing prayers —all except Maria's biggest fan. He just stared—first at Bambi's boobs and then he gawked at Ava who couldn't help herself and encouraged him by blowing him a kiss. Finally, he locked eyes with Maria, clicked his tongue, and drooled as he ogled her.

Maria felt herself gag and forced a swallow. She turned away, leaned into Bambi, and tried to count blocks as they crept along. She inched back in the seat, but his hot breath on her back made her skin crawl.

She tried to direct her thoughts away by re-viewing the evening and her unusual encounters. The first in Buddakan with the slick Mr. Too-white-teeth Old Guy, the second her slamming into the Princely Dude in the train station, third, the cowboy on Broad Street, and now this. She added this guy to her mental diary, sighed, and decided that this might qualify for an all-time record for the most strange and disturbing but memorable encounters to happen to her in one evening. Even though this was not normal for most people, Maria chalked it up to just another night.

Maybe my mother was right to worry.

Counting blocks was no longer a distraction. Maria imagined ranking her life events in cringe worthiness order as she wiggled forward in the seat trying again to put distance between her and the guy, but the very crowded van made it impossible. She closed her eyes and tried to concentrate on meditation basics. She focused on her breath and being in the moment, but the only thing she could hear was others sniffling and coughing.

Maria squirmed. *I've got to get out of here.*

Ava leaned across Bambi and whispered, "We're almost there," as she grinned and then sat back, pulled out a lipstick, reapplied, and then turned to Bambi and said, "How's my hair?"

"Oh my god. You're fine," Bambi fired back.

The van finally stopped. Maria was thrilled to see the once elegant but neglected building had been restored to its former glory and was given a second life as a grand event space. Decked out for the festivities, the limestone building looked almost magical. With the glitz, the expensive line-up of vehicles, and the very fancy crowd, it now looked as if this was *the* place to be in the city.

Bambi and Ava squealed.

"Oh, look, Ri," Ava said as she nudged Maria.

Their driver muttered something, slammed the emergency brake to the floor, hopped out, and slid open the door. Bambi and Ava spilled out together, hand in hand. Maria pushed her way out and followed. Her suitor trailed after her, reached out and again slid his finger across her shoulder. She had had enough. She twirled, smacked his hand and said, "Ewwwww. Gross. Stop. Never happening. Ever. Go away."

"He's praying, Ri," Ava said as Maria pushed his hand away.

"Yeah? Praying that I'll let him live tonight," Maria barked as she leaned in, and nose to nose, continued, "What? Did you miss out on your Rumspringa? News flash. Cancun. Spring Break. Get wild. Go for it. Get out now, while you still can, little man. Live a little. Run. Run. Run. Go. Now."

Bambi winced and whispered, "Little harsh, Ri."

"Go," she added as she waved him away, and added just in case he missed it, "Go on."

"You tell him, Ri," Ava added. Her cousins, the yin-yang twins, had spoken.

Maria fumed.

One of the older women grabbed the man by the arm and escorted him away. She shooed him along as they moved, pushed him back inside of the van, hopping in after him and sliding the door shut. He leaned in to the window, doe-eyed and palmed the glass. Maria watched as a tear rolled down his cheek and he mouthed, "*I love you.*" She cringed as he pressed his lips against the window as the van made a sharp U-turn and drove off.

The three of them stood frozen for a second or two, taking a moment to shake off the ride and to absorb the crowded spectacle. Maria wrapped the Pashmina around her shoulders. Bambi stood up straight.

Ava said, "Wow," and took a step forward as Bambi and Maria followed. "Oh my god, it's gorgeous," Ava added. They moved ahead and joined the mass of bodies snaking to the entrance.

"C'mon," Ava grabbed Maria's hand and pushed through the crowd toward the top of the steps. They got stuck mid-way up the grand staircase mashed in the middle of the mob. A group of guys stood shoulder to shoulder a few feet in front of them creating an impassable wall of testosterone. All but one was dressed in tuxedos. The odd one wore a top hat and tails and a large cloth diaper, clearly, in the spirit of the night and ready for the festivities.

Amused, Maria giggled and watched him bounce from one person to another saying, "Happy New Year, to you and you and you." He seemed to repel most of the women as he went and the men shrugged or pushed him away. Maria wished she possessed an ounce of his abandon.

The crowd seemed frozen in place, inching forward slowly. A loud, "Dude! You made it," rang through the din of background noise. A large burly barrel-chested man wove his way through the mob, pushing people out of the way as he approached the group of men. He slapped one of them hard on the back, wrapped his arms around the man lifting him off his feet while yelling, "H! Good to see you, buddy. Long time, huh?" He laughed loudly as he lifted the guy up and down until a stunning woman inserted herself into the mix.

"Ingram," she said. "What are you doing? Put

the man down." She extended her hand to the other man and said, "Sorry. I'm Barbara."

The one on the end shook her hand and said, "My pleasure, Barbara."

Maria tilted her head to one side as she eavesdropped. The voice sounded strangely familiar as she stared at the back of his head.

Ava fidgeted and jumped trying to see over heads to judge the length of the line. She wedged herself between an older couple and the velvet ropes and was inching her way forward, motioning to Bambi and Maria to come along. They followed, inch by inch, squeezing between bodies, fielding cold stares.

An older woman barked, "Hey, where you think you're going?"

"Watch it," was heard as until they pushed their way through and made it beyond the group of men and up several steps.

Someone blurted, "C'mon, this really sucks. We're out of here," as a group of young men pushing the opposite way knocked into Maria. She wobbled at first, then grabbed onto something, someone. It was too late; her stiletto rocked on the edge of the step and she felt herself fall backwards. She closed her eyes, sucked in a breath, bracing herself for the inevitable, until…she landed softly.

Her eyes were still squinched shut when she heard, "You really have to start watching where you're going." She opened her eyes and saw—his face.

Oh. My. God.

"Me?"

He smiled and said, "Yeah, you," as he righted her. "Are you okay?"

She glanced at his tuxedo shirt still covered with newsprint smears and cringed. She felt her face flush warm and all she could manage to say was, "I'm sorry." *How could this possibly happen? I wasn't ever supposed to see him again. Oh. My. God.*

"You say that a lot," he said and smiled a crooked grin.

She opened her mouth and once again could not make audible sounds come out.

He was still holding onto her arms as Ava bolted over and grabbed her hand, "What are you waiting for? Would you please come on? We are going to miss the whole thing." Maria glanced over her shoulder at him as Ava dragged her away, through the crowd, up the last few steps toward the entrance.

"Who's that?" Joey asked as he watched Hunter let go of the girl being whisked away by her friends and into the party.

"Missed opportunity, my man, missed opportunity. As usual. Let's go," Hunter said as they inched inside.

"Seriously, Hunter? She was a babe."

"True that, Joe. True that."

"What were you thinking?" Joe said and then added, "I wouldn't have let that one go. Better luck, next time."

Hunter laughed, knowing this was very true; Joey wouldn't have let her go. He shoved Hunter forward and said, "C'mon, man. Let's go. Time is running out."

Ava yelled, "Nikki!" and dragged Maria to an entrance where her BFF, Nicole, was stationed wearing an EVENT STAFF tee-shirt and a rhinestone tiara. Bambi was impatiently waiting at her side.

Nicole slipped event bands on their wrists, "Hurry up before my supervisor sees you. Go on. It's 11:45. You sure are cutting it close."

Ava started to explain, "Our cab got a flat..."

Nicole opened her eyes wide, looked around, and ordered, "Go, already. Tell me later before I'm busted," and then added, "Happy New Year, Bitches."

They bolted inside and merged with the crowd inching toward the bar. Ava yelled over the noise, "Who was that guy, Ri? Did you know him?"

"Never mind," Maria snapped.

"Well, he was checking you out, Ri. Big time."

"No, he wasn't," she insisted.

"Ah, yes, he definitely was," Bambi added. "Did you get his name? He's hot."

"No. I didn't get a name. How was I going to get a name?" The last thing she was going to tell them was that this was the second time in one night she hadn't gotten his name. She'd never admit to them that this handsome guy with the kind face had caught her at her typical clumsy worst—twice. She sighed. *Who gets a re-do on a meet-cute? Was fate playing games with her?*

Before she could think it through further, Ava interrupted, "You should have gotten his name so you could at least Google him later."

Maria shook her head, no.

"Okay, okay, only if you wanted to, Ri. Geez," Ava chided impatiently.

Ava and Bambi both rolled their eyes at her as they budged their way through the mass of people at the bar. Ava waved at a bartender and drinks appeared. Ava turned and handed Maria a glass, "Vodka soda. You should maybe switch that up once in a while, Ri."

Maria narrowed her eyes and took a gulp of the drink.

Ava handed Bambi a martini that she quickly downed and quickly motioned for another one. Ava knocked back a shot of Jack Daniels, hoisted a beer bottle into the air, and shimmied into the crowd checking out the availables and yelling, "Come on, you two. We have to dance the rest of this year away. We don't have much time. What are you waiting for? Woooooo! It's almost midnight."

Bambi shrugged at Maria and pushed her way into the crowd following Ava.

Chapter 14

The excited party crowd looked to be a mash up of happy revelers and eager hook-ups. Hunter took it all in and watched as Joey bee-lined to a group of women and, as expected, within minutes was passing out drinks and putting names and info into his iPhone. Goose, Elmo. and Frankie had disappeared, sucked into the party vortex, he was sure. Hunter inched to the bar and raised a hand trying hard to get the bartender's attention as he served a glass of champagne to the woman in front of him. The dude was pouring and mixing drinks and hitting on her, ignoring Hunter. As the song ended, the mass of people on the dance floor oozed in his direction. The wave of bodies pushed him into the barstool in front of him. The seated woman jolted forward, her glass tipped, and champagne spilled onto the bar.

She spun around to face him.

Stunned, he said, "I don't think we've been properly introduced," as he grabbed two champagne flutes off of a passing waiter's tray. He handed one to the woman and said, "Hunter Reed."

"Hunter, we really have to stop meeting like this," she laughed, nodded her head, and added,

"Maria."

"Well, it's a pleasure to *officially* meet you, Maria. Finally."

She raised an eyebrow and tilted her head, "Hunter. Yes. Finally."

An Event Staff girl rushed over to the bar, her hands full of hats, glow-in-the-dark necklaces, and noisemakers. She plunked a glittery top hat on Hunter's head and handed Maria a rhinestone tiara motioning to her to put it on. As she moved down the line of people hugging the bar, she screamed, "Five minutes. Five minutes everyone. Five freaking minutes. Get your party on. Now. Woooo-oooo! Let's put this year out of its misery. C'mon, people."

Hunter looked at the tiara, then up at Maria. Her eyes glittered. He wanted nothing more than to pull her close. He carefully slid the rhinestone crown on Maria's head and thought even wearing a fake headpiece, she was stunning. She touched the top of her head, pushed the tiara in place, and made a silly face. He lifted his glass and motioned to her. They clinked glasses and sipped. She looked at his shirt again, bit her lip, shook her head, and said, "Yeah, I'm really sorry about that. So, my fault," pointing at his dirty shirt. "Can I have it cleaned for you?"

Hunter laughed and said, "It's all right, really." He offered her his hand and asked, "Would you like to dance?" Not wanting to chance a no, he didn't wait for an answer and said, "C'mon," took her hand and steered her onto the dance floor. The vocalist crooned a slow romantic song as couples held tight and moved around the dance floor. "At least I don't have to embarrass myself with my awkward dance moves, yet." The room was swaying as he took her in his arms and they moved easily with the crowd. The moment passed by too quickly, the song wound down, and they slowed to a stop until the music shifted suddenly and the crowd started jumping. Hunter slipped an arm around Maria's waist and together they glided off of the dance floor dodging people as they moved.

The emcee's breathy voice growled into the microphone, "And now. It is time. Time to forever say goodbye to this year and all it held, good, bad or otherwise."

Midnight. The moment of the year with the potential to be magic, or that lonely, dreaded, epic fail. The moment of the year that has more than its share of angst attached to it for most people. Some say that this is the moment that sets the tone for the whole year. Hunter never bought into that, but he agreed there was a certain amount of disappointment to feel if you weren't attached.

The crowd broke into a rowdy cheer. The emcee continued, "AND say HELLO to all of the possibilities of the next. So, let's hear it. Come on. Say it with me...Come on. Ten. Nine. Eight..."

Hunter looked into Maria's eyes as the crowd counted down with the emcee.

"Seven. Six. Five."

Maria looked up at him and forced an unsure smile. They both shuffled their feet. Anticipation or anxiety? Hunter wasn't sure. He looked for a clear sign from her and felt like an idiot. Should I? Then he thought, if he hesitated, this could really suck and end right here. He floundered, as usual, weighed the pros and cons in his head as the year ticked away. He quickly concluded that he *was* an idiot.

"Four. Three. Two...Happy New Year."

All around them, couples kissed. Some singles grabbed the nearest willing partner and went for it, some tentatively, some with gusto. He paused at first, but then he leaned in. They both bobbed and weaved for a second, unsure. He pulled her close and felt her lean in as he kissed her. It was an awkward first kiss, but it was a kiss. At least she didn't pull away, he thought. As the kiss ended and he pulled away he couldn't help but notice again how adorable she looked with the silly tiara on her head.

Balloons and confetti drifted down from the ceiling and fell on them. Her face lit up as she batted a silver balloon back over the crowd and laughed. Streamers shot across the room as people cheered. It was close to pandemonium. *Auld Lang Syne* blared. People were going crazy. Hoots and hollers mixed in with the cheers and yelling. Hunter grinned wide.

Goose, still dressed in his tails and diaper, ran up hand-in-hand with Ava and slapped Hunter's back hard and screamed, "Happy New Year, dude!"

"Ri! Look what I found. Isn't he cute?" Ava blurted. Goose grinned wide and preened. "I think I'll keep him." Maria giggled as Ava looked Hunter over from head-to-toe. "Ohhhhhh, look what you found.

Good girl. Way. To. Go. Ri-Ri."

"Hunter, this is my cousin, Ava. Ava, this is Hunter."

Ava looked him over again and shot back, "Nice, Ri," as Hunter shook her hand.

Over the noise, Hunter thought he heard a cell phone buzzing. Maria heard it too and opened her evening bag. Ava shot her a look, opened her eyes wide and shook her head "*no.*" Maria closed the bag and glanced in Hunter's direction.

"Where's Bambi?" Ava asked as she scanned the crowd. "Oh, Ri, Look." Ava pointed at the stage where Bambi was dancing up a storm behind the band with Joey and Elmo. Ava grabbed Goose by the lapel and dragged him across the dance floor, screaming, "Bam. Bam! Look. Isn't he cute?" Bambi didn't miss a beat. She nodded at Ava and kept dancing with Joey.

Goose grinned a lopsided grin and puffed up his chest. He tugged on his lapels, flapped his arms like wings, and circled Ava who just stood there and giggled at his goofy act.

Bambi paid no attention to Ava. She was shimmying and dancing around Joey who just stood there, drink in hand watching. Hunter glanced around for Frankie and spotted him on stage lip-locked with one of the back-up singers. Just like old times, he thought. His friends were the life of the party. Maybe it's good that some things never change.

Hunter spotted an empty bar table and steered Maria to it. They sat. He motioned to a waitress who brought them two glasses of champagne. Maria's evening bag buzzed again. She looked agitated by the sound. He squinted at the bag and said, "It's okay. Answer it. It must be important," wondering if it was an out-of-town boyfriend, or somebody waiting to wish her a Happy New Year.

"I'm sure that it's not, important, that is," she said as she picked up the bag and stood up. "Would you excuse me for a minute? I have to find the ladies room."

As she moved away quickly, Hunter thought, yup, here we go, dumped again.

Hunter sat alone and studied the happy chaos around him. His friends were having a blast.

He downed his champagne.

Chapter 15

"Start the year with a bang, because what you do on New Year's, you'll do all year." Another one of Antonetta's ridiculous rules bounced around in Maria's head, taunting her.

I don't have to answer it. Maria was trying to convince herself she could ignore her phone when it buzzed again. Great, just great, she thought. Except for one crying girl being consoled by a small group of friends, the bathroom she had found was empty. Ha, she thought, midnight. People were moving on to more important things, she guessed. She pulled the lipstick out of her bag and tried not to glance at her phone. Of course, curiosity got the better of her and she glanced at the screen. Six missed calls from her mother. *Really?* They had been gone for less than two hours. *What now?* She stared at her tired faced reflecting back at her. The contrast of the glittering tiara and her depressed face looked pitiful. She reached for the crown, straightened it, snapped her bag shut, stood up straight, and marched back to the party.

Just outside of the restroom she spotted Ava and the diaper guy lip-locked, hands moving all over each other. Maria was sure she must have looked at Ava like she was nuts because she barked, "What? I am not letting this one go." She leaned in and whispered, "He went to Penn," then she giggled, winked and whispered, "Smart, Ri. Among other things," as she raised an eyebrow.

Maria shook her head and watched as he grabbed Ava from behind and kissed her neck.

Ava was mouthing, *Oh My God,* as Maria's purse started to buzz again. Ava stared at it, wide eyed. As Maria began to open the bag, Ava grabbed her hand and said, "Don't, Ri."

"I have to. What if something's wrong?"

"What could be wrong? We just left. And, nothing's ever wrong. Your mother's a control freak, drama queen. Let it go to voice mail. You're an adult," she scolded.

"You're right. You're right. I know you're right. Why don't I ever listen?"

"You gotta' live a little, Ri," Ava added.

"Live, baby, live," the guy said.

Maria must have been squinting at this short pear-shaped man with the unusually long neck dressed in a diaper wondering, *What the hell...* when Ava said, "Oh, Ri, this is Goose."

Maria nodded, speechless.

"Hey," he grunted toward Maria and then said to Ava, "C'mon, baby. I wanna show you the Rolls."

Ava squealed as he took her hand and led her away. She looked over her shoulder, opened her eyes wide and mouthed, "A Rolls Royce?"

Maria's purse chimed again. "Damn it." She pulled out the phone, and glanced at the screen. Her eyes opened wide and she felt a chill run through her when she saw her mother's text: *Daddy fell on ice at Lucky Strike. At Pennsylvania Hospital. Getting tests.* "Great, just great," she said as she bolted out of the ladies' room and dialed her mother. The call went straight to voice mail. She scanned the room for Bambi and Ava and found them near the bar with Goose and Hunter. She plowed her way through the stream of drunk people. She shouted "Excuse me, excuse me..." over the noise of the exiting party guests. After pushing and shoving her way across the room she made her way through the craziness to them, and said, "I've got to go."

Bambi sighed and rolled her eyes. "We. Just. Got. Here. Ri."

Ava said, "No. I am not leaving."

"Yes," Maria said as she pulled her Pashmina off of a barstool and wrapped it around her shoulders.

"I knew I should have thrown that freakin' phone of yours into the Schuylkill River," Ava said.

"What now?" Bambi asked.

Maria bit her lip as her imagined her father in the hospital, and felt tears starting to well.

"Come on. What? The girls didn't get home from bowling? She's out of flour for cookies? No more gold paint in all of Eastern P.A. again? What? What? It can't be that big a deal. Not tonight," Ava said as she stamped a stiletto. "Not tonight."

Again, Maria was at a loss for words. She opened

her mouth as Bambi took hold of one of her arms and said, "Breathe, Ri. Just breathe."

"Who died?" Ava asked.

"Nobody died," Bambi said as she shot Ava a look that said *Shut up*, and then turned back to Maria and said, "Huh, wait. Nobody died, did they? Oh, god...Ma?"

Maria finally spit out, "My father fell, on some ice, or something."

"Oh, no," Ava said.

"He's in Pennsylvania Hospital."

"Oh, no," Bambi said.

"Yes. They are doing tests. I don't know anything else. I have to go. I have to go now."

"We have to go," Bambi said.

"Go?" Ava asked.

"Yes, we have to go. Well, I have to go," Maria said and then added, "You stay. It's fine."

Ava sighed and said, "No. We have to go." She hugged Goose tightly, they locked lips and when they broke apart, Ava said, "It just figures."

"Baby," Goose said as Ava grabbed his face with both hands and went in for another kiss.

Maria looked at her cell phone and frantically dialed. Again, the call went straight to voicemail. As Maria listened to her mother's awkward message, the call was dropped and she heard an "All Circuits Busy" sound pulsing in her ear. She stared at the phone. *Huh? Why?* She watched as Ava held onto Goose's lapels with both hands as Bambi tried to yank her free. She looked up at Hunter. He extended his hand. She took it. He leaned in and kissed her cheek. "I'm really sorry. I have to go. It's…" was all she could manage to choke out as she held back tears.

"It's okay. I hope everything turns out all right," he said.

Bambi pulled on Maria's arm. "Family. It's family. She's got to go. We've got to go."

Hunter nodded. Maria locked eyes with him and held onto his hand for a moment until Bambi yanked her loose. Maria wobbled and grabbed onto Hunter's sleeve. She felt something rip and then pop. She looked over her shoulder at him as Bambi dragged Ava and her toward the exit. They paused at the doors, pushed their way to the top of the steps, and looked at the swarms of people moving everywhere.

"Great," Maria said as she pushed further through the crowd, hopping up and down to see over heads, "Where are the taxis?" she demanded.

Hunter caught up to her and said, "Wait. Maria. Wait. We have a car. We'll drive you."

Maria scanned the scene and the massive crowd. The line for the valet was at least fifty people deep. The wait would surely take over an hour. She shook her head "no" and said, "It'll take too long. Thank you."

Maria pushed through the crowd, making her way down a few steps at a time. She felt her heel hit the edge of a step hard, jolting her as one of the stilettos snapped off. This time, as she lurched sideways, she caught herself before she fell. *Could this really be her life? Could anything else possibly happen to her to-*

night?

Angry and determined, Maria gathered up the flouncy skirt in her hands and kept going, glancing over her shoulder periodically, her eyes darting, searching for her cousins. Somehow, she moved fast, settling in to a motion of limping and hopping, an awkward irregular speed walk. Ava and Bambi wriggled and tried hard to walk as fast as they could in their tight dresses and high heels, but couldn't keep up. Hunter pushed his way toward them. Maria spun around and saw him stop, bend over, as if to pick something up off of the ground.

She pushed her way down the rest of the huge staircase onto the circular driveway weaving through moving and honking cars making their way into traffic. Ava and Bambi finally caught up to her and together they made their way across the great lawn toward the subway entrance where they were stopped by a dense mob of waiting people. "Ugh. We don't have cash, or a Septa Pass," Maria blurted as she remembered their ridiculous ride here. She clenched her fist. Something stabbed the palm of her hand. She looked down, opened her fist and saw a gold horseshoe shaped cuff link in her hand. "Oh my god, Hunter." A stabbing sense of guilt made her stomach ache. She felt really bad for this poor guy and his unfortunate luck, crossing paths with her, today.

Maria looked up at the several horse-drawn carriages waiting in the Ballroom's driveway. She bolted toward one, hoisted up her dress and climbed in. Bambi and Ava wobbled in the direction of the driveway, but were surrounded by a swarm of people and stopped.

Maria grabbed the reins and felt a blast of panic run through her as she realized that she'd never done this before. The closest she had ever been to a horse was the couple of times that she rode a pony at the Jersey shore at some long forgotten, until now, Children's Zoo.

She took a deep breath in. The cool air soothed her. Trying hard to come up with rational thoughts, she wondered aloud to the horse, "Okay. I've read a lot of books. What to do? What to do?"

She nudged the horse with the reins. The horse moved a few steps backwards and then forward. She smacked him hard and he took a step up and over a curb and yanked the carriage onto the Ballroom's grand lawn toward the street.

"Oh no. Easy there."

The carriage bounced up and down over the uneven grass, tossing Maria back and forth. She was nearly thrown out of the seat when the carriage skipped over another curb and landed in the street. Horns blasted as cars screeched to a stop as they got close. Traffic parted slightly to let the horse move into the flow.

Maria was shocked that she was somehow maneuvering this animal into wall-to-wall traffic on Broad Street *and* guiding him forward, though guiding him was generous. She wasn't lulled into believing she was in control, or the horse was responding to her. He was clip-clopping along doing what he knew how to do.

She thought she heard someone yelling her name in the distance, but she was trying hard to concentrate on the massive horse and was really afraid to turn around. Out of the corner of her eye, she saw a buggy driver wearing a top hat and tails running across the street, his hands full of McDonalds' takeout, yelling, "Hey. What do you think you're doing? Get out of my carriage."

Maria turned for a split second, afraid to take her eyes off of the road and the horse.

"Ri?" he screamed.

"Vince?"

"What the hell?" he yelled.

"My father. He fell. I'll be right back."

"What? Be right back? Are you crazy? That's my horse. My carriage. Get outta there, Ri," he screamed as he tried to dodge cars and cross the street. "I mean it."

Maria shook her head defiantly.

"Ri, have you lost your friggin' mind? Stop."

"No," she said as she moved around another car frantically urging drivers, "Look out. Coming through. Oh. Sorry, so sorry. Look out."

Maria glanced back over her shoulder and saw Vince stuck in the middle of four jammed traffic lanes, trying to weave through a mass of people and cars not able to move. He dropped his McDonalds and pulled out a cell phone. She thought she heard him scream, "You don't know the first thing about that horse, any horse. Maria. Stop. Let me go with you. You don't even drive a car, Ri," Vince yelled.

"No time. Sorry."

She pulled the reins to the left and the horse slowed down. "Whoa, baby. What's happening? Not you, horsie. Secretariat. Giddyup. C'mon, you, giddy up."

Vince was right. She had no idea about what she was doing. She smacked the horse with the reins. He didn't react well. He neighed, shook his head, and tugged back. Caught off guard, Maria was yanked forward. She grabbed the front of the carriage, steadied herself, and smacked the horse again. He was clearly confused, but finally lunged forward again. People in the crosswalk dove out of the way. She smacked the horse again. This time he whinnied and sped up. She could barely make out Vince's exasperated scream in the distance, "Maria, give me my horse back. NOW."

This night, and her life, had gone to a whole new level of in-over-her-head, but as always, Maria was committed to forward motion. One of the carriage wheels hit a curb. She lurched sideways in the seat, but hung on as a car cut them off. The startled horse reared up in the air, his front legs pumping frantically. She pulled on the reins, "Easy now. Easy," she urged. Somehow, he seemed to settle down. "That's it. Attaboy. Girl. You a boy? A girl? Sorry," she cooed, then shook her head. *Why am I apologizing to a horse?* She looked over her shoulder and thought that she saw Ava and Bambi stutter-stepping through traffic to catch up to Vince. Bambi waved her arms frantically. Vince appeared to be on his phone. Ava was bent over trying to catch her breath.

"Wait. Wait. Maria, wait," she thought she heard one of them scream. "What about us?"

"I'll call you from the hospital," she yelled as loud as she could, sure that they couldn't hear her anyway. She glanced back again to see both standing with their hands on their hips as the celebrating and drunken mob surrounded them.

She smacked the horse again and flew backwards in the seat as the horse trotted up Broad Street, the carriage rocking as they went. Cars screeched and tried to pull over. Stunned people quickly moved aside to let them pass. Maria glanced at the chaos and winced. She wasn't prepared. She didn't have a plan. And she had no idea why she had reacted and stolen a horse. Borrowed. Technically, she had borrowed the horse from Vince, but it was too late to worry about it now.

If he had to admit it, Hunter felt rejected. He didn't like feeling discarded. His first reaction to Maria's escape was complete confusion, but when Hunter and the group had caught up to Ava and Bambi and watched the horse and carriage disappear in the distance, he laughed out loud. He admired her tenacity, impressed that she took the situation into her own hands and decided nothing was going to stop her from doing what she needed to do. This was a take-charge girl with guts. Her quick thinking, hell-be-damned outlaw reaction to the situation was pretty remarkable. Okay, if he was being honest, her running, high-heeled escape in a ball gown, stealing a horse, and taking off was just plain hot. He wasn't sure that he completely understood her devotion. In his family, they kept everything and everyone at arm's length. But Maria's father was in trouble and she was all in. Hunter admired that.

A guy dressed in a top hat, tails, and riding boots paced frantically next to Ava and Bambi. He panted and screamed, "What the hell? What the hell? What the hell?" as he dialed his phone and sputtered "Come on, Maria. Damn it. My horse. That's my horse."

"Oh my God," Bambi said.

"What was she thinking?" Ava shrieked.

Bambi glared at Ava and then turned to the guy and snapped, "Who are you calling, Vince?"

"I'm calling 9 1 1, Bam. What do you think? She's got my horse. She's got my life. She doesn't know the first thing..." Vince stepped away and into his phone said, "Uh, yeah, I have to report a stolen horse."

Bambi stomped over to him and grabbed his arm. "Vince, stop. Hang up. Now. We'll get your horse back. Do it, now," she ordered as Vince disconnected the call.

Judging by the speed of the hang-up, it was clear that there was history here. Whose, Hunter wasn't sure yet, but Vince paced furiously, kicked at the ground, and fumed at all of them.

"Your cousin's crazy, Bam. Cra-cra crazy. She's been in New York way too long. What does she think, this is Saratoga or something? Belmont? I need that horse back here, now."

"You'll get your horse back, Vince. Chill," Bambi ordered.

"Chill? Seriously? She's out of her mind, Bam. If anything happens to my Roxanne, I swear to you on my mother's life, somebody is going to pay. Big," Vince said.

"God, Vinny. Blow things out of proportion much?" Bambi fired back.

"I can't afford vet bills or to lose that horse, Bam," Vince said.

"You are not going to lose the horse, Vinny. Get. A. Grip."

"We have to get to the hospital, Bambi. We have to get to the hospital, now," Ava said frantically.

"Hospital? What hospital?" Vince said.

"Oh my god, will the two of you let me think?" Bambi said.

Vince stomped away yelling, "I'm calling the cops, you two. I'm calling the cops. No frigging way she's getting away with this."

Ava and Bambi stepped toward the subway entrance, stopped and frantically looked around. "Where are the taxis tonight? I can't believe this. One taxi. That's all we need. One friggin' taxi."

"C'mon," Joey said to Ava and Bambi. "I'll drive you."

"Oh, thanks, but that's going to take forever," Bambi insisted.

"Don't worry. I've got this," Joey said.

Hunter watched the mob of people move in waves away from the Ballroom and wondered how they were ever going to go anywhere. They pushed against the chaotic mob and walked back toward the Ballroom steps and the valet to retrieve Joey's car. Hunter glanced around at the madness. Maria and Bambi were right. Getting out of there was going to take a long time.

"No worries. I always have a plan," Joey said as he tapped his fingers to his forehead, moved to the front of the line, spoke to the valet, and motioned to the Rolls. Hunter watched as Joe slipped the guy something. The guy looked a little surprised as he looked the bill over, flipped it, and held it up to the light. Perhaps thinking that Joe would change his mind, he shoved the bill into his pocket, quickly retrieved the keys, and tossed them to Joe.

Joe waved the keys in the air, and yelled, "Ladies and gentlemen. Let's roll."

"Let's go," Hunter added.

Everyone squeezed inside of the car. The valet motioned to other exiting cars to stop and waved Joey out. Joey eased into the gridlock on Broad Street where they sat...and sat...and sat. Joey had successfully positioned the car for a fast exit, but the volume of traffic had beaten them.

They were stuck.

Chapter 16

"You don't know what you can do until you try."
Maria always thought she'd dismissed this bit of advice wrapped in one of her mother's rules. However, when she thought about it...she had never shied away from a challenge.
Ever.

Being a horse thief was never on Maria's list of things to accomplish. This was completely over the top for her. Even so, a slightly smug feeling teased a crooked smile on her face as she maneuvered the carriage, the horse clip clopping around people and cars for several blocks. Her newfound unskilled equestrian moves stunned her until traffic ground to a halt. Her momentary cockiness faded as she anxiously waited, surrounded on all sides.

An impatient driver laid on a horn. She jumped as the horse pawed the pavement and rocked his head back and forth. The traffic noise increased as frustration multiplied, horns blared, and people yelled at each other. "Easy, now," she said, not sure if she was soothing the animal or herself.

Billy Penn peered down on the scene from his

perch on the top of City Hall as if taunting her. She could almost hear his famous words rattling around in her head. *Rarely promise, but, if lawful, constantly perform.* She had memorized and never forgotten a ninth-grade oral report that she had titled *William's Wisdom.* His noteworthy quote was the cornerstone of her presentation and quickly became her own life motto. At thirteen, she was certain that she would be the girl who could and would perform at a level higher than most other people. She knew that she would always be the girl who would remain within the lawful part of society, always doing noble works as she progressed through life. Of course, tonight, his words taunted her. *Why am I always trying to be such a goody-goody?*

She hadn't guaranteed her mother she would come home tonight. She had tried to explain that she wasn't promising only hours earlier. Now, here she was, a full-on law-breaking criminal, good girl. At least I'm performing, she thought as she fought back tears and sat in standstill traffic waiting.

"Do you like this corner, Mr. Horse, huh? It's nice, don't you think?" she said as she fought the desire to jump out and let the horse fend for himself. She bounced her feet up and down trying to stretch out her aching arches. She thought better of the escape plan when she glanced at the broken shoe. "It's okay. I can't walk anyway. I could hardly manage walking in these shoes with both heels, let alone one. Bare feet are not an option."

I can't just abandon an animal that I "borrowed."

Maria bunched her lips. Oh, crap. The horse. Vince's horse. She was never, ever going to hear the end of this. She was sure that this would be a story long remembered, told and embellished going forward. She covered her face with her hands as the realization sank in. She was now going to be the subject of the next family story told year after year.

Vince grew up a few houses away from Maria. Their mothers, lifelong friends, had delivered their babies within days of each other. They had fantasized that their children would grow up and fall in love, forever cementing the women's bond. If only the bond had lasted through Vince's family's move over the bridge to New Jersey. Antonetta's loyalty and allegiance had a fifteen-block radius. She didn't take it well when her best friend's husband convinced her to leave the neighborhood to put down roots in the Garden State. They had timed a few vacations together at the Jersey shore, but that tradition wore thin as the families expanded and children didn't get along.

When Antonetta reported that Vince started his business in Philadelphia, she insisted he wasn't good enough for Maria. Antonetta had her own set of rules and a loyalty line that moved whenever she felt slighted, often realigning just as fast with no explanation. Maria explained many times that Vince was never an option. Maria watched her mother's eyes glaze over when she showed her examples of the life that she imagined as illustrated by her vision boards.

And now this, this…His horse.

Maria groaned as traffic crept forward. She

looked over her shoulder as the cab next to her also inched forward. "Excuse me. Pardon me." The cab squeezed closer to the car in front, boxing her in. "Hey, c'mon," she screamed as she pointed, "Going that way."

The driver smiled a missing tooth grin at her and stood his ground.

"That way. Trying to turn here. Onto Pine," she said and pointed again.

The cab crept forward once more; the driver clearly determined not to give her an inch.

"Please?" she said as the horse whipped his head back and forth. With her limited horse-whisperer sense she interpreted the horse's reaction as hostility aimed at the cabbie and the too close car. Maybe it just was her frustration, but she was sure that the horse was now on her side. She reached forward and patted his hind quarters. "Easy there," she whispered as the horse calmed. The cabbie tapped his horn at the car in front of him making her jump and the horse whinny.

"Seriously? Happy New Year to you too," she shot at him.

The taxi driver laughed and blew her a kiss.

She guessed she should be glad that he only faked a kiss and not something else, but it only made her angrier. "Are you kidding me? Where do you think you're going to get to? Huh? Nobody is moving. Nobody." *Why are people so competitive when they're behind the wheel?* She screamed, "I'm driving a carriage, idiot." This was slow motion road rage, each of them jockeying for position inch by inch.

The taxi driver shook his head as he crept forward.

Maria looked around as if for an answer. As she did, the next car paused to give her room. She waited and guided the horse, or so she thought. When the animal slowly maneuvered into the right-hand lane, even she was surprised. "Good boy!" she squealed as they finally turned onto Pine Street. She waved to the car as they rounded the corner and yelled, "Thank you." She had no idea if they heard her but was relieved by the gesture. "We did it, boy," she squealed, surprised by the fact that she had performed a completely *legal* turn with her stolen horse and was now comfortably out of Billy Penn's sight.

She sat up straight, pulled her Pashmina tight, and shivered as snowflakes began to flutter out of the sky. They were clip clopping down the street past beautiful townhouses and stately old row houses. Pine Street, Philadelphia, at its finest. Beautiful. Quiet. Peaceful. Serene. She blinked as snowflakes landed on her face. For a split second, she imagined being transported to another time, another century, to a time that she would have most definitely known how to handle this horse and, maybe even this carriage...until...

She was forced out of her serene fantasy by a car screeching around the carriage, blowing past her, honking a horn. The horse's ears flicked back and forth at the noises. Silly String blasted out of one of the car's window in their direction. The animal shook his head side to side as the sticky foaming strands landed on him. A large moon hung out of the rear passenger side window as the group of teenagers in the car howled with laughter.

"Oh, grow up," she yelled as the car cut the carriage off, skidded around the corner, and continued north on Eleventh Street. Maria shivered and reached down to the floor of the cab for a blanket. She wasn't sure why, but she sniffed it. "Oh, god," she said as she recoiled from the revolting smell. She was desperate, freezing, and close to tears, but she draped the smelly fabric across her lap anyway and settled back into the seat.

Maria guided the horse to Seventh Street and continued a block. She couldn't believe her luck as the traffic light turned red. She tugged on the reins and said, "Whoa, boy," as the horse stopped. "We're so close," Maria said as she tapped her foot and waited, the hospital's Emergency Sign taunting her from a block away. She shifted in the seat worried about her father and thought about her uncharacteristic outlaw behavior of the evening and cringed. Despite the lack of traffic on this corner, she lawfully waited until the light finally flashed green, then snapped the reins. They moved forward onto Spruce Street and slid into to the hospital's emergency entrance.

Maria pulled back hard on the reins and said, "Whoaaaa," as the horse closed in on a parked ambulance stopping just short of the rig. "Good boy. Maybe I'm getting the hang of this. Maybe this can be my Plan-B if New York doesn't work out." She shook her head at her ridiculousness as she dropped the reins, hopped out of the buggy, and limped one heeled into the emergency room.

She scanned the space. At the reception desk, a chirpy nurse was busy flirting with a young cop. Maria wasn't sure if she should interrupt, but was too agitated and had no time for the Meet Cupid scene unfolding in front of her. She shot across the room and blurted, "Uh. Thomas Vigliano. My father. He was brought in a little while ago. He fell."

Lucy heard her voice and screeched, "Riiiii."

Maria spun around.

"Ri. Where were you?" Lucy asked. Maria glanced across the room and spotted Aunt Sylvia comforting Connie, an arm around her shoulders as Lucy stood nearby. Tears streamed down her sister's faces when they spotted Maria. They bolted to her and they hugged tight, melding into one massive group hug.

Lucy said, "It's not good, Ri. It's not good. It's our fault. He had to come to pick us up. Our designated driver wasn't..."

Connie interrupted, and added, "He couldn't drive...They mentioned..."

"Surgery," Lucy said.

Maria's eyes zig-zagged between them, trying to keep up.

"It's our fault. He's gonna die, Ri. If he goes under the knife, they'll kill him. You know what Mom always says..." Connie said.

"...about doctors and hospitals," Lucy said.

"Shhhhhssssshhh." Aunt Sylvia shot at them as she approached, making the sign of the cross and then said loudly, "Don't even," to the girls.

"Lucy. Stop," Connie ordered as an upset toddler wailed in the background trying to escape his mother's grasp.

Maria was trying very hard to follow what each was saying, and at the same time trying to assess the situation to see what she could do to help, if anything.

"Don't tell me to stop. You know that I'm right," Lucy said.

"Do you always have to be right? Give it a rest for once," Connie said.

"Girls. Stop. For just a minute. First of all, it's probably not that bad. You know how Mommy always blows things out of proportion. Always." She squared her shoulders and stood up straight trying to defuse the situation and limit the bickering between the two. Connie shook her head yes, then no. "It's going to be fine. Okay. C'mon. Yes. It will. Okay. So, now, where's Daddy?"

They pointed to the examining area. "Exam twelve," Connie said through sniffles and added, "Nice tiara, Ri."

Maria felt the top of her head. It was still there. Midnight already seemed like a lifetime ago. She felt her shoulders slump. She closed her eyes and took a deep breath in to try to calm herself when she heard a familiar voice in the background, "Maria, Maria, Maria. Girl, where have you been? Where is your father? Good god, your Mother has been calling me all night. Where is Thomas?"

Maria opened her eyes, pivoted and shrieked, "Lyndon?" Her mouth hung open when she saw him in front of her.

"Is he all right?" he asked.

"Lyn, what the—?"

"I spoke to your mother, several times, and got here as fast as I could," he said.

Maria shook her head, trying to decide if she had lost her mind or if she was somehow trapped in an odd nightmare that wouldn't end, getting more and more bizarre, adding level after level of non-sensical events as it moved along. She blinked hard, opened her eyes again. Lyndon was still standing there. "What? How? Are you kidding me? How did you get here?" She was certain that she had imagined him or was hallucinating until he spoke again.

"Facebook, honey," he said.

"What?" Maria shook her head, confused. Not only because he had just answered, but also because he was explaining his travel through Facebook. "Huh?"

"News feed," he groaned and continued, "O. M. G. Let's just say, I know a guy, who knows a guy, who knows someone," Lyndon said and winked. "He posted that *someone* was diverting a chopper to Philly for some other hotshot who wanted to be home in Philly for midnight. That *someone* was on his was to A.C. You know, Atlantic City, for some high roller-only party," Lyndon winked again. "A party that I should have been invited to, B.T.W."

Maria squinted at him trying hard to keep up, but this was Lyndon. She was not drunk. This was not New York City. This was not her office. This was Pennsylvania Hospital and she was at a complete loss.

"A. C.," he was waving his hands at her now motioning catch up. "Let's just say, someone owed me... him...us. I called in a favor, honey so that I could be here for you and your mother. I got air lifted. Ooo-la-lah." Lyndon laughed and winked at her again.

"Is there something in your eye?"

Lyndon put one hand on his hip and scrunched his face.

"Oh my god." Maria struggled to find words. She was kind of glad to see him, but could only look at him, eyes open wide, deer in the headlights like, as she walked away towards the exam area.

"B.T.W., Ri, nice tiara. Can you get me one?"

She pulled the rhinestone crown off of her head, twirled, slid back over to him and plunked it on top of his, kissed his cheek, and said, "Thank you."

Lyndon cooed, "I love you too."

"Back 'atcha, Lyn," she said as she spun and marched into the exam area searching for curtain twelve and the rest of her family.

The antiseptic hospital smell made her woozy as she approached the treatment area. She took a deep breath, steadied herself, pulled the curtain back a few inches, and peeked inside. She saw her father looking uncharacteristically small and vulnerable, lying in the bed wearing only a hospital gown. His ankle was elevated and encased in a splint that reached almost to his knee. Her mother sat next to him, stroking his arm. She stood and fluffed his pillow as he winced from the motion. She paced, grabbed a cup, and pointed a straw toward his mouth. He pulled away at first, but then relented, taking a sip. She watched her mother caress his face, wipe his forehead, then kiss him gently. Maria took it all in and smiled as a tear rolled down her cheek.

It must have been that maternal GPS of hers, Maria thought, because somehow her mother had sensed her presence. Antonetta looked up and immediately started to cry when she saw her. "It's about time," she said as she bolted across the small space, squeezed Maria tight and between sobs said, "Where were you? Why didn't you answer your phone? I needed you."

Maria reached for her father's hand, squeezed it, and said, "Daddy."

"Toni, enough. Stop. I'm okay," her father said, trying to stop his wife's waterworks. He could tolerate a lot from them, but crying pushed him into another dimension of helplessness. When tears and tantrums from Antonetta or the three girls would inevitably start for one reason or another, he would retreat into the living room to his chair and turn up the volume on the television to drown out the emotional uproar. Here, now, he was stuck, and this was not going to go well if he didn't put a stop to it quickly. "I'm okay," he repeated.

"For the moment," Antonetta said to him.

"You're okay for the moment, Tom."

"It's a sprain. It's no big deal."

"It's a high ankle sprain." She turned to Maria and added, "That's serious."

Her father groaned and looked to Maria for assistance.

Antonetta continued, "Didn't that quarterback have that? He was never the same. You said so yourself, Tom."

"I'll be okay. I'm not starting on Sunday."

"No. You're just marching in the morning. You could throw a clot," she spit back. Maria listened and smiled, somehow comforted in her mother's ability to take everything to the extreme. "That damn parade," Antonetta added for good measure even though it wasn't lost on Maria or her father that the upcoming Mummer's parade wasn't optional for any of them.

Maria sniffed, grabbed her mother by the shoulders, looked her in the eye and ordered, "Mom. Stop. He's not going to die. Not tonight anyway. Let's take a breath." For once, her mother listened. Antonetta breathed in deeply. Maria took a breath at the same time. "That's it. Good, breathe."

Maria watched her father smile in the background enjoying this role reversal as a young doctor entered and scanned his chart. Antonetta didn't miss a beat. She checked out the doctor, looked at Maria, raising an eyebrow, and motioning toward the doctor with her head. "Breathe, Mom, breathe. I mean it," Maria said and then mouthed, "Don't."

"Handsome. No ring," Antonetta whispered.

"Mom."

"Mr. Vigliano. Everything looks good," the doctor said as he dropped the chart on the bed, listened to Thomas's heartbeat and checked his pupils. "But I am going to admit you. Keep you overnight. Falls like this can be tricky," he said matter-of-factly.

"Oh my god," Antonetta blurted.

Maria grabbed her mother's arm attempting to defuse the outburst and said, "Mom."

"I knew it," Antonetta continued. "I just knew it."

"Mrs. Vigliano, for observation. Overnight. Just to be safe," the doctor said.

"Doctor—" Maria glance at his name tag, "Webster. Um, is that necessary? Is there something else? Something you're not telling us?"

"Miss?"

"Vigliano. Maria, Maria Vigliano."

"Our daughter. Our eligib—"

Maria elbowed her, "Mother."

"Maria. Your mother thinks your father may have hit his head when he landed on the concrete. Your father can't confirm for us one way or the other. So, we're going to keep an eye on him tonight. We'll see how he feels in the morning."

Maria looked at her dad. He bunched his lips, shrugged and then smiled at her.

"Head injuries can be…" the doctor continued.

Antonetta gasped, started to cry again, and as she paced, she said, "Like that Kennedy. Or that actress."

"Ma'am. Do you need something? We can give you something so that you can calm down if need be," the doctor said.

Antonetta grabbed her chest, breathed in hard, and looked at the doctor as if to say, *Really?* The doctor ignored her. "Thomas, we should have a room for you soon. Hang in there, okay? We'll be moving you any minute. I know it's a holiday and I'm sure that you probably had other plans. Let's see how you do overnight," he said and then slipped through an opening in the curtain partition and was gone.

Maria held her mother's arm, guided her over to the chair, and helped her sit as Connie, Lucy, Aunt Sylvia, and Lyndon tiptoed in and gathered around the bed crowding into the too small space.

Tom motioned for Maria to come closer. She squeezed in close as he whispered, "Ri, you have to go over to headquarters. Make sure that they have everything under control. Uncle Bruno should be down there by now, but I need you to check over everything. Okay? I'll get down there as soon as I can."

"Daddy, I should be here."

"Ri. I need you to do this for me."

"But..."

"No buts."

Maria motioned to her mother, the pillar of strength and overflowing fountain of emotion and said, "But, Mom..."

Thomas shook his head, "I'll take care of it, of her. Don't worry. Your aunt can take your sisters home. I need you to go down there. Keep everyone in line. Make sure they are ready for the morning. I promise I'll get there as soon as they let me out of here. Okay?"

Maria leaned in, kissed his cheek, and said, "Everything will be fine."

And, there it was, she had promised again without thinking.

"I know, baby," he said as she moved away from the bed.

Maria watched Lyndon interacting with the family, smiled, patted his arm, and whispered in his ear, "Thank you, and good luck."

Lyndon smiled and turned back to Antonetta who was instructing him on the importance of a balanced diet. Thank god she had something else, or someone else, to distract her, Maria thought. Lyndon seemed to understand his role as he explained in detail his disastrous attempt at making Pizzelles over the Christmas holiday.

Her mother was all too happy to review his fail with him. "Did you melt the butter?" she asked. Lyndon nodded. "Did you leave them on the iron until the steam stops coming out like I told you? Twenty seconds or so. That's all," she said.

"I think so," Lyndon said.

"Think so, or know so? It's important."

Maria smirked as she watched Lyndon squirm under her mother's inquisition. She had the ability to do that to everyone, even Lyndon. Imagine that.

Chapter 17

Maria took a few steps toward the waiting area, hesitated and remembered...

Rule number One. Always take a moment to compose yourself. Take a breath and pause...

Her mother's instruction ran through her mind. She had already made one unforgettable entrance. There was nothing she could do at the moment about pulling herself together or fixing her lipstick. The intensity of her wacky race up Broad Street to the hospital and into the E.R. was overwhelming her. She caught her breath, sucking air in and blowing it out as she clutched her stomach and fought back the deluge of tears threatening to burst out. She leaned against a wall and heard Bambi's voice, "Maria. Ri, where..."

Ava interrupted, "...Is he? Did he?"

Maria looked at their shocked faces and teary eyes and realized that she must have really looked like a wreck. "He's fine. It's a bad sprain. That's all," she said as she pointed toward the exam area.

Her cousins blasted towards the door, wobbling on their stilettos. Ava yelled over her shoulder, "Hey, Ri, I think you one-upped Nonna Mary with this one." Maria looked at her and shrugged. "Stealing Vinny's horse. You way out-did the gold paint fiasco. Ha. This one's for the books."

Maria groaned and closed her eyes.

"Watch out for the cops. They're onto you," Bambi added cocking an eyebrow and motioning toward the entrance, laughing.

Ava yelled, "Uncle Tom? Aunt Toni? Ma?" as they both wiggled inside.

Hunter, Joey, Frankie, Goose, and Elmo watched them leave then walked over and surrounded her. "Is he okay?" Hunter asked.

Maria's lip quivered. She nodded and said, "He may not survive my mother tonight, but otherwise, he's going to make it."

"That's good news," Joey said as the others nodded.

Maria turned toward the Emergency Room entrance and saw flashing red and blue lights illuminating the driveway near the horse and carriage. She felt an overwhelming sense of panic run through her body again. She walked outside to see a Police Animal Van parked in the E. R. drop-off area. An officer had unhitched the horse from the carriage and was guiding him into the van, securing the animal inside as another cop hitched the carriage to a tow. "Wait," she said.

The cop looked startled as she approached. He defensively put one hand on his holstered gun, and said, "Stand back, Ma'am."

Maria wasn't sure if she was more startled by the fact that she was really worried about Vince's poor horse, that he had reached defensively for his gun, or the fact that he had just addressed her as Ma'am. "Ma'am? Huh? What? Wait."

"Please stand back, Ma'am," he ordered.

"But, I..." she stammered.

"Is this your horse, Ma'am?" he asked.

Again, with the Ma'am. Geez, I must really look like crap.

"I asked you if the horse belonged to you, Ma'am," the cop barked.

"Well, no, um, not exactly." She wasn't ready to eagerly admit her unlawfulness and wind up in jail. She had too much work to do.

"Then what exactly do you want me to wait for?" the cop asked.

"It's... I. I need. Just... Nothing. Never mind."

The cop barked into the walkie-talkie on his shoulder, "Yeah, abandoned horse at Pennsylvania Hospital matching the description of the animal and vehicle stolen from the Ballroom. Transporting now."

Maria watched as he signaled to a driver and the horse trailer and the carriage moved forward, thumping over a curb and onto Tenth Street. The other officer slid into the squad car and rocketed out of the driveway. His siren blasted as he skidded around the corner and was gone.

Exhausted, Maria sat on the curb and covered

her face with her hands. She heard footsteps and sensed someone as they sat down. She wasn't prepared to be chastised by her cousins and was surprised to see Hunter when she looked up and opened her eyes. She thought to herself that this can't be. Did this amazing looking, really sweet guy have to enter her life tonight, of all nights? This had to be some kind of karmic joke. Maybe she was stuck in her own little fractured fairy tale. She thought she must be starring in an episode of *Punk'd*. Where was Ashton Kutcher? She actually glanced around looking for cameras expecting someone to announce that she had been had.

She thought the exhaustion was making her a little paranoid at this point because she started to wonder if her mother could have somehow orchestrated this whole crazy series of events. Maria knew it was complicated, even for her, but Antonetta was the queen of situational "hmmmms" and "coincidences."

She remembered back to Christmas Eve, just a week ago…She had returned to Philadelphia by train as usual. At the last minute, her mother had called and asked her to stop at Esposito's Market to pick up a couple of extra pounds of shrimp she had ordered. Antonetta had insisted she was desperate. She was sure she wouldn't have enough for everyone later that evening when she served her Twelve Fishes dinner for the extended family. Maria had thought it a little odd then. She knew that her father, or Uncle Bruno, could have easily gone for the seafood, but she asked Maria to do it on her way home.

Maria arrived with the dripping bag of seafood

and found her in the kitchen whacking a whole flounder into bite-sized pieces for her Bouillabaisse. After she chastised Maria for taking a cab, she grabbed the bag and steered Maria into the dining room where Sonny, a slightly balding UPS man, was feasting on a plate of her famous homemade Christmas cookies. Antonetta had just smiled, pleased with herself for having pulled this off perfectly. Maria's arrival flawlessly coincided with Sonny's hectic Christmas delivery schedule.

Maria had thought then that her mother had reached new heights in her ability to embarrass her. Maybe Maria was wrong. Maybe she had somehow one-upped herself. "You just need a little nudge in the right direction, Maria. Sometimes you just don't even see what's right under your nose," she had said later that night when Maria busted her on the unnecessary two pounds of crustaceans used to stall her arrival.

Maria blinked hard trying to shake off the Christmas Eve memory and recounting all that had happened so far today. This day was simply too complicated even for Antonetta Vigliano. She was good, but this, this crazy chaos was beyond her capabilities, Maria was sure. At least she hoped it was so. She tried to remember what she ate this morning at that breakfast meeting with Hal and their client. She was sure that she was in the middle of some kind of weird nightmare, about to wake up any minute at her desk at R.H.T. and Associates to gratefully realize and accept that she had somehow slept through the whole big bad night. Her thoughts were suddenly interrupted by Hunter asking, "Do you need a ride?"

Maria nodded.

"Can I help?"

She shook her head "no."

"It's okay to ask for help," he said.

She nodded again. "You know you'll be aiding and abetting. I'm kind of a criminal now. You shouldn't put your reputation on the line."

Hunter smiled and said, "Yeah? I think I'm okay taking a chance." He stood, took a few steps into the street, and whistled loudly. Another horse drawn carriage rounded the corner. "C'mon," he said as he extended his hand.

Maria took his hand and said, "Seriously? Are these guys the only people working tonight?"

"I guess so," he said, motioning to the carriage and then added, "C'mon."

Maria stepped onto the cab's footboard. Hunter held her hand and helped her into the carriage. This climb was more elegant and far from her earlier clumsy hop and belly flop into the seat. He jumped in and settled in beside her.

Yeah, my dream, ummm, this dream, was clearly being influenced by all of the rom-coms I've watched and re-watched in my life. She made a mental note to expand her viewing habits and switch to thrillers or action adventures for a while.

"Where to, folks?" the driver asked.

Hunter looked at her wide-eyed and waited for her to answer.

"Pennsport. Corner of Second and Moore will

do."

The driver swatted the horse's rear and the carriage glided onto Spruce Street.

"Oh sure. He makes it look easy," she said and they both laughed. For some reason, she thought to herself that she probably should pay close attention to how he handled the animal. Then, she shook her head and wondered if this was really all a dream, why did she even care? If in this situation again, she would simply perform, and perform lawfully, she hoped, next time.

Hunter reached for the blanket next to him and unfolded it. She flinched and leaned away, but was surprised when he moved the heavy wool blanket toward her and nothing pungent wafted up to her nose. Hmmm, I'm going to have to take that up with Vince later...if he's still speaking to me, she thought. She hoped that his horse was okay and wondered if those cops wrote him a ticket. This was going to cost her in more ways than one. She'd reimburse him, she thought, as her mind pinged around, flashing through the evening's events.

"It's okay," Hunter said as if he was reading her reaction, "It doesn't smell. And, it's cold. Here." Hunter covered their laps and moved in a little closer.

She'd have to admit that it felt really nice to have someone do something for her for a change. She took a deep breath, relaxed a bit as she felt the exhaustion move through her, and remembered that it *had* been a really long day. She watched as Hunter stole a look at her and moved a little closer. "What?"

she asked.

"Are you hungry?"

"Starved," she admitted as she remembered that breakfast meeting again.

"Me too," he said as he leaned forward and whispered something to the driver.

"As you wish, Sir," the driver said as he steered the carriage north to Chestnut Street and then east towards the historic district.

As the horse clip-clopped through Old City on an even keel, something she couldn't accomplish earlier with Vince's horse, Hunter texted someone on his phone. Maria couldn't help but wonder who. Her imagination went wild again. *Girlfriend? Wife?* She wasn't sure what she was thinking, or why. Oh my god, he's probably just talking to the friends he left behind at the hospital when he offered to help me. *I'm such an idiot.* The snow flurries had stopped, but a sudden chill knifed right through her. She shivered.

"Here," Hunter said as he took off his jacket and put it around her shoulders.

"But you're going to freeze," she protested.

"I'm fine," he said as he slipped an arm around her shoulders. She leaned back and snuggled in, feeling safe and comfortable for the first time in a long time even though his text hung over her, troubling her.

They crossed Fourth Street and the carriage slowed to a stop. Maria looked up and felt her shoulders slump when she saw that they were in front of Buddakan. She couldn't help but wonder if there was also karmic significance in ending up at the same place that she had started her night yesterday in New York. *Damn you, serendipity. Joke's on me.*

"Here? I...I don't think that I have time." She glanced at her phone. It was 3:00 a.m. "Oh my god. It's late. I really have to get going."

"It'll only take a minute. Really." As Hunter stalled, a waiter bolted out of the restaurant with two large Chinese take-out containers and handed them to him.

"Your Dip Sum doughnuts, Hunter. Happy New Year, Dude. Glad you texted. Good to see you again. Make it a good one," the waiter said, pointing at us.

"You too, Nick. You're the man," Hunter said as they fist bumped. "Say hey to everyone in there," Hunter said to the waiter, then turned to her and said, "I tended bar here one summer," he laughed and continued, "The tips were really good."

"I've heard that," she said and immediately felt bad for assuming the worst about the text.

As the carriage continued down Chestnut Street, Hunter opened the containers and handed her one. She balanced the box full of cups of dipping sauces. They ate the warm round doughnuts, taking turns dunking them into the creamy sauces.

"I'm still not sure which I like better. Gingered cream cheese. Nope, Chocolate. Definitely the chocolate," Hunter said.

"They're good. All good. Sooooo good," she said and giggled. "Chocolate is my number one for sure, but that blackberry jam is pretty awesome too." She couldn't remember the last time she had eaten anything so delicious. And, try as she might, she really couldn't remember eating anything since yesterday's meeting. She took another doughnut and dunked it into the chocolate and took a bite. "Oh, this is amazing."

"Amazing," Hunter said, laughed and popped another doughnut into his mouth. "Mmmmm." He tapped the driver on the shoulder and said, "Bradford, would you like another doughnut? We have a ton."

"Much appreciated, but no thank you, Sir. Can't do the carbs. Watching the waistline, I am. My better half says I'm putting on the pounds. It's just my winter coat, I like to tell her. She doesn't buy it. Thank you for your kindness, though," the driver said.

"Anytime, Brad. Anytime," Hunter said.

Hunter dipped a doughnut into the chocolate and put it up to Maria's mouth. She tried to bite it as the carriage turned south onto Second Street and rocked side to side. She grabbed onto Hunter's arm and he bumped her cheek with the goo. He laughed and said, "I'm so sorry."

She giggled as he wiped her face with his finger and then popped the morsel into her mouth. "It's okay," she said as she glanced at his ruined shirt, "I think I deserved that."

The mass of New Year's Eve revelers was gone, only a few stragglers shuffled along. The horse clip clopped on the cobblestone streets of Old City as they made their way through the quiet Society Hill neighborhood, then through historic Head House Square.

The small brick buildings and houses dating back to the late 18th century were dark and silent. Maria watched Hunter glance around. He said quietly, "I'd forgotten about the charm of this part of town. It's been a long time..."

Maria stole a look at him and reached her hand toward his collar.

"What?" he said as he turned to her and caught her looking at him.

She blinked and asked, "You're not really real, are you?"

Hunter laughed, turned toward her, leaned in, and slowly brought his lips to hers. She closed her eyes. His lips were soft and warm. "Real enough for you?" he whispered.

This was a sweet first kiss and even though it was technically their second, this was a real kiss. She was a little startled and not sure how to react, but for the first time, she felt herself unwind. She opened her eyes, nodded, and said, "Mmmmm. Yes. Real enough, I think. I could be dreaming. Who knows? Maybe I just made you up."

He grinned wide. He looked exquisite.

Maria turned away, worried the whole montage was too picture-perfect. She was sure that any minute she would wake up and be incredibly disappointed that this was all a dream. Her alarm or Lyndon would certainly blast her out of this flawless vignette and back to her lonely world. This...this, was surely the power of her imagination toying with her emotions. She was positive of it until he slipped his arm around her waist and pulled her close, reached over for her face, held it in her hands, and kissed her again.

There was no mistaking it this time.

This she felt through and through.

The carriage continued through Old City, and traveled south on Second Street. The after-hour partying had wound down, the streets near empty. As they neared Moore Street, the middle of the night silence was pierced by music, an occasional String Band warming up, banjos twanging and saxophones tuning up, the sound drifting out of clubhouses as they passed by.

Last-minute rehearsals were being squeezed in. Maria heard the familiar, "One, two. One, two. Left. Right. Right. Right. Left." The Mummer's Parade and zero hour was definitely approaching. People were stirring. Busy groups were heading in and out of buildings up and down Two Street. She could feel the familiar energy starting to ratchet up. She was sure now that she wasn't dreaming.

The driver slowed the horse and parked at the corner of Moore Street. Hunter hopped out and reached up for her hands and helped her down to the ground. Forgetting about her heel-less stiletto she wobbled to one side as her feet landed on the sidewalk. Hunter caught her. Her face flushed pink. She laughed and said, "This is just getting silly"

"Hey! Silly's good, at times," he said as he surveyed the activity. "Okay then. Here you are."

"Thank you. I really have to go in. I'm sure they're a mess. Even when my dad is here it's always a last-minute scramble. Always."

"Do you want some help?" he asked.

Maria heard the bells and whistles going off in her head as panic started to ooze into her brain. The last few minutes had been perfect, too perfect. She wanted to keep it that way for now. She wasn't ready to bring this man into this part of her crazy life.

"It's okay," she said with a shrug.

Hunter nodded, leaned in. She leaned in too as they kissed, wishing that this could last a little longer, but realizing that this one moment was perfect for now. She was sure that she had made the right choice to keep this, whatever *this* was, separate for now.

"Good night," he said.

"Night," she said as she took off his jacket and started to hand it to him.

"It's okay. You've got almost nothing on."

"But I'm going inside," she insisted.

"Keep it. I'll have an excuse to find you tomorrow."

"Today," she reminded him.

"Today," he said as he took a step backwards, "On Broad Street. Mummering," he added.

She pulled the jacket tight and watched him shove his hands in his pockets and walk away in the other direction glancing over his shoulder at her as he moved.

"On Broad Street. Mummering," she muttered feeling more than a little judged. She watched him walk away for as long as she could.

A loud, "Ri. Where's your father?" cut through the air, interrupting her thoughts.

She turned to see Christian, a big, barrel-chested Longshoreman with a shaved head, wringing his hands and shuffling his feet. He held several brightly decorated jackets over one arm. "We're in big trouble, Maria. Your Uncle Bruno and Iggy are missing in action. I can't find them anywhere. Rudy says there are costumes missing. Missing. Gone," he said, huffing, puffing, and shaking his head violently while waving his free hand at her to make his point.

She sighed, and turned back toward Hunter who was a block or so away. She watched him turn around, and wave. She smiled and waved back, not paying any attention to Christian.

"Ri? Ri! Help. Where is your father?" Christian yelped, sounding desperate.

Maria smiled as she watched Hunter disappear in the distance, ignoring Christian.

"Maria? Your father?"

"Yes."

"Maria!" Christian snapped and stomped a foot.

"Hospital. In the hospital. He's in the hospital," she said matter-of-factly.

"Wait. What? Something happen? He sick? Is he okay? His voice raised an octave as he continued, "What are we going to do? Oh no. Ri, do you know how to find Iggy or Bruno?"

"Yeah, of course. No problem," she said as she opened her clutch. Something dropped and pinged the sidewalk as she pulled out her phone. She reached down for the object she had let fall and was surprised to pick up Hunter's cuff link. The gold horseshoe had wound up in her hand a few hours ago...no, a lifetime ago.

She looked up, realized that he was really gone, stared at the shiny jewelry, sighed and smiled. She was more than a little relieved that maybe, just maybe, she had real evidence that she didn't imagine the whole night, the whole thing, whatever this thing was.

Christian cleared his throat and shuffled his feet and said, "Ri, we've got problems here. Real problems."

Maria was jarred back to reality, this reality. There was no time right now to pine for a guy or to feel any sentimentality, perfect man or not. Still, she couldn't believe that she had simply let him walk away. *I'm such an idiot.*

She glanced at her phone. It was 3:30 in the morning. She knew that she had to move, and she knew that she had to move fast and get down to business. She entered the Clubhouse alone. Christian shuffled in behind her, waiting for her to do something, anything.

Chapter 18

Hunter walked fast with a bit of a skip in his step north on Two Street re-running the night's events in his head. Maria. He had finally learned her name. His first impression was on point. She was charming.

To ignore the coincidence of their meeting after crossing paths three times in one day would seem foolish. He wondered if someone was trying to tell him something. Not a real fan of anything woo-woo, he chalked it up to chance. Sorry he had left her, he wanted to prolong the evening a little bit to get to know her more. He should have insisted on staying, was the only thought looping nonstop through his head.

Oddly, his life in Washington seemed lifetimes away right then. He was glad that he had listened to Joey and had sprung for the train even though spontaneity like this usually made him uncomfortable. It was not something he had ever excelled at. It was all of those straight lines that his father had laid out for him from day one of his life, always hammering his tried and true model, "Stay on course. Stay on track." He was sure that for once in his life this was a time that he was really glad he had taken the shot and gone for it.

Maria seemed his opposite, and versed in spontaneity. Maybe she could teach him a thing or two. He smiled, recalling her taking the horse. Okay, she knew the guy, but still, it took guts to grab the carriage and run. He chuckled and shook his head as he remembered watching her jump into the cab, swat the horse hard, and take off on a wild ride up Broad Street dodging traffic. He wasn't even sure how she had made her way through the gridlock that boxed them in as they tried to follow her.

Mummers' clubhouses were coming to life, groggy people hauling instruments, supplies and costumes out of vans and into warehouses and meeting spaces. The amount of activity on Two Street at this time of the day surprised him as he moved along. He watched the enthusiasm grow as people gained steam prepping for the day's big show. Being away from this city for so long, he had forgotten about the significance of the tradition and the importance of this day for so many. A lot of people would be nursing hangovers or watching the Rose Parade happening three thousand miles away, but here there was another time-honored tradition about to happen.

And, here he was in Philly, with his boys, having just met this amazing girl on this really crazy night. His gut somehow told him the night wasn't over. He was sure of that. He fished his phone out of a pocket, slid his finger across the screen, and dialed.

"H, where'd you go?" Joey asked.

"Hey. I'm on Two Street heading up to South."

"Is Maria with you?" Ava yelled in the background.

"Tell her that she's at the clubhouse checking things out. Joe, I'm starving. South Street diner is still open. Wanna…"

"Diner?" Joe asked, stunned. "Are you kidding? Did D.C. convert you to the pancakes and waffles in the middle of the night type?"

Hunter laughed, "I lost my head for a minute there. Cheese steaks?"

"You really need to ask that? Say no more. We are on our way. We're still at the hospital. Be there in ten. Pat's or Geno's?"

Hunter said, "Geno's."

Joey shot back, "Pat's. Dude, really?"

Hunter laughed and said, "Whatever. Pick me up. And hurry. I'm freezing," secretly really glad that nothing had changed.

"On our way."

Hunter was waiting at the corner of Second and South when the Rolls appeared in Headhouse Square, slid around the corner, and screeched to a stop in front of him. He hopped into the passenger seat and glanced in the backseat at Ava sitting on Goose's lap squeezed in with Elmo, Bambi, and Frankie. Ava was cooing and fawning over Goose who was eating up the attention.

Hunter was relieved to see Ava and Bambi were in the car and grateful that maybe these two would lead him back to Maria later. Maybe things were not a lost cause after all. "Is your uncle okay?" he asked.

They nodded in unison. "He'll be out tomorrow," Bambi said.

Hunter was still thinking, *what a night* as he glanced at Joey who grinned and smashed the accelerator to the floor and said, "Pancakes? Dude, seriously?" The car lurched forward. He chuckled, yanked the wheel, and turned south. As they sped towards South Philly and the Mecca of cheesesteaks, Hunter realized that he was really, really hungry.

Minutes later, Joey eased the car into a parking spot near Ninth and Passyunk. Even at 5 a.m. the corner was busy with people looking to satisfy their cravings for Philly's famous gooey cheese steak sandwich. Groups of rowdy partiers mixed with couples still dressed from the evening's parties lined the sidewalk eager to be making the pilgrimage to the legendary corner.

"We made it. Time to eat, boys. Let's go," Joey said and pointed. "Some things never change." A few limousine drivers were returning to cars with out-of-state license plates holding armloads of sandwiches and beverages for occupants who didn't want their identities revealed.

During a few previous late-night pilgrimages, the group had tried to get a driver, or two, to reveal his passengers' names. Answers always ranged from the unbelievable to the absurd. Bill Clinton and Ben Franklin were yelled more often than not. Joey and Hunter once spotted Bruce Willis in town for a movie shoot sitting on the corner with his entourage eating a cheesesteak. He had nodded and said to them, "Good morning."

Goose, Frankie, and Elmo popped out of the back seat and helped Ava and Bambi out of the car. Joey got out, looked up, and said, "Awesome," as he and Hunter high-fived and joined the others on the corner where the group gazed up in awe at the competing glistening neon signs piercing the dark sky—The Oz of South Philly.

The two narrow buildings seemed to jut out of the narrow sidewalks. Their take-out windows competitively faced each other, pumping the scent of sautéing beef and onions into the morning air, firing up their appetites, making their stomachs growl, and reminding them of their other all too frequent late-nights visits. Goose and Elmo threw their hands up and high-fived as Frankie inhaled deeply and said, "Man, I love that fried onion smell first thing in the morning. Mmmm-mmmm."

Chapter 19

"Nothing good happens after 3 am, Maria. Ever. It's a witching hour, the spirits are communicating. Some believe someone could be watching you."

Another rule forever embossed onto Maria's brain began to taunt. She had heard her mother say this to the family more times in her life than she could have ever attempted to count. Antonetta and Maria had often argued bitterly over this as her teenage curfew was negotiated. Explaining away her sleepy college weekends after late nights trying to justify her need to sleep away a Sunday afternoon were unsuccessful and always fell on deaf ears. She didn't know why she had catalogued this mantra, except that most of the time when it came to this particular point, her mother was usually right.

She was definitely right tonight, or this morning...today. Nothing good was going to happen at this hour.

Overwhelmed and filled with dread, Maria walked into the Brawlers Clubhouse, a large open converted warehouse space with a full bar lining the perimeter on two sides. On most nights every bar stool was filled with a colorful assortment of people laughing and carrying on. The interior of the massive room was usually occupied by tables used as workbenches lined up row after row filled with busy volunteers working on costumes and props, precisely following her drawings and Thomas's instructions. Once the marching routines were planned and finessed, and regalia finished, the tables were moved out of the way to make space for the dance rehearsals.

Maria glanced around the room and watched for a moment or two, frozen in place, unable to react. This couldn't be happening. Not now. Not today.

There was chaos everywhere: feathers, headdresses, and costumes hung on large garment racks haphazardly. Props were leaning against walls, most still needed painting. Towers of beer cases were stacked up shoulder height around the room haphazardly like a maze. People rushed back and forth, creating what seemed like a lot of activity and movement. But, despite the bouncing around, and cheerfully greeting each other, nothing seemed to be getting done. Nothing.

It was unsettling and disturbing for Maria to watch this unfold and not see her dad acting like an air traffic controller holding his clipboard, pointing people in the right direction, defusing emergencies and assigning last-minute tasks to ensure everything ran smoothly until game time. He was a master at orchestrating and overseeing people and problems, something he had learned from his father over the years. Clearly without her dad there, there was no one in charge *and* there was no order.

Maria scanned the room for Uncle Bruno. He was nowhere to be found.

Maria felt the panic start to take over, her ears buzzed, and she began to feel dizzy. This was a mess. No, she thought, they had passed mess and hot-mess. This was a mess with a capital M. This was a *Royal Mess*. They were screwed. She felt doomed and sensed her shoulders sag as she took it all in from one disordered end to the other. Not sure where to turn or start, her mind raced. *What would my father do?*

Maria had spent most of her life here on New Year's Eve watching him assemble this event; surely by osmosis, if not by direction of her DNA, she should have some idea of what she should do or where she should begin.

She crossed the room, grabbed her dad's clipboard and studied it, feeling a sense of dread seep into her brain. She flipped through the pages of lists, tucked the board under her arm, put two fingers in her mouth, and whistled loudly.

Stunned people froze in their tracks, some spun around confused, and stared. Christian and several other men surrounded her, standing completely still in a semi-circle waiting for her to do or say something. Certain they were waiting for her to start barking orders like her dad, she did. "Listen up," she yelled. Heads turned toward her. She pointed at a group of men and said, "Props. Go. Finish the painting, now. And hurry it up. We don't have a lot of time to let everything dry so get a few fans pointed on them as you finish each one."

Maria watched the group dash across the room to grab cans, rollers, and brushes, quickly applying fresh coats of paint onto the large plywood cutouts.

"Christian, can you and Rudy please, please recount those costumes. Double check, no, triple check your numbers." Christian nodded and moved to the garment racks.

She turned to the last man, "Bobby. You get a couple of coffee urns started. We're going to need caffeine, and lots of it. Did anyone order food? If not, get going. Somebody, find something. People need to eat before we kick off."

It dawned on her that barking orders was in her DNA, but frustration was taking over. Maria took a deep breath, rubbed her eyes, and started to pace. As she zig-zagged the room, she screamed, "Will, count those headdresses, please. Tell me how many are complete. They should have been finished a week ago. Figure out what supplies you think we're going to need to wrap up the unfinished bunch. And, Will, remember I needed that info, like yesterday."

She smiled and watched Walt, one of the oldest members of the club, bring out several trays of coffee mugs and carefully set them up on one of the bars. One by one, people jumped into action, moving around the warehouse working with fervor.

Jackets were sorted and hung on racks and headdresses were lined up as they were counted as complete. Unfinished ensembles were being worked on. One by one, things were coming together. Soon the room seemed a little less frenzied and haphazard.

As Maria watched the activity, she was grateful things were getting done even if it was at this late hour. While reluctantly in charge for now, she was at least in command of these last-minute details, hopeful the time she could hand things over to her dad was approaching.

As she sized up the frenzy, she knew there was too much to accomplish before parade time. She arched her aching back and cracked her stiff neck, and squinted at her feet. She was still standing off balance and her feet throbbed. She kicked off her broken stilettos and crossed the room to a table where rows of boots: Uggs, Timberlands, and an assortment of sneakers were being sprayed with gold paint by an older woman wearing goggles and a painter's mask. "Morning, Amy, thanks so much for painting. I need a pair of shoes. Are there any extras?"

Amy flicked the mask off of her face, pointed to the end of the table, and said, "Take those, honey. The ones at the end are dry now."

Maria forced a smile, took the boots, and bent over to slip them on. As she stood up, she caught her reflection in a large full-length mirror propped against a wall. She pulled Hunter's tuxedo jacket close. Sadly, the blue tulle skirt hanging below the jacket looked dirty. Nonna Mary's vintage dress looked as if it had seen better days. *I've ruined it.* Maria sighed. She vowed to take it over to Nunzio's Dry Cleaning as soon as she could, hoping it could be cleaned and restored to the state she'd found it.

Nunzio was a magician, Nonna Mary had always told them. They make everything look brand new. Right now, there wasn't any time to worry about how she looked or if she had destroyed Nonna Mary's dress.

Maria rolled up Hunter's sleeves, crossed the room to a workbench, plugged in several glue guns, and waited for them to heat up. She pulled open a bag of brightly colored peacock feathers and started to work, attaching them to an unfinished costume. Her father taught her how to work with the feathers years ago, explaining how fragile the quills were and showing her how to carefully insert and attach them into the base material. Over the years, she had become skilled at not destroying the delicate beauty of the fluffy barbs as she attached them, finding her own rhythm in the careful but fast assembly.

She once again worked quickly, attaching the colorful fluff to the ornate back piece and then secured the large feather fan to a harness. She took a step backwards to check her work. "Okay. You're not perfect, but this will have to do."

Once Amy had finished painting the shoes and boots, she joined Maria at the table and began to assemble feathers. She worked quickly and had the other plumes filled out in no time. "Wow," Maria said.

"Go. I'll finish this," she ordered and waved Maria away.

Maria walked to the perimeter of the shop where her costume sketches were pinned up on the wall. She squinted at the drawings, studying them and thought that something was indeed missing from the jackets. She thought back to her conversation with her mother this morning. Something was definitely off. They did need something. They needed more glitz. Maria sighed. *She's always right.*

The pageantry of this extravagant tradition had nothing to do with appearing subtle in sound, color, or dazzle. In fact, it was the quite the opposite. Maria opened a bag of tiny mirrors and started gluing, one after the other in rows onto the jacket cuffs. She decided to add rows of rhinestones and other colorful bling to the sleeves too. Slowly but surely, they were coming close to her original vision.

She was frustrated by her slow speed and trying hard not to let panic take over. She wiped her brow with the back of her hand, then turned her attention back to her task, adding additional decorations to her third jacket when a woman approached and said, "Can't have too many mirrors, huh?"

Maria smiled and looked up to see a short round woman with soft, kind features grinning wide and holding a glue gun in the air. She moved the gun close to her mouth and blew on the tip as if she was a gun-slinger in an old cowboy Western and went to work. Maria furrowed her brow and watched. This was the first time since college that she had pulled an all-nighter. She was tired, worn-out, a little confused, and more than a little groggy. To say that she was out of practice putting these costumes together was an understatement. She was afraid she'd pass out if she sat down. She rubbed her eyes, squinted at the woman, and tried to force a smile, grateful for additional help.

Maria's smile looked more like a grimace; her lips pulled into a lopsided line. The woman continued, "You can't do it all yourself you know, honey." She took the jacket from Maria's hands and continued, "You need to delegate a little more. It's okay, really. People are more than willing to help out. All you have to do is ask."

Maria nodded, recognizing this had always been one of her shortcomings, noted on every one of her early grade school report cards. Clearly, it was still an area to be worked on if this stranger could readily see this.

"You're only one person, sweetheart. Everybody needs somebody by their side. Pulling when they're pulling. Pushing when they're pushing."

Maria raised an eyebrow and shrugged. She didn't like being judged, ever. She especially didn't like being judged by a stranger even if she might be right. *What did she know even about me?*

"You have to know when to pause. Take a breath," the woman said softly, a sense of kindness projecting from her.

Maria wasn't sure why, but she took a deep breath in and rocked her head back and forth, her neck cracking as she moved.

"Good girl. Go on now. I've got this. You go."

"Thank you. I'm sorry. I didn't get your name."

"Olympia, honey. You remember me...from Reed Street. My father's old shop. The hardware store. On the corner. Shriver's. Ask your mama," she said and winked. "She'll remember. Her mother…"

Maria giggled and nodded. Ha, yes, legendary Nonna Mary. Like the family always said, it was historic. Everyone knew the story. Maria warmed, felt a kinship to Olympia immediately, and judgment or not, this chore was progressing a lot faster with her assistance. Maria and Olympia continued gluing. They worked quickly together until their supply of mirrors and rhinestones was quickly depleted.

"I'll be right back," Maria said as she headed to a supply closet. Inside, she grabbed a couple of plastic bags of the reflective bits and returned to the workbench. She was stunned to find the rest of the jackets were all finished and neatly hung on a garment rack.

Maria spun around, searching for Olympia. She was gone.

Her mind raced. *How? Where?*

She was exhausted and more than a little bleary-eyed, but moved on to another workbench. She picked up a large feather plume and was struggling to attach it to the wire frame. Denny, a large bearded man wearing jeans and a green plaid flannel shirt and a wide brimmed hot pink fleece Happy New Year hat, approached. He held the large harness still as she snapped the last couple of plumes in place. The feathers fanned out in a glorious peacock-like semicircle that would frame the performer beautifully. Surprised at how easy it was when Denny helped, she jumped in the air, high-fived him, and yelled, "Yes!" Pleased and more than thankful that this piece was now done, she shoved her fist in the air. Denny winked at her and walked over to the next table to assist someone else.

Maria glanced at the clock above the bar that read: 4:30 and tried to fight the panic that was setting in. She knew that they needed to be in line for the beginning of the parade in just a couple of hours. They were nowhere near being ready to go. She tried to size up the room and jumped in to assist two women hunched over another table sewing rows of gold sequins onto the costume pants.

Maria was finishing sewing her first row as Tony burst through the clubhouse door, frantic, eyes opened wide, his half purple, half green painted face sweaty. He huffed and puffed, sucking in air and wheezing, trying hard to breathe and speak. His perspiration was smearing the face paint into a sickly brown as the colors blended and dripped down his cheeks. He blasted toward Maria yelling, "Big Manny forgot that he had costumes in the back of his Eagles bus. Stunod. How does that happen? Every friggin' year. I don't get it. Give me a break. Every year. Where's your father, Ri? Where's Tommy?"

Maria continued to sew, shook her head, and said, "Not here. He's in the hospital. I'm in charge for the time being..."

As Tony's wheezing worsened, he pulled out an inhaler and sucked on it. Maria looked up as he grabbed his hat and started to fan himself, as he spoke, "Crap. Geez-o. Hospital? Oh no. Oh my god, what's wrong? That can't be good. Ri, is he all right?"

Maria pulled a chair over and shoved Tony into

the seat motioning for him to breathe and said, "Calm down, Tony. Breathe." As Tony took a breath, she continued, "That's it, good. Breathe…My dad's going to be fine in a couple of days. He fell. That's all. It's just a sprain, we hope. And, Manny, breaking down pre-parade, well, you know that's kind of his tradition. Breathe," she said again as she nodded in time with his breaths. "Right, Tony? Right? You know what I mean? What would New Year's be without a little agita?"

"A little agita? That jerk, Manny's got that mastered. And, Ri, this tradition's one I could do without, if you know what *I* mean," he said as he took another deep breath. "Big Manny's stuck on the Walt Whitman this time. Flat tire. Again. Fourth year. In. A. Row. Ri. Fourth. Idiot. He's such an idiot. Should've left them here. Why did he take the costumes home?"

Maria motioned for him to breathe again, gulped, and said, "Wait. Costumes?"

In between breaths, Tony nodded and continued, "I can't find any wheels to go over there and get him, or the costumes. We're in trouble, Maria. Big trouble."

The entrance door opened with a loud bang. Rowdy, drunk-singing, blasted in from near the entrance. "Here we stand before your door. As we stood the year before. Give us whiskey. Give us gin."

Maria spun towards the door to see Uncle Bruno and Iggy, arm-in-arm, swaying and singing louder and with gusto now, "Open the door and let us in. Or give us something nice and hot, like a steaming hot bowl of pepper pot. Pepppperrrr Poooot."

Oh good, my family has arrived.

"What the—? About time you got here, boys," she said through gritted teeth. "Get some coffee," she ordered. "Somebody get these two some coffee. Fast," she yelled to anyone close by. Several people sprang into action at the bar. "Uncle Bruno, call Big Manny, ASAP," she barked. "Get his exact location. And, I mean his exact location. See who's closest and get them there. Now. We're missing costumes and we are running out of time."

Tony looked over at her, nodded appreciatively, and then headed towards the bar continuing his deep breathing as somebody tossed him a water bottle that he opened and chugged in one pull.

"C'mon? Really, Ri? What are you saying? That bus of his? Again? Will somebody please make him leave that Partridge Family hunk of junk home, for god's sake, already. Geez-o. I'm really sooooo tired of his last-minute commotion," Uncle Bruno said.

Iggy added, "Yeah, boss. You're right. What's he thinking?"

It was all she could do not to smack both of them both hard. She shot them a look that she hoped said, *you're kidding, right?* She added a wave in their direction as she tried to make her point. "Let's go. CHOP. CHOP. No arguing," she said and added, "Go," to make sure they understood she was serious and meant business.

And, there it was. It was happening. She stood there with her mouth open, raging and barking orders. She had become her mother. Bruno and Iggy straightened up and quickly moved away and got to work. Bruno pulled out a cell phone, dialed and yelled into it, "Yo, Big Manny. What are you doing?"

Maria couldn't make out what Manny said on the other end, but Uncle Bruno's face was now turning purple without the benefit of paint. She was grateful for his help, though she was still really angry that he had only just arrived minutes ago.

"MANNY, what are your coordinates? Manny?" Bruno shouted into his phone, shrugged at her and then continued, "C'mon, Manny. You over the side of the bridge? 'Cuz, I got a couple a navy seals that are real, real bored right now. They're just itchin' to get back in the river like old times. You could make their day." Uncle Bruno looked at the phone and then at Maria, shrugged and said, "I think he hung up."

Iggy pulled a bolt of fabric off of a shelf and quickly unrolled a few yards. He grabbed scissors and started to cut. "Iggy, not this year. We're out of time," Maria said.

Iggy hung his head and muttered, "Dang."

She patted his back and said, "One of these years, Ig, one of these years," then turned to Uncle Bruno and said, "Somebody must be coming over the Walt Whitman. No?"

Iggy added, "Yeah, yeah. Oh, maybe Enzo! He usually takes the bread truck over about this time, right before we start, right Bruno?"

"Really? Uncle Bruno, see if he's out there. Can you call him and find out if he's on the road? Maybe he can find Manny's bus, grab the costumes, and bring them over here," she said, trying hard to mask her desperation as she glanced at the clock. "Oh, great. It's almost 5 a.m. already. We are so out of time. Tell him they'll have to meet us in line if they can't get back over the bridge and down here. We'll improvise."

Maria collapsed into the closest chair, face palmed her head into her hands, and thought, this was it. It was over. The team was not going to pull off competing this year. This would be first time ever in her family's history that they wouldn't march in this parade and it was now her fault. All of her fault.

This was an epic fail.

This was her epic fail. She was going to go down in history just like Nonna Mary, but this story was beyond missing gold paint for the shoes. This was complete and total annihilation.

They were doomed.

And, worse yet, she'd let her father down.

Chapter 20

The group stood facing a take-out window and several bright orange picnic tables taunting from Geno's on one side of the street, and a take-out window and red tables beckoned from across the street at Pat's. It was a Philly cheesesteak crossroads of sorts. Geno's versus Pat's with fists in the air, dueling as always.

Joey once explained allegiance to one or the other of these beloved places was almost a birthright in this town, assigned to you when you left the hospital for the ride home with your family. Joey shared this during freshman orientation week with such conviction that Hunter couldn't argue, or be bothered to fact-check him. He'd learn later cheesesteak loyalties were passionately argued across town. Several other popular spots were always in the running for "Best of Philly."

As first-year students, they had been sent out on a scavenger hunt with a map and a list of Philly icons to be located over the course of an evening to familiarize them with the city. Together they had managed to breeze through most of the list, easily finding Boat House Row, running up and down the

Rocky steps at the Philadelphia Museum of Art, taking photos at the Love Statue and the Clas Oldenburg Clothespin sculpture, and locating the goat in Rittenhouse Square. The Liberty Bell, Independence Hall, and Ben Franklin's grave were also not a problem to find due to the streams of tourists also snapping pictures.

They had left this famous South Philly corner for their last stop that night. They eagerly taste-tested sandwiches at both places and pocketed evidence to prove that they had been there. They argued then on the perfect thinness of the steak, which cheese to order—American, Provolone, or Cheese Whiz—whether to add onions, and most importantly how to order as if you knew what you were doing. They learned that Whiz wit translated in South Philly speak as a cheesesteak with Cheese Whiz and onions and seemed to be universally accepted as the most popular. They hadn't agreed on one thing that night or any night thereafter, each of them insisting their choice was perfection.

Hunter had once made the mistake of taking Joey to an authentic "Philly Cheesesteak" place in Foggy Bottom during one of his D.C. visits. To this day, he would not let Hunter forget that he was once forced to consume a bastardization of the renowned sandwich. He made Hunter promise then they would only eat this particular delicacy at home.

Hunter already knew that they wouldn't see eye to eye tonight either, but he was all too happy to deliberate the pros and cons once again with Joey for old time's sake. It was sport. It was what they did. They enjoyed fighting this fight and knew that there would never be a winner, not that it mattered to either of them.

Traditions come in all forms. This one was theirs.

The group stood there, heads turning back and forth until Joey said, "Breakfast of champions. Pat's."

Bambi corrected, "Geno's."

Hunter agreed, "Geno's."

Goose nodded and said, "Geno's."

And, there it was, allegiances by birthright, or experience. Goose, Bambi, and Hunter headed to Geno's and the rest to Pat's. They stood in line with a few of the other New Year's Eve stragglers and waited to order. A wall of celebrity photos prominently displayed near the window caught Hunter's eye again, a who's who of people that have made the pilgrimage. This time, front and center right next to Danny DeVito's autographed photo, was a picture of Geno's founder, Joey Vento, shaking hands with a Mummer, handing over a giant check for forty thousand dollars donated to the "Save the Mummers" campaign when the parade itself was once in danger of ending.

Bambi kissed her fingers and reached up to the photo, "God bless his dear departed soul."

In South Philly, there were loyalties and devotions of all sorts, sports, neighborhood bars, Sunday red sauce, and the never-settled debate as to whether it is called sauce or gravy, and especially cheese steaks.

The man taking orders at the window tapped his pen on the counter as he waited for Hunter's order. "Whiz wit," he said quickly. He always ordered his steak sandwich with Whiz, not provolone or American cheese. It wasn't exactly health food, but he ate enough kale and organic green stuff in D.C. so he deserved the splurge. And, he was hungry.

Bambi didn't need to verbalize an order. She just smiled at the guy who nodded at her, said, "Hey," and motioned to the pick-up window. Her sandwich was there waiting with a side of cheese fries, on the house.

Hunter and Bambi joined the rest of the group at one of the picnic tables where everyone was silently devouring their food. Ava took a sip of Diet Coke and picked up her phone. Her eyes opened wide and she said, "Oh no. Bam, check your phone."

Bambi said, "What? Why?" and picked up her phone and gasped.

Hunter looked over Bambi's shoulder and saw: Maria—Three Missed Calls.

Bambi and Ava locked eyes. "Oh no," Ava said. "What time is it?"

"5:15," Hunter said and stared at them blankly.

Bambi and Ava both started dialing.

"Voicemail," Bambi said.

"Same," Ava said.

"This can't be good. We've got to move. I've got a bad feeling," Bambi said.

"Me too. Six calls? Ava said as she and Bambi stood up, gathered up the remnants of the snack and looked at the group. "C'mon," Ava said as she grabbed Goose by the lapels. Joey, Frankie, Elmo, and Hunter shoved the rest of their sandwiches in their mouths. Ava motioned hurry, both hands circling in the air as they guzzled soda and quickly ate their French fries, not quite sure of the urgency.

They bolted to the Rolls, piled in as Joey started the car, and revved the engine. "Hurry," Ava wailed. Seconds later, they were tearing up Ninth Street careening around a corner at the Italian Market just missing a vendor unloading produce boxes to set up his outdoor display of fruit and vegetables.

"Where are we going?" Joey asked.

"Just drive," Ava said as she dialed her phone again and looked at Bambi's panicked face.

"This isn't going to be good, Ava. I've got a bad feeling," Bambi said.

Chapter 21

"You need to spend the first day of the year reviewing the last twelve months and then resolve to do something to improve, Maria. New Year's is like getting a clean slate. What are you going to change, Ri? Start small. This way you'll feel like you accomplished something," was Antonetta's motto for her daughters for as long as Maria could remember. *"I prefer to go big, but you do you, Maria. Do what you are comfortable with."*

Antonetta and her resolutions usually made Maria crazy, but at this moment she resolved never to be put in any situation unprepared ever again.

The snow flurries were gone and temperatures had crept up. A thick fog eerily hugged the ground just above the street as dawn approached. It felt a little bit warmer to Maria as she stood on the sidewalk watching the neighborhood slowly come to life. It would be better for the performers if it wasn't a frigid day, better for the massive crowds that turned out to watch too, she thought.

She pulled out her phone and tried to call Ava and Bambi again. Neither was picking up. "Great, just great," she muttered. They were never unavailable, ever. Why now? Why today?

A sudden chill and a surge of sadness hit her. She folded her arms and pulled Hunter's jacket tightly around her waist as she felt tears well again. *I will not cry, not now.* She blinked hard and sucked the damp early morning air deep into her lungs, trying hard to fend off the breakdown that she really wanted to have right now. A good cry might be cathartic, but she knew she couldn't give in. She stood there a moment more, not able to turn and face what was inside.

"Morning, Maria," and a few "Happy New Year, Ri-s," flew at her as people approached the Brawler's clubhouse and the others up and down Two Street. Scruffy hung-over men and women carrying costumes and instrument cases shuffled up the block and entered buildings. A few groups of parents and grandparents carried sleepy kids into the Brawlers headquarters, deposited them into chairs, and propped them up with pillows and blankets to sleep until start time. They nodded hello as they went inside averting Maria's attention and tears, at least for now. She knew she didn't have time to fall apart and wouldn't want to in front of these people. She'd never live it down.

As she walked back inside, Grace, an older woman whose own father was once a captain years before her grandfather, approached, handed her a steaming mug, and said, "Coffee's up, honey. It'll do you good." Maria watched sleepy people fill up mugs, one after the other at several coffee urns that had been set up on the bar. People were fueling up and waking up. Chatter filled the room and her brain with static and noise. It was all she could do not to turn and run.

Uncle Bruno and Iggy had successfully located food and were busy opening tubs of cream cheese and slicing bagels arranging them on trays. Boxes of Tastycake Donuts were ripped open. A delivery man carried stacks of bakery boxes in and was escorted to the food setup. Iggy pointed at an open spot next to the bagel trays. Grace quickly emptied the stacks of boxes, setting up pastry trays and arranging them on the tables. Hungry people helped themselves to the food. A man deposited several cases of Philly Soft Pretzels in front of Uncle Bruno and handed him a shopping bag full of bottles of yellow mustard. Maria felt a wash of relief that at least something was on schedule and on track.

Her phone buzzed. She looked at it and saw Ava's name. Maria clicked accept and heard rapid fire yelling, "Ri? I just now heard your voicemail. Are you kidding me? Who gave Big Manny costumes again? Again? Really? Doesn't anyone ever learn in this family? Ever? Geez. What do we have to do? C'mon, already."

Maria couldn't get a word in. She knew better. She let her finish.

"Ri? You there?" Ava asked.

"Yup. I'm here. And yup, I know, I know. Ava, where are you?"

"We're on Tenth Street. Almost to the stadiums," Ava said.

"Manny's on the Walt Whitman. Stuck. He's got

a flat or something, again. Any chance?" she asked.

"Walt Whitman. You got it. We'll take care of Manny. Believe me, we'll take care of Manny."

"Be gentle."

"Oh. I'll be gentle," Ava said as tires squealed and an engine raced in the background.

"I owe you."

"Don't mention it," Ava said. "We're in this together."

Maria heard someone yell, "Watch out, Joe." And she heard tires squeal again.

"Ava? Are you guys okay? Ava?" she asked as the phone went dead. She closed her eyes and wished that her father was there. The comforting sounds of banjos being tuned and scales being played on several saxophones in the distance pierced the din.

Maria opened her eyes and watched as costumes were sorted and claimed. Lines of people pushed their feet into gold-painted Timberland boots, gold Uggs, and gold sneakers. She joined the women at the workbench sewing sequins and tried her best to assist, but her hands ached. She couldn't stitch a thing.

Uncle Bruno pushed a plate toward her and said, "Eat something, honey. It's a cinnamon raisin, your favorite," he said as he kissed the top of her head and handed her a bagel.

"Thanks, Uncle Bruno," she said softly.

"It's going to be okay. You'll see," he said as he patted her shoulder. She shrugged and managed a weak smile as he moved away. She knew there was no way they were pulling this one off today. Maria moved over to the bar and took a seat. Somebody plunked a fresh cup of coffee in front of her. She picked up a remote control and clicked on the television.

Breakfast with the Mummers, Philly's local parade "pregame" show flashed on the screen. A PHL-17 reporter talked animatedly at the camera, surrounded by a group of Mummers, a Fancy Brigade, wearing massive plumed back pieces and ornate costumes. Maria turned up the volume as the reporter faced the camera and said, "Ten thousand costumed Philadelphians are about to parade up Broad Street from South Philadelphia as they have done for more than three hundred years. As most of you know, Mumming is a grand family tradition handed down from generation to generation."

Maria hung her head as he continued. She knew that the team was finished.

"Hold on," Joey yelled as he blasted the Rolls down Tenth Street toward the stadiums, turned past Lincoln Financial Field, then whizzed by Citizens Bank Park, and onto the expressway.

Within minutes, they were gliding up and over the Walt Whitman Bridge heading to New Jersey. "Do A.C." billboards advertising the casinos taunted from the both sides of the bridge. Any other night they might have just kept driving east to the Jersey shore to hit a poker table, play a little blackjack, feed a few slot machines, and overindulge in free cocktails, but tonight, or rather, this morning, they were on a mission, a Mummer's mission. This was not something Hunter ever thought he'd say, or think, in his lifetime, but today they were united on this crazy task looking for some guy named Manny who had apparently really screwed up.

As a group they were not easily deterred by any scheme they'd attempted together, no matter how absurd. They had enthusiastically embarked on a few ridiculous capers during their time together. Hunter was sure they would not be overcome tonight by these circumstances, despite Ava and Bambi's concerns and worried faces.

"There. Over there," yelled Bambi as she pointed at the broken-down bus waiting on the shoulder of the road. A white flag was tied to the antenna and whipped violently in the wind, ironically signifying Manny's reluctant surrender.

Manny's Eagles' Bus was on the other side of the bridge pointed toward Center City. It was an old school bus painted Philadelphia Eagles green that had seen better days. More *Magic School Bus* than a Sunday afternoon tailgating palace, the bus was decorated from end-to-end with the Eagles logo, NFL helmets, a rudimentary cartoon drawing of the team mascot, Swoop, and words from the team theme song: FLY, EAGLES FLY. Big Manny had worked hard to pimp this bus out. Hunter was sure under other circumstances he and the guys would have shared a beer or a roast pork sandwich with Manny at a tailgate party, but today their mission to locate him and the missing equipment was paramount.

Ava pointed at the bus, "Oh crap. We have to get over to the other side of the bridge. Joey, you're going to have to go over to Forty-Two and turn around. Slow down a minute first, Joe, please."

"You got it, babe," Joey said.

Ava rolled down the window and yelled, "Big Manny. Yo. Big Manny. What are you doing?" as Joey slowed, stopped, and put his hazard lights on.

On the opposite side of the bridge was a huge, brawny man, dressed head-to-toe in Eagles team gear, leaning against the front of the broken-down bus, head hanging, arms folded.

"Manny!"

The big man looked up and waved sheepishly at them.

"Again, Manny? Seriously? You ever going to learn?" Ava screamed.

Hunter watched the man's shoulder slump as he cowered and shrugged sheepishly. Clearly, he had experienced Ava's wrath before. Hunter felt bad as he watched Manny hang his head, shuffle his feet, and move to the back of the bus.

"Don't move. We'll be right there," Ava continued.

"Where am I going, Ava? I mean, really. The Bird Bus ain't moving, babe. It ain't rolling anywhere right now," Manny shouted.

"Not news, Manny. Not news. It never rolls anywhere. Ever. When you gonna give it up already?" Ava said.

A tractor trailer barreled up the bridge behind

them, laying on its horn and careening around the Rolls just in the nick of time, narrowly missing Joey's car. A chorus of, "Floor it, Joey" and "Oh my Gods" were screamed as Joey floored it over the Walt Whitman Bridge into New Jersey. And then as fast as he could, he exited and reversed course back over the bridge towards Philadelphia.

Joey parked behind the Eagles bus. Ava bolted out of the car towards Manny, smacked his arm hard a few times, and squealed, "Really? Manny, really? What were you thinking? C'mon. Every year? Do we have to do this *every year*? Give up. Get rid of this piece of junk."

"Look, Ava. I'm sorry. It's not like I planned this. It's not ever, ever my intention to hold the guys up on purpose. It's not my fault," Manny said.

Ava and Bambi groaned.

"Not your fault? Really?" Ava said.

Hunter was sure that it probably was Manny's fault, despite his protests.

The group did their best hoisting instrument cases and costumes, gathering Manny's other necessary flotsam and jetsam from the bus, quickly jamming everything into the trunk of Joey's car as a large tow truck rumbled up.

"Be careful with her," Manny pleaded to the tow truck driver as he hooked and hoisted the Eagles Bus into the air.

"I ever let you down, Manny?" the guy asked.

"No, you never have," Manny tearfully admitted as he climbed into the tow truck's passenger seat.

The group watched and flinched as the bus lurched and jumped as it hit several potholes and drove away, back into the city. They squeezed back into the car and headed back over the bridge following the bus. "You've got to step on it, Joey. It's really getting late," Bambi said.

Joey floored it.

Chapter 22

"If it's not one thing, Maria, it's fifty others. That's life. One step at a time. Remember that. First things first." Somehow, her mother threw this wisdom at Maria when she was overwhelmed. Antonetta always made it look like she was impeccably juggling challenges and somehow kept everything under control.

Another of her mother's nuggets zig-zagged through Maria's cluttered brain as she tried to gather her scattered thoughts. *One step at a time. First things first. If only.*

The massive surge of activity in the warehouse created enough noise to completely drown out the Mummers' pre-game show on the television. Maria could no longer hear the scripted recap of the parade history. Not that it mattered, she couldn't bear to listen to the reporter's cheerful patter. It was too upsetting a reminder of her impending doom and the impact it was going to have on The Brawlers' personal parade history.

Most of the team and their families had arrived. Merriment and camaraderie buzzed in the air as they packed into the space chatting, eating, organizing costumes, and changing clothes. Besides the obvious problems and the already averted disasters, something else just didn't feel right to Maria. She could feel it deep in her gut. Counting heads was complicated by the size of the crowd and the bustle. Her intuition, another happy circumstance that she had inherited from her mother and the other women in the family, was nagging her. Something was telling her to pay attention. If only she had a clue about what was needed.

She glanced at her dad's office where an antique brass sign that read, CAPTAIN'S QUARTERS hung on the door. She needed a quiet minute to think. She headed inside, closed the door behind her, and leaned against it, wishing that her dad was there.

What would he do?

She glanced at her father's organized mess of an office and took a minute to take it all in. Detailed plans for this year's performance were randomly taped to the walls. A collection of her drawings from years past were carefully framed and hung around the perimeter of the room. Her very first attempt at costume design, a crayon drawing of a Mummer that she had carefully scribbled when she was about eight years old was ornately framed and displayed front and center with the rest of her later designs.

Maria walked behind her father's simple metal desk to a row of battered filing cabinets. She stared at several family photos lovingly displayed on the top of cabinets as they had been for years. She picked up one of the frames and studied the snapshot of her dad proudly wearing Mummers' regalia holding a young

Maria. She put the frame down and picked up another —her mom pushing a baby stroller and holding a toddler. Maria smiled as she put the photo down and scanned the line-up of trophies, each one symbolic of the years that made up their history. Her family history. Her history.

An old-fashioned clanging bell sound cut through the silence. Maria jumped and reached across the desk, grabbed the office phone, surprised to hear her father's voice bellowing, "Ri. I'm hung up here for a little while longer."

"Oh hi, Daddy. Is everything okay?"

"Yes. We're waiting on the doctor to come back with my paperwork. How's it going down there?"

"Oh. Fine. Everything's fine. Uh-huh. No problem. Nope," she lied as he questioned her, hoping she sounded cheerful and reassuring. "I'll talk to you soon, okay. You just rest. Bye," she said quickly as she hung up, not giving him an opportunity to grill her further on the details of what was actually happening in the clubhouse. She couldn't bear to tell him that everything was a complete mess. She knew he didn't need to hear that now. She was determined that somehow she was going to find a way to make this work. She had to make this work. She had to fix this.

First things first.

She spotted her father's freshly pressed costume carefully hung on a garment rack ready and waiting for today's march. The ornate fruit-covered head piece was sitting right next to the rack cradled in a cardboard box.

She put on the jacket. It was huge on her tiny frame. She found the pants and put them on, cinching a belt as tight as possible to keep them up. She tried as best as she could to roll up the cuffs on the long pants. She shoved the giant fruit-covered headdress on her head and tried to balance it, knowing she must look ridiculous. She spun towards a full-length mirror to see her reflection and gasped. She looked like a little kid playing dress up; the jacket's sleeves were too long, the bottom of the pant legs puddling on to the floor. She could hardly move, but took a tentative step forward anyway. The huge headpiece tilted to one side; a loose feather fell over her eyes. She tried to blow it out of the way. It wouldn't budge.

She looked like a huge Lucy Ricardo fail.

She took the headpiece off, tucked it under her arm, and tried to walk back out to the workshop, sliding her feet across the floor and tripping on the pants as she went.

It's over.

She scanned the crowd. There was chaos everywhere. People dancing, eating, fooling around. This wouldn't be happening if her dad were here, she thought. She wondered why she believed she could just step in for him. Why did *he* ever think that she could take over? There was no way she was pulling this off.

At that moment, she accepted The Brawlers would not be winning a prize this year, but the realization they might not even make it out to Broad Street hit her hard. It would be a first.

She felt the weight of generations past crush her shoulders. She slumped on a bench, knowing in her heart that they were sunk. Her cell phone rang. She didn't recognize the number, but sighed, and answered it anyway. "This is Maria," she said and listened to the person on the other end.

Bambi, Ava, Joey, Elmo, Frankie, Hunter, and a very guilty-looking Big Manny burst into the clubhouse carrying costumes and instruments. Manny circled the room handing out costumes to the people still dressed in street clothes and not yet Mummered up and earnestly apologized to each person as he distributed supplies. Most of them just nodded and shook their heads, a few patted his shoulders knowingly as they were handed their stuff.

Bambi and Ava spotted Maria and rushed across the room.

"Ri, you okay?" Ava said as she looked her over head-to-toe. "What? What are you thinking?"

Maria leaned her head back, closed her eyes and ran her hands over her hair and sighed. She looked up at them, opened her mouth, but couldn't speak.

"Ri," Ava said again.

"Ri! Are you okay?" Bambi asked.

"Okay?" Maria said. "What am I thinking? Thinking? Who said I'm thinking? I'm not thinking. Who can think? I'm reacting. I'm doing what I do best. Right? Fixing? Pleasing," she rapid fired as she tried to stand. The weight of the costume yanked her back down to the bench. "Gravity. Got to love it," she spit out as she plopped back down. "I was going to try to step in for my dad. Do the routine. Uncle Bruno's still smashed and doesn't know dad's part anyway." Tears began to pool. She sniffled. "I can't even stand up. I just can't do it anymore. I'm done. It's done. We're done."

Confused, Ava and Bambi exchanged looks. Unable to respond, they stood there and stared at her. Ava sat next to Maria, understanding that at this point she might completely lose it. She put her arm around Maria's shoulders and said gently, "We got here as fast as we could, Ri. Really." She pointed to Big Manny. "And, Manny gave out the costumes already. Look. We can do this. It's going to be okay."

"Yeah, it'll be fine," Bambi added.

"No. It's not. It's not going to be okay. It's not fine. Not today. It's over. Over. Little Paulie just called. He and old Mikey-bag-o-doughnuts and Little Stevie are in jail," she blurted and then added, "We're done."

"Ri, we're not done. No problem. Send Iggy over to the Roundhouse to get them out. We've got plenty of petty cash in the back, don't we? This isn't the first time somebody got—," Ava said.

Bambi scowled. "Wait. They couldn't stay out of trouble for one weekend?" she hissed and started to pace.

"It doesn't matter. They're in Paoli. They're in jail in *Paoli*." Maria said.

Bambi stopped and spun around. "Paoli? What were they doing in Paoli?" she asked.

"Ohhhhh. They were probably chasing after

that Wendy girl. Little Stevie's got it bad for her," Ava said.

"What difference does it make why they were out there?" Bambi snapped at Ava and then turned to Maria and asked," Why were they out there, Ri? Wendy? Really? Her?"

"Oh my God. How do I know? I can't keep track of everyone. I'm only one person. Big Stevie is on his way out there now to bail them out, if he can. But, it's a holiday. So even if he can manage to find a judge and get them out, there is just no way they'll make it back here in time. No way."

"Can we do it without them?" Ava asked.

Bambi sat down on the other side of Maria and said, "Geez. That's three instruments. Three performers. Kind of messes up the routines. No?"

Maria pursed her lips and nodded.

"I didn't think it could ever happen, but this is worse than the debacle of seventy-four," Ava said.

"Way worse. Nonna Mary was the only one who was in jail and she never marched, only cooked," Bambi added.

"Yeah, look at us now. Woo-hoo. And you two thought I'd outdone her *just* because I stole Vinny's horse," Maria said.

"Borrowed," the three of them said, laughing and nodding in unison looking like a strange line of giggling bobble head dolls.

"Yup. We're done," Ava said.

"Definitely done," Bambi said as they laughed hard enough that tears started to roll.

If this was some kind of a dream, Maria thought that she had now blasted right into nightmare status, the South Philly edition.

Maria looked up. For some reason, Hunter and his friends were still standing in front of them, watching.

Hunter moved in closer. She looked up at him, at that kind face, and wondered what he was thinking. Why was he still there? Why wasn't he running out of the door to get as far away as possible from her and all of this nonsense?

Maria almost fell off of the bench when he said, "We can help."

One step at a time.

A short time later, Maria stood in front of Hunter in complete disbelief, wondering why this man was willing to jump into this mess, her mess, something that no one had ever done for her, ever. "You don't have to do this, you know. This is really above and beyond what you should do, or should want to do for someone you've only met hours ago."

"It's okay. I want to help, Maria," he said as he stood tall and tugged at the sleeve of her father's colorful and a little over-the-top Captain's costume. It was a far cry from the way he looked when she first plowed into him at Thirtieth Street Station, ruining that perfect look, his elegant tuxedo, and, she was quite sure, his entire amazing night.

The costume looked only slightly less ridiculous on him. He too somehow resembled Lucy Ricardo auditioning for a spot in Ricky's Club Babalu show. The huge headdress sat on his head cocked a little to the right, and the feathers poked crookedly, this way and that. She reached up, straightened the hat on Hunter's head and tried to bend the feathers back into place. Her few quick adjustments weren't working. She stepped back, not satisfied with her quick fix, and realized that they were out of time. *What was I thinking?* Her creative inspiration long forgotten, she decided that this was as good as it was going to get right now.

Hunter scrunched his lips, raised his eyebrows, and looked for some indication of approval. Maria was about to attempt some reassurance when Ava interrupted, "Maria," she said as she pointed at Hunter's shiny black dress shoes.

"Oh, no," was all Maria said as she grabbed a can of gold spray paint, shook it, and yanked up his pant legs. She didn't wait to ask, or wait for him to protest, or offer an alternative. She aimed the can and spray painted his perfect black leather shoes a glittery gold then blurted out, "I'm sorry, really, sorry."

There it was.

She had now completed total devastation by ruining his expensive shoes too.

Crashing sounds diverted Maria's attention and her heartfelt apology for a split second. She shook her head at the sight of Uncle Bruno splayed on the floor surrounded by a fallen wall of beer cases and wondered what could possibly go wrong next. Uncle Bruno sat up straight, laughed, held a can of beer in the air, and screamed, "Game time."

Maria glanced at the television above the bar. Peppy music blared from the speakers. She watched the parade kick off on the screen. A group of comics stepped off first, leading the way, strutting up Broad Street, and pumping colorful parasols enthusiastically up and down in the air.

She heard Joey yell, "Oh. My. God," as the group joined her to look at the screen.

They were all speechless, mouths hanging open, staring at the television above their heads as the camera zoomed in on—Goose, still dressed in his diaper/tuxedo get up, but now also wearing gold Timberland boots strutting up a storm, and triumphantly leading off the parade.

"It's Goose! Look," Joey said as he pointed at the screen. "I can't believe it. It's Goose." Joey and Hunter scanned the room searching as if there could possibly be two guys that looked like this funny little man and their Goose would suddenly appear across the room with them.

They stood frozen and watched as...

Goose stepped three steps forward and then two steps backward. He pumped a parasol into the air, smiled wide, and spun around and around. He pumped his arms out, again, pushed the umbrella to the sky, strutted some more, and spun around again, and again. He cruised across the street from side to side working the excited crowd. Women posed for photographs with him, men slapped him on the back, and people laughed at his performance. Goose strutted some more, eating up the attention. He stopped on a corner and locked lips with an older woman. She fanned herself as another comic yanked Goose back into the street in front of the group.

The group, mouths open in disbelief, watched the television in silence. As...

Goose ate up the attention, grinned wide, and shoved his face close to one of the television crew's cameras. The crowd's screaming, hooting, and hollering and clapping fired him up. He went nuts, stomping his feet and flapping his arms.

"I thought he was with you," Joey said to Hunter.

"It wasn't my turn to watch him. I thought he was with you. How'd he get all the way to the front of the line?" Hunter asked.

Ava jumped up and down, grabbed Maria's arm and shook her. "Ri, look. Look. That's my man!" she said and screamed at the television, "Honey, I love you."

"Dang," Elmo said.

Iggy and Bruno approached. "Maria," Uncle Bruno said.

Maria, still glued to the television, wasn't able to look away. She didn't react. She couldn't react, or believe her eyes.

"Maria. Ri! It's time," Uncle Bruno said louder this time, shaking her arm to get her attention. "Hey. We should move out."

"Great. Just great. One minute, Uncle Bruno." She grabbed Ava and Bambi and they flew into the office searching for boxes of Brawlers sweatshirts.

They quickly changed into their blending-in ensembles, black hoodies, yoga pants, and puffy down jackets, then headed back out to the workshop.

The chaos had now reached new heights of bedlam, people moving around with no sense of purpose. She had stood there in that spot year after year and excitedly fallen in with the troops, knowing her responsibilities. She had watched her father take command of this bunch, and witnessed the team dutifully act on his orders. Maria looked around, wishing she could run out of the door back to her little apartment in New York to escape.

She couldn't move.

"Ri!" Uncle Bruno snapped.

Yanked back to this reality, Maria's eyes popped open wide, she stuck two fingers in her mouth, and whistled loudly. The room froze, everyone suddenly completely silent and attentive. *Hmmm. Okay, then.*

She pointed to the door and yelled, "Let's do this. Now. Go. Go. Go."

People moved fast, grabbing gear and lining up. The Brigade poured out onto Two Street and they took their place in line, assembling with the other bands where they waited…and waited.

Chapter 23

Joey, Elmo, Frankie, and Hunter exchanged looks and a "let's do this" nod as they moved into the street and took their places with the band. "We've got this," Joey said, as he grinned, and plucked the strings on the banjo he was holding.

"I'm not so sure," Hunter quipped, "but a challenge is a challenge. No turning back now." As foolish as it seemed, they were committed, and not about to quit before they started.

Joey fell in with the other strings. Elmo gripped a saxophone and moved toward the brass section. He ran through scales with the other musicians. Frankie slid into line with the men and women hugging accordions that rounded out this group. Frankie rocked back and forth and launched into an oompah-pah chorus, nodding his head with the music. He added a few Beatbox sounds, creating a growly hip-hop version of the song as he stomped his feet. His street beat fired up the group's attention and they enthusiastically joined in on his fresh take on the old polka standard, adding their own versions of wild noises.

Hunter glanced at Maria as she surveyed the crowd and twirled her hair with her finger. The seriousness of this act was written on all of their faces.

Hunter winked, smiled, and gave her a thumbs-up, hoping to reassure her as he moved up front and took his place in the Captain's spot, front and center. He squared his shoulders, trying very hard to look confident and in charge, knowing the importance of this day to her, and to the extended family that made up the Brigade.

The enormity and significance of this long-standing family tradition wasn't something Hunter was schooled in. In his family, his mother and he were treated as necessary props, used only when his father demanded they be present for public events. They weren't an integral component of his existence or even an important part of his life. They were put in place when he needed a living illustration of his moral compass and his family values. Hunter always felt like an extra, in the background to fill space when it suited his father's needs, not put there because he wanted him present. Eventually, Hunter and his mother were discarded and replaced by another set of willing characters. *That* reality was the only family tradition he knew. They weren't now, or ever, the get-together just to be in each other's orbit kind of family. This level of commitment was foreign to him.

The band trudged along, kidding and cajoling each other as they made their way up the street. Hunter was surprised to see performers and props lined up as far as he could see snaking around the corner in the direction of the official beginning of the parade route. He glanced at Joey and said, "Whoa."

"Dude!" Joey laughed and high-fived him.

Hunter had never experienced this event in this way. His viewing had traditionally been while nursing a hangover splayed on the sofa in front of a television miles away, and once in person when he and Joey had stationed themselves in front of a Center City bar on Broad Street. The magnitude of this spectacle doesn't translate to the television audience and was lost on him until now as he watched Brigade after Brigade ready themselves waiting for their cue to move ahead and perform. "This is nuts," Hunter said, and shook his head.

They inched forward bit by bit as the morning wore on. He wasn't sure of the frantic urgency of earlier, but supposed that meeting this deadline and being in line on time with last-minute details fine-tuned was a necessary part of this tradition too.

Men, women, children of all ages, and even a few dogs, all dressed in their best Mummers finery waited patiently. Some older folks were ceremoniously perched in chairs riding high on flatbeds, poised for the chance to be center stage, and their yearly moment to shine.

Hunter nudged Joey and said, "This is like Mardi Gras on steroids."

Joey chuckled and shot back, "Carnival gone crazy."

"Boo-yah madness on Broad Street. Go figure," Hunter said as he fist bumped Joey.

"Dude! We're Mummering."

They understood this long-standing ritual exemplified *tradition* here. It was Maria's tradition, and they were now on a mission. At least Hunter was on this mission for the girl he had just met hours ago. The rest of this group, these guys, his friends, had never ever turned down a challenge, no matter how big or small. They were in it to win it, if he was. And, he was all in. They were back together as if their college days had happened just yesterday. Truth be told, he was really happy to have them there by his side now.

He was aware that if any one of his family, friends, or acquaintances, besides this core group of guys, saw him they'd be sure that he had completely lost his mind. He didn't know what he was thinking exactly, or if he was thinking at all, but for now, this moment felt right. It was as if this was the most important task he could've taken on. Of course, his competitive side had won. Hunter was approaching this event like it was any other goal he needed to conquer. For some unknown reason, this crazy endeavor felt as important to him as anything he had ever done. He knew it sounded foolish. Maybe it was the lack of sleep. Or, maybe it was the fact that he was back with the guys that could be counted on to goad him to do things he might not otherwise try—good or bad.

Whatever it was, he wasn't about to lose now. He wasn't going to screw this up.

Not now, not for this girl, even if he had only just met her *twelve* hours ago. This simple fact wasn't lost on him, but it was a detail that didn't seem to matter at all in the moment.

I've got this.

He glanced over at Joey and yelled, "Hey, Joe. We've got this, right?"

Joey cupped his ear with a hand and yelled back, "What?" and laughed.

One by one, the bands slowly crept along and made the turn onto Broad Street. Before them was a miles-long, noisy mash-up of riotous color and feathered costumes, loud music, controlled chaos, and lots of enthusiasm. The marchers were lively—singing, dancing, cheering, critiquing, and yelling. It was jubilant but also felt more than a little ruthless.

Hunter took it all in. *Game on.*

Banjos strummed, *Oh 'Dem golden slippers.* Saxophones wailed. Arms pumped accordions. The crowds watching from the sidewalks were buzzing with excitement and cheering raucously. The audience strutted to the music; off-key voices belted out lyrics, enthusiastically singing along.

Vendors zipped through the mobs of people selling Happy New Year paraphernalia,
sing-songing, "Souvenirs. Souvenirs, here. Get your souvenirs," as they pushed shopping carts overflowing with colorful keepsakes—large hats, feather boas, silly string, invisible dogs on leashes and hot pretzels —up and down Broad Street from corner to corner.

The Brawlers inched forward slowly until they paused in front of an ornate stone church.

Hunter watched a group of African American women standing in front a colorful handmade sign taped to a banquet table that read: Red Beans and Rice—$2.00. The women stirred several large steaming pots warming on camp stoves. One by one, they punched fists in the air and moved to the beat as they cooked and waited on the hungry and cheerful crowd lined up with bills in hand. The women happily served bowl after bowl of food, wishing each person a hearty, "Hello. Have a blessed and Happy New Year."

As they moved further along through the route, clusters of bawdy morning happy hour crowds spilled onto sidewalks on numerous corners, drinks in hand, cheering. Full tables set up outside of bars and restaurants added to the buzzing cacophony of noise. In the street, band after band inched forward and performed, dancing and strutting up Broad Street at designated corners to the excited and supportive crowd.

Hunter suddenly wondered about their opposition and tried hard to size up the other competitors, attempting to decipher The Brawlers chances. It struck him that as a Mummering virgin, his only experience having been watching this from one of those crowded bar tables or on TV, didn't exactly give him cred or anything to compare to.

Given any thoughts to your next steps? Great. Now Dad, really?

He wasn't sure how he thought that they would pull off their never practiced routine to appear synchronized enough to compete with these other groups, let alone win. He guessed he was delusional, or possessed, or something, because for some reason, standing in the middle of this craziness he decided worrying was pointless. He glanced at Maria. Their eyes locked. Her lips pulled in a tight line and she shrugged.

Hunter instinctively knew there was no turning around now. They were just going to have to go with it. He, Joey, and the guys had always taken pride in their spontaneous and nonsensical endeavors in their younger days. During their senior year, Frankie, Elmo, and Goose had overslept, woke up hungover, and raced to class to give their final group presentation still dressed in the Santa costumes they'd passed out in the night before. Since then, they were always game to add another experience to their shared history to one-up that story. This might just do it.

With no time to hesitate, and in too far, Hunter wouldn't waver. He knew that the guys wouldn't either. Whoever had coined the phrase "older and wiser" hadn't met this group.

They moved along, improvising as they paused at each of the performance corners. They faltered. They missed cues. They bumped into each other. They were awful. "Eh, don't worry. The only time it really matters is in front of the judges up at City Hall," Uncle Bruno shouted over the noise trying to encourage them.

Hunter felt himself shuffling his feet in anticipation, trying to slow the inevitable as they neared the judges. Maria walked over. Her face said it all, she was worried. "Ummm," she said. Hunter grinned wide trying to reassure her. "I mean, how are you—"

"Relax. You worry too much," he interrupted.

Then, he said, a little too confidently, "It'll be fine. Really. We've got this." Her expressionless face said she wasn't buying it.

He knew that they didn't have this. They had no clue, but that had never stopped them before and this factor wasn't going to stop them today.

Chapter 24

"There's always a lesson, Maria. What's your take-away? What did you learn?"

There were many days she wished she could tune out her mother's rules, her advice, her lectures. Antonetta was sure that her girls never heard her messages, and told Maria that as many times as she offered her precious nuggets to her. Little did Antonetta know that Maria always heard them. Apparently, she had carefully catalogued them away to torture herself at any given moment.

The lesson...today...

We're screwed.

She wasn't sure what would be worse—having this group of lovable knuckleheads she'd just met go forward with this plan, and bomb, having the supreme public debacle televised to the entire Philadelphia viewing area *and* The Brawlers becoming the biggest never ending joke in the neighborhood, or her going down in history as being the responsible Vigliano family member who had been entrusted with this responsibility and failed. Not participating would be a first, shattering uninterrupted years of performances and wins. Either way, she knew she was letting everyone, her father, the family, her ancestors, and these guys down.

Falling short wasn't something Maria was accustomed to. She was an overachiever, always had been. She excelled at anything and everything that she'd ever set her mind to from day one. All anyone had to do was ask Antonetta.

She looked around at the group. Hunter stood in the middle of the band. They were goofing around, nudging Uncle Bruno, and egging on Ziggy. There was nothing she could do. It was too late. She knew in her heart they were just a group or two away from total embarrassment.

Two rival string bands, The Fanatics and North West, had stepped off in front of them. Maria was sure they had already wowed the judges with their routines, as always. Most teams had been together as long as the Brawlers and were well-oiled machines every year. There had always been a friendly but heated rivalry between all of the bands going back to her grandfather's days.

I'm never going to hear the end of this. She was sure that The Fanatics boys would be merciless for the rest of the year. And, she knew that the North West gang would construct carefully worded sound bites full of sarcasm and snark for 6ABC and NBC10 reporters as they gleefully recapped the post-game highlights. Maria was sure their competitors would chide, explaining that The Brawlers were just not up to the challenge without her father at the helm. The

Fanatics would put together GIFs and memes and post them on multiple Facebook pages and YouTube channels just to taunt through the next three hundred and sixty-five days.

She was never going to live this one down.

Ever.

Maria's knees felt weak as she saw her father's face in her mind. She could once again hear him asking to make sure everything was okay with the performance. She knew that he put all of his faith in her being able to wrangle Uncle Bruno and Ziggy and handle this challenge.

She felt her throat close as she imagined him sitting in his hospital bed watching the pre-game on television waiting for the parade to begin, anxiously waiting to see all of them on screen. She could sense his anticipation and his counting the music beats. She was even sure that even though his foot was immobilized and he was unable to move much, he'd be waving his arms and perfecting some sort of stationary Mummer's strut. She was also quite sure that her mother was beside him doing a novena or two on her behalf while trying to bribe the doctors to give her something for her nerves.

"Oh no," she muttered out loud as her hands began to sweat at the memory of Lyndon's arrival hours earlier. She hoped he'd gone back to New York by now. She didn't want to endure his ridicule for forever too. *I'm going to have to quit my job too.* So much for her fabulous career, DOA before it ever got off the ground.

Maria thought back to the day that her grandfather handed over the Parade responsibility to her father. She remembered the look on his face. Anxiety. Pride. Hope.

She felt her shoulders slump. She knew that her disregard for the complexity of this event left her ill-equipped to carry this responsibility forward. She felt her breathing go shallow.

Her father had always made this look so easy.

It was not.

They were up next. She tried very hard to breathe, but felt something churn in her stomach. She thought she might just throw up. Her lesson?

They were most definitely screwed.

Chapter 25

Hunter watched as Joey and the guys were horsing around with the old timers. The long night and morning had started to take its toll. *I need a minute to sit.* He glanced down the street. The judges seemed at least a block away and the other teams were taking their time performing and moving off stage. The cumbersome costume was heavier and warmer than expected and he was exhausted. He pulled the headpiece off and wiped his wet forehead with his hand. He took a couple of steps toward a building, leaned against the brick wall, and slid down to sit.

He took a deep breath, rubbed his eyes, and pulled his knees close. His head bobbed until it rested on his arms. His ears rang. He took another breath in and thought he heard someone call his name.

Hunter walked across a street and up to a small stage just outside of a picture-perfect gazebo. His mother in tastefully curated professional clothes looked glamorous standing next to his father as he shook hands with people. Hunter watched as a little boy sat off to the side alone. Hunter stood in the background and watched. It took a minute for him to realize the boy was seven-year-old him. A small orchestra sat off to one side and played *America, America...* Notes drifted into an unrecognizable beat as Hunter watched the boy stand and walk away from the gazebo and fade into the distance as Maria and her cousins dressed in evening gowns walked toward him. He blinked hard as his parents dissolved and his assistant, Laurel, came into focus as she pushed her face close to his.

Maria spun around searching for Hunter. It was time to nudge him forward and in place. She felt her stomach fall as she realized he was gone.

Joey plucked the banjo strings hard, spun around, and then posed rock star-like behind Maria. She was not amused. She glanced behind her, her lips pulled in a straight line, her jaw jutted out. Elmo jumped in, wailed a quick scale on his saxophone, and grinned. Frankie squeezed his accordion, ran his fingers up and down the keys, pumping out his nuanced Oom-pah-pah with his added Beatbox drum beat and high-hat sounds.

Maria shook her head and motioned for them to gather around. Her eyes darted from face to face. "Where's Hunter?"

"He's right—" Joey looked to his left and then his right. The guys spun around, searching.

"Whoa," Frankie said, realizing that Hunter was missing.

"Great," Maria took a deep breath and said, "Okay, look, we're here. It's game on. There's nothing else to do, so let's try to do the best we can. We're going on without him. It's all we can do at this point."

Maria rushed toward a man about her size, holding an accordion, and barked, "Gabe! Give me your jacket."

Eyes wide with fear, he stammered, "What? Why?"

"I don't have time to explain. Just do it. Come on," she ordered.

Gabe unbuttoned his jacket and handed it to Maria who tossed her jacket to him, "Here."

She slid into the jacket and raced to one of the backgrounds, ripped down several palm branches, and moved center stage in front of the band as the group looked on confused. With branches clutched tightly in her hands, she bowed her head and crossed her arms over her chest, screening her body with the green fronds.

Hunter felt someone grab his shoulder and shake him.

Hunter watched as a woman grabbed the boy's hand and turned him back to his parents. "Go on, Hunter. Child…"

"Hunter! Child. You have something important to finish. Now," Olympia whispered. Groggy Hunter forced his eyes open, to see Olympia's smiling face nose to nose with his. "Child. Now. That's it. C'mon. Wake up. You've got to go," she said gently as she shook his arm.

The sun warmed Hunter's face. He opened his eyes and looked around, not understanding where he was as a mass of legs floated by. Swarms of people surrounded him, walking as if one large block of humanity, pushing toward the street and the parade frenzy. Hunter looked up expecting to see his father. He rubbed his eyes, confused. As his jumbled mind shook off the grogginess of sleep and his dream, he bolted up, and looked around for Olympia. She was nowhere to be seen. Certain he had dreamt her too, he searched the crowd for Joey and the guys, panic flooding his mind and his face.

He leaned down and scooped up the headdress and plunked it back on his head. "Excuse me. Pardon me. Look out," he yelled as he pushed people away and ran through the crowd up Broad Street. He spotted The Brawlers almost a block away, hopped over a police barrier, mouthing "I'm sorry" to a cop who just nodded and waved him in and he raced toward the group.

"I'm here. So sorry. So, so sorry. It's okay, Maria. Sorry," he stammered, hoping to reassure her as he squeezed back in with the band, confused by her costume.

"They've worked on this stuff together for years," Maria barked, worry written across her face as Hunter arranged his headpiece and took his place in the circle. Maria focused her gaze on Hunter as he shrugged and mouthed, *Sorry*. A twisted feeling of both relief and dread settled in her stomach.

Joey exchanged looks with Frankie and Hunter,

shot Maria a look and said, "And, we haven't? Okay, game on."

"It's okay. Relax. We've got this. Really. I promise," Hunter blurted out. Hunter looked around, shrugged, and shot her an apologetic look and said, "It'll be fine. Trust us."

Maria frowned, still angry at him and clearly not buying his bravado. "The Brawlers are a well-oiled machine. Okay. Sort of. Maybe, uh, okay, well, most years," she shot back and then pursed her lips.

"Well, the challenge is on, then. You really shouldn't dare us. Pep band. Rock band marathons. Mummer's strut? What's the difference?" Hunter tried to sound sure of himself knowing that even he didn't believe his own words.

Exasperated, Maria fired back, "What's the difference? Pep band? Rock band?"

"Yup," he said and nodded, knowing that they really didn't have a clue and he was trying his best to reassure her while also convincing himself.

"Seriously? A difference? Where do I even begin?" she said and looked at him wide-eyed as she shrugged.

"Uh. You two ready? I mean, if you're finished having your first fight, we have a show to do," Joey said as he arched an eyebrow, laughed at Hunter and Maria, and motioned to the judges. Maria, frozen in the middle of the street, glanced over her shoulder and realized she was now part of the show. Knowing she couldn't just slink off, she shook her head at them, threw her hands in the air, crossed her arms, and faced front with the palm branches in front of her.

Joey, Elmo, Frankie, and Hunter traded looks. "I've got nothing," Hunter admitted. He knew their big plan was to wing it. He was sure that they would look like idiots, but he wasn't sure what else they could do. They couldn't turn around now and say, "Just kidding."

"We've got this, H," Joey said.

Elmo nodded.

Frankie said, "No problem, Hunter. Really, dude. C'mon. Piece of cake," and added a Beatbox *pah-dum-pah* drumbeat.

Hunter studied the group. They looked dead serious. Their eyes locked. He glanced at Maria and then said to them, "I'm ready," and nodded. Joey, Elmo, and Frankie nodded their overconfident responses.

They had nothing to lose and nowhere to turn.

Hunter turned and took his place up front behind Maria. He put his hands on his hips and waited. Behind him, Joey and Elmo pulled Ray Ban sunglasses out of their pockets, put them on and stood shoulder to shoulder, Blues Brothers style. They looked like they meant business. Hunter glanced over his shoulder at them and took a deep breath.

Uncle Bruno teased a few bars.

Maria tapped her foot and counted, "One. Two. Three."

The music picked up, the notes circled and rose, floating far and wide...*At the Copa, Copa Cabana*...

Maria pulled her arms apart, the palm branches

waved as she moved them in opposite directions revealing the band. She pushed the greens behind her back and skipped off to the side.

The old-timers hit it hard. Uncle Bruno and Iggy were crazed, heads and saxophones bobbing up and down fast as they played. They swayed and they moved. They strutted, moving a few steps forward, then backwards and then from one side of the street to the other.

Hunter hesitated for a split second. He could see Maria out of the corner of his eye. He nodded in Joey's direction and then...

Joey, Frankie, Elmo, and Hunter moved in step with Uncle Bruno and Iggy. And they were off. They were playing, strutting, moving back and forth across the street, and back again. Hunter and the guys worked the crowd, approaching people on the sidewalks as if they had done this together for years. The people loved them.

Hunter heard cheering erupt. He was pumped. He moved front and center, hamming it up for the crowd. The more they screamed, the faster he moved. It was as if he was possessed, overcome by the experience. The band made their way forward in front of the judges, and stopped dead center surrounding Hunter.

Hunter paused, aware that everything was on the line at that moment.

Elmo and Joey knew it too. They extended the song's hook, repeating the music over and over, and then they exploded, stomping their feet creating a dance all of their own. Frankie added a few more Beatbox sounds and the other accordion players jumped in. Hunter could feel the vibrations of human drum beats surrounding him. He paused and watched out of the corner of his eye as the group's movements erupted. He felt the headdress slip to one side of his head. He adjusted it and stood tall.

After a minute or two, Elmo and Joey wound down and...

It was Hunter's turn. He went for it...

He pumped his arms, lifted his knees. He took three steps forward and then two steps back, spun around, arms stretched out wide, and then did it again. He was strutting, pumping his arms and his knees. His knees bounced higher than he thought they could go. He slid back and forth across the street from side to side, working the crowd. Joey, Elmo, and Frankie followed Hunter's lead. They rocked. Knees pumped. Saxophones bobbed up and down. From the sound of the cheers and applause, Hunter knew they were bringing it. He also knew that simple applause was not going to be enough for this crowd and these judges. He knew that he had to wow them.

He hopped into one set of viewing stands, motioning to folks to stand and dance. As soon as the crowd was moving and stomping to the music, he hopped out and moved to the other side of the street, shaking his body as he strutted. Now people were screaming and cheering him on. Hunter saw Maria for a split second out of the corner of his eye. He thought that he saw her smile and mouth, "Oh my god," as she and her cousins moved the colorful prop backgrounds behind the band.

Something took over. Hunter was overcome with the feeling that he was strutting for his life. His legs burned as he pushed once more to give everything he had left to the crowd.

Hunter watched Uncle Bruno jump up on one of the metal crowd barriers and wave his arms to the audience asking for cheers. Iggy did the same on the other side of the street.

Hunter pushed. With every last ounce of energy, strutting harder and faster.

The crowd loved it. They were screaming and tossing things. Confetti rained down on them. A woman jumped the barrier and bolted at Hunter; her arms spread wide. A cop stopped her just inches from him and dragged her back kicking and screaming to the sidewalk.

He saw her clearly now...Maria was smiling wide as she, Bambi, and Ava moved the large plywood cutouts. Two-dimensional palm trees and beach scenes swiped back and forth behind the band. They stopped suddenly. The backdrop was in place.

Hunter glanced up at the announcer's booth and saw a man hand a piece of paper to someone. He thought he heard his name, or what sounded like his name. Hunter stomped and pirouetted until he was dizzy. The announcer leaned forward. Hunter couldn't hear what he was saying. A *wha-wha-wha* noise, something like cartoon speak bounced off of his eardrums. Between the loud music unrolling into the air and his heavy breathing, he couldn't hear a thing. He couldn't think. All he could do was keep moving.

Chapter 26

"Expect the unexpected. Something great can happen at any moment, any day, Maria. You are born on one day and you die on one day. Anything can happen in just one day. Believe me, one day can change everything."

Maria groaned every time Antonetta said it. She preferred to interpret this nugget of her mother's advice with her own spin, "No expectations. No disappointments." Except that she somehow still had expectations every day, but was realistic about what might, or might not happen. More often than not, even when she tried to anticipate something positive, she was usually disappointed.

This was one of those times she really hoped her mother was right, but again she had no expectations. She had already accepted the inevitable doom. There was no way around it. These guys were in over their heads.

Maria, now back with Ava and Bambi and the prop team, stood motionless. The team stopped moving and Hunter took his place to perform the Captain's solo, the centerpiece of the routine. In all of the confusion, Maria couldn't remember if she'd even taken a minute to explain to him about his responsibility or the magnitude of this segment. This was the most important few minutes of competition every year, the portion of the dance when the bulk of the team's score was on the line. The solo and the ability to wow the judges and bring the whole routine together makes or breaks an evaluation. This was where numbers counted, and winners and losers were separated.

Maria inched closer to the announcer's booth trying very hard to hold her rolling plywood palm tree stationary. She sucked in a breath and held it, remaining motionless near impossible. Her foot bounced franticly as she worried about the ramifications of her decision to enlist this group of guys. *What have I done?* On top of carrying the burden of the team's demise, she worried that Hunter wasn't clear that this was his big moment.

This was it, his cue. It was time for the Captain's solo.

Maria nodded at him and whispered, "Go!"

Hunter wasn't sure if he had anything left. He paused for half a beat, sucked in a long breath, and then he started to move. His arms. His legs. Everything pumping as fast as he could go, nothing feeling connected to his body. He was in the flow, was somewhere else.

He was a Mummer.

Hunter spotted a Philly cop or two crack a smile as he felt he was somehow in another dimension and strutting for his life.

Oh. My. God. What did I do? No expectations, Maria thought. She was too tired to even react. Let's just get this over with. There was nothing she could do, no turning back. They had nothing to lose. Maria knew that this group of guys had gone above and beyond anything that anyone in their right mind would have done at this point for her. Given that they'd all just met hours ago, and she knew virtually nothing about them, she couldn't comprehend why they stepped in to try to save her. For what? Bragging rights? She didn't think so. These guys seem reasonably successful in their own worlds. She couldn't imagine why they would do this for virtual strangers? They had heart, a lot of heart, was all she could think.

She thought back to all of the people from her past that scoffed at this ritual. Her college friends couldn't grasp her devotion to this family tradition when she turned down the group ski trip every year over Winter Break. Her refusal was met with blank stares when she tried to explain this custom was handed down through bloodlines in all of the families she knew. She had to be home and not on a mountain somewhere sipping champagne. She wasn't sure why, but she always apologized to them.

Her one and only semi-serious college relationship had been repulsed by her explanation of the costuming. Her protests and clarifications only seemed to further confuse him. "Like Mardi Gras, sort of," she had tried to explain once. "But this party came first, hundreds of years ago." His puzzled expression made her press on further, "It's the oldest folk festival in the country."

He didn't get it, or her. The relationship was over in January of their senior year when they returned from break. Her roommate insisted it just was pre-Valentine's Day dumping for a cash-strapped guy, insisting that they all did it. Maria wondered if it was the fact that her South Philly roots were just too alien for his central Ohio genes. After a good cry, or two, in her dorm room, she repeatedly, and silently, told him to go home to his white bread world to drink vodka gimlets with mummy and daddy. She wished her naive freshman self had never rushed up to his dorm room after an impromptu sledding party in Central Park with a group of his friends. *Expectations. Disappointments.*

Maria was breathing hard and watching as someone handed a piece of paper to the announcer. *Oh no.* She was convinced that they were going to be kicked out of the competition for some obscure rule violation. Panic and fear ran through her like a jolt as she waited for the epic rejection. *Great! On camera. On the air. For everyone to see.* She was thankful this couldn't reach the New York market and her boss, or clients. She was sure they were being booted out of the competition and would soon be escorted off the street. She muttered, "Damn it," under her breath, hoping that the judges wouldn't catch on.

The announcer squinted at Hunter and then said into the microphone, "Gee folks, I don't think that's Thomas Vigliano. Tom's been the Captain of the Bella Vista Brawlers since he took over for *his* father in 1989, I believe. Isn't that right?" he asked his co-host.

"Right you are," his co-host chirped and nodded.

Maria felt her cheeks flush and waited for him to broadcast the announcement of their disqualification on live television.

The announcer looked at the paper again and said, "Yes. Yes, folks. I've just been told that there's been a last-minute substitution. Seems Tommy's hurt and in Pennsylvania Hospital." Maria watched as he looked up at the TV camera trained on his face and said sincerely to the camera and audience below, "Get better, Tommy. We miss you and we are thinking about you." He glanced back at his script again and read, "Filling in for Captain Tom Vigliano is Hunter Reed. Hunter must be new to the Brawlers this year. Let's take a moment to watch."

Maria's stomach fell, and she sighed.

The announcer looked over at his co-host who had bolted up out of his seat and was standing up to get a better look at Hunter.

Here it comes. She watched the co-Host lean over the edge of the booth and adjust his glasses, squinting at Hunter. *Oh no. This can't be happening, not now.* She bit her bottom lip and braced herself, waiting for the inevitable.

"Hunter? Reed? *Hunter* Reed?" She heard the co-host say in disbelief.

"That's what I've been told," the Announcer said back.

"Are you sure?"

The announcer nodded and said, "That's what it says here."

Maria watched as the co-host became visibly excited, animated almost, as he shifted side-to-side. He asked again, "Really?" Not waiting for an answer, he pointed and yelled, "H. Yo, H." He tapped his chest near his heart with his hand, and looked more excited. He pointed at Hunter again, screaming this time, "H. It's I, man. It's I. Ingram. From the train. I'm I. Dude!"

She watched Hunter glance up at the booth and squint at the co-host.

"You're the man, Hunter. You're the man!" Ingram screamed.

The announcer squinted at Ingram. He looked a little befuddled at his co-host's outburst, but continued to voice the parade's narration trying to steer the conversation to the band, "You know, I don't think Tommy's missed a parade in forty years, maybe more. Is that right, Ingram? It must be serious. Be well, my man. Be well. Let's hope that Mr. Reed can pull this off. He's got some mighty big shoes to fill. Mighty big."

"No problem. H's got this. He's H. Noooo problem. He's H," Ingram added as he sat down.

"Ooo-kay. Let's watch," the announcer said.

Maria felt herself cringe, sorry that she had allowed this really sweet guy to put himself in this predicament for her. Now he was doing this fully I.D.'d on television and in front of someone that actually knew him. She looked to the sky and thought, "O*h no*," then crossed her fingers and bowed her head for a moment. When she looked back at the street, she couldn't believe her eyes.

Hunter was moving like a strutting pro.

Ingram bolted up from his seat in the judge's booth and mimicked Hunter's moves, then screamed, "Go, H, go, you maniac!"

Maria bit her bottom lip and glanced at the wall of judges fearing their reactions.

The stone-faced group stood motionless studying Hunter. She could not sense a tell from any one of them. *We are doomed.*

Glittery sunlight bounced off of a poufy and very curly grey-blonde hairdo and caught Maria's eye. Next to the judge's booth, in the VIP area, she spotted a beautifully dressed woman with long sparkling Botticelli curls framed by sunlight. She was bundled up in a fur coat standing with a city councilman, the mayor, and the mayor's wife. Hunter's friend, Goose, still dressed in his tuxedo/diaper costume as baby New Year was standing between the woman with the glistening curls and Olympia, his arm draped around Olympia's neck. The three of them were grinning ear to ear and jumping up and down, cheering and applauding Hunter.

The woman with the curls stuck two fingers in her mouth, whistled loudly, and screamed, "Go, Hunter, go. That's it, baby. I knew you had it in you. Go, baby, go. That's it. Have some fun. C'mon. Make us proud. C'mon. Uh-huh. Uh-huh. You've got it.

Gooooo. That's it," she said as she pumped her arms in the air. "You can do it. Strut it, honey. Strut it. Uh-huh. Uh-huh. Goooooooooooo. That's it, baby."

Wait. What?

Confused, Maria cocked her head to one side and watched as the woman and Olympia exchanged glances and winked at each other. The councilman watched the excited woman, grabbed her arm, and yelled, "Mother? Contain yourself, please. You are making a fool out of me."

"Oh, Wayne, you are such a stick in the mud," she said as she pushed her way out of the row of seats and made her way down to the street with Olympia following close behind.

Goose jumped out of the booth, stomped over the tops of seats, pushing people out of the way as he made his way toward the women and into the street where he pointed and howled at Hunter. Joey spotted Goose and waved his hands to the other musicians to pick it up. The band pumped up the music. As if on cue, Goose started to strut alongside of Hunter, flapping his arms, pumping his legs and moving his head back and forth bird-like and stomping his golden Timberland boots in time with the rest of the performers.

Maria glanced around, convinced that nobody was quite sure whether or not Goose was supposed to be there. To the audience, his unusual entrance seemed planned and part of the routine. Most had probably assumed that his jumping from above was theatrically designed by the troupe, so nobody stopped him. She watched as Goose punched the top hat into the air and marched in circles around Hunter.

The judges studied him, exchanged glances, and looked a little confused.

Expect the unexpected.

Oh well. We've made it this far. She was sure this couldn't get any worse if they tried. Maria glanced around at the smiling faces as the audience exploded in applause and whistles. They loved Goose.

Hunter looked unsure. At first, he did his best to ignore Goose. Maria wasn't sure if it was the audience's reaction, or Goose's strutting, but something incited Hunter to push to a new height of manic moves. His lips pulled tight into a straight line. She wondered if the look on his face was serious determination or something else. She watched as he was now strutting as if this was the most important thing he had ever done.

Maria couldn't help but grin.

Joey, Elmo, Frankie, Uncle Bruno, and Iggy were standing behind Hunter and as he began to hit the crescendo in "his" routine. They fell into tempo with him and manically moved alongside. A huge web of arms and legs flailed, crisscrossing the street back and forth. Knees pumped and feet moved, fast. When it seemed that Hunter needed a beat to catch a breath, the guys instinctively took turns jumping into solo performances. First, Joey wailed on the saxophone, the group moved to mimic the notes he blasted out of the horn. Frankie and Elmo then each followed suit. After each riff, Uncle Bruno and Iggy broke into a frenzied strut with the rest of the band until Hunter could once again jump in and take over, working the crowd and hamming it up in front of the judge's stand.

The crowd was now wild, screaming, applauding. Streamers, Phillies caps, and a few undergarments blew through the air at the band, and landed in the street.

Maria was convinced that she had never, ever seen anyone strut like this before. This was a pure show of emotion and grit. True spirit. True devotion. *Sorry, dad,* she thought as she wondered if she was somehow being unfaithful to her family's history and the band's past award-winning performances.

The judges smiled, made notes, and conferred as they tried to tabulate a score.

The crowd was on their feet, applause out of control. Maria looked up at the mob. She couldn't believe it. They were getting a standing ovation at the Mummer's parade. The crowd loved him.

Hunter took a bow. The headdress fell off of his head and plunked onto the street. He quickly retrieved it as the applause grew louder and people stomped the bleachers.

She felt relieved and proud. Her stomach fluttered.

The woman with the curls, moved near the curb, close to Hunter and whistled loudly again, waved, and screamed, "That's my boy. You did it. Hunter, you did it." She pushed pass the barrier into the street, and made her way next to Hunter. She leaned in next to him, posed, took a selfie with her cell phone, and then kissed his cheek. "I knew you had it in you, Hunter." Hunter smiled wide, took another bow, and tried to catch his breath. She kissed his cheek again and they hugged.

Maria looked around, searching for Olympia, and spotted her in the distance. She winked, at Maria, waved and then moved away, further into the crowd, and was gone.

Watching Hunter smile and work the applauding crowd again, it hit Maria hard that no one had ever once done anything like this for her in her life. It was all she could do to not run over and throw herself at him right there in the middle of the street.

The brigade moved further up Broad Street to a waiting area as the applause continued and then slowly wound down. They moved the props off to the side of the street as a team of judges approached. One of the men handed Hunter a trophy. Hunter hoisted it into the air as the band surrounded him. The guys slapped his back and fist-bumped him.

Maria's wide grin made her face hurt. Maria watched Ava and Bambi screaming and jumping in the air. Goose grabbed Ava and kissed her. Joey grabbed Bambi. Ava launch into a loud "Wooooo-ooo-oooooo!"

As Hunter handed the trophy to Joey, Maria blasted across the street, pushed her way through the group, and jumped into Hunter's arms. He picked her up and twirled her around.

"I can't believe it. I can't believe it. You did it," she said. She slid down and planted her feet firmly back on the ground, their faces still close.

"We did it," he said.

They were nose to nose, both gasping for air when she leaned in and kissed him—hard. His hands slid down her back and he pulled her close. Their lips broke apart; she took a breath and kissed him again. This was a real first kiss. At least, Maria counted it as their first real kiss. She was excited, happy. And, she never wanted to let go of him.

"You did it. We did it. They did it," she said giggling.

"We came in fourth!" Hunter said laughing.

He wasn't thinking about the prize as Maria had jumped into his arms. All he wanted to do was kiss her. The only thing he could think about was that he didn't want to let go of this girl as she pulled away a little. He held her face in his hands. They were nose to nose. He was still breathing hard and his muscles burned more than they had in years. His ears were still ringing as he heard her say, "Thank you. Thank you. Thank you."

"You're welcome," Hunter said as he winked, pulled her close, and kissed her again. He held her close for a moment, then he put his arm around her waist, and together they turned and looked at the giddy group standing in line in front of them watching. Joey, Frankie, and Elmo were still holding instruments and grinning ear-to-ear. The group exploded into applause, laughter, and high fives.

Chapter 27

It took Hunter more than a few minutes to calm down enough to allow his brain to process just *what* exactly they had all pulled off. He wasn't even sure about what he had done. For once, he was actually really glad that there would be filmed evidence to confirm that this experience had happened. The whole episode felt more than a little out-of-body to him. He was surprised that he wasn't at all worried about the possibility of professional blowback. In fact, he was actually looking forward to seeing the replay and hearing his friends and associates bust him for this one.

Wow. As things came into focus, he was a little puzzled by a couple of things that he thought he had experienced. First, he thought he saw the woman from the train. And, he was sure that at one point he saw Olympia's smiling face in the crowd cheering him on too. He remembered his odd dream and tried to recall if she had been the one to wake him? *How was that possible?* It's funny how the mind works, he guessed, especially the exhausted mind, he justified. As far he knew, Olympia was from the D.C. area, not Philadelphia. Though truthfully, he couldn't confirm that fact given he'd bumped into her in his office building only a few times and had only spoken to her briefly for the first time yesterday. *Was that yesterday?*

He watched as numerous iPhones and cameras were still being pointed in his direction to record his face. He huffed and puffed trying to catch his breath as he wiped his brow. He disregarded the throngs of instant paparazzi and what seemed like massive interest in capturing a photo. He really didn't care if this wound up on Facebook and that realization surprised him more than a little bit. He might live to regret it down the road if it wound up on some morning show in a throwback segment, but for now this experience seemed completely removed from his life in D.C., and harmless.

He glanced at Maria. She looked happy, relieved, and pleased. He smiled, guessing that they did okay, hoping they did okay. They had tried their best. Fourth place. Not exactly his highest of honors, but he'd take it for her, for all of them. He had no idea how they had somehow it pulled off, improvising and faking it enough to blend in with the rest of the competition.

Joey pointed and rushed over first, ringing his arm around Hunter's neck, messing his hair with his knuckles. "Dude! Were you keeping something from us all of these years? Where'd you find that? You were awesome. You're a Mummer, you maniac. You're a Mummer."

Bambi nodded and said, "Really awesome," as she inched toward Joey.

Hunter laughed, as he breathed in cool air still trying hard to catch his breath.

"No, really, you were amazing," Maria said, "Really amazing."

"Damn right," he said chuckling.

Goose and Ava circled Hunter. Goose pointed, laughed, flapped his arms and pumped his knees high, and said, "Dude. You're a Mummer, man. How'd you do that?"

"How'd you do that?" Hunter pointed at Goose's get-up. "And that," he pointed over his shoulder at the area that they had just lit up, and laughed.

"Never would have predicted you had it in you," Elmo added.

Elmo and Frankie launched into a lively riff with their accordion and banjo. Frankie added some Beatbox noises. Clearly, this group was not done. And, clearly, he was not going to live this one down right now, or ever, with them. They began to strut circles around Hunter who moved with them shuffling his feet back and forth, flapping his arms and twirling until he was spent. He stopped as the exhaustion crept in.

He looked around at the crowds in the stands wondering about the last few minutes. The whole experience seemed more like a dream to him than any reality he had experienced in his life so far. Another fragmented bit pinged his mind. He thought that he had spotted Ingram in the announcer's booth *and* he was now positive he did see the bag lady from the train. *Wait. Did I take a selfie with her?* Like a dream that starts to reveal itself in cloudy memory bursts, he remembered now that he definitely saw Olympia's face in the crowd. None of this made any sense. He thought that he must have spaced out and rocked into another dimension, not at all sure what was real or if any of it had actually happened.

"C'mon. We should load everything onto the flatbed and head back to the warehouse," he heard Maria say.

"Plenty of celebrating to do, boys," Uncle Bruno added. "C'mon. You've earned it."

Goose spun around, looked at Uncle Bruno, and burst out laughing, "We've earned it. Dude, you're speaking my language now. I've been saying that all night. You have any pretzels?"

Uncle Bruno nodded and added, "Plenty of pretzels."

"Do you have any Grey Poupon?" Goose asked.

Uncle Bruno laughed and rung his arm around Goose's neck, "For you, man, anything."

"Finally. Cool, man," Goose laughed as he shot the group a raised eyebrow look that said, told you so.

Iggy chimed in, "Big party back at Vigliano's, too."

Maria nodded and said, "Please. Uh, if you have time, of course. I don't even know how to begin to repay you. Do you have time? I mean, I…"

"We've got time," Joey said as he elbowed Hunter, "Right, Hunter? Plenty of time."

Ava and Bambi waited, glanced at Maria, and then to Hunter.

"Plenty of time," Hunter said as the group moved toward the waiting truck, "Plenty of time."

Chapter 28

"The first person to visit your home on New Year's Day is very important. It is significant, Maria. And, it's good luck if it's a man. Don't give him a key, but invite him in. Always invite him in. It's even better if he's tall, good-looking, and has dark hair, honey."

At least I haven't broken all of her silly rules. As always, Maria wasn't ever sure where her mother got this stuff or came up with such specific details, but for once she was happy to have remembered this one. She was even happier to be executing on this particular rule.

They slowly wound through the jammed Center City Streets and back to South Philly waving at cheering spectators as they crept along. Explosive applause greeted them as they entered the warehouse. All of the extended families were already there and waiting. Champagne bottles were shaken and popped open. Showers of bubbles rained down on everyone. Maria took a few steps into the room and looked around. She saw big smiles and chests puffed up with pride. She saw big happy families overlapping with other big happy families. Lastly, she saw joy, lots and lots of joy filling the room. She watched as beverages were handed out to the spent performers, and food quickly followed.

Ava and Bambi led Joey, Goose, and the rest of the guys toward the bar. Bambi and Ava opened beers and handed them to the group.

"Ri, you want one?" Ava asked.

"Not yet. Save me one, okay," she said. Maria looked at the exhausted Hunter. She wanted to give him back his tuxedo so that he could at least get out of the sweaty costume. She felt her heart racing, not sure of what to do or say. She tried to calm down just a little bit, still worried about Hunter and more than a little worried about what he thought about all of this.

She moved toward her father's office door, motioning for Hunter to follow, and entered.

He followed her inside, closed the door behind him, and handed her the jacket. She hung it up on the garment rack and took the headdress from him and placed it back into its box. Putting this stuff away made her feel emotional, as if she had crossed over some strange boundary. Memories of parades past flooded her mind.

She watched as Hunter slowly sized up the office, her drawings, the trophies, the photographs... all of it. He studied a framed picture of her father and a six-year-old Maria and then placed it back on the filing cabinet, turned and said, "This is something, really, something."

She nodded, mostly because she wasn't sure

what to say to that. *Something could mean a lot of things, good, or bad? Bad good? Good bad?* Maria was over analyzing every word coming out of his mouth. *This is not good.*

She suddenly felt really awkward with the man that had just helped her save this year's show and helped her to keep this important tradition alive. And, most significantly this year, kept this family tradition uninterrupted one more time. A man she hardly knew. She was not sure she could verbally express how much this all meant to her. She wasn't sure that she should, just yet. She really was afraid this admission would just make this guy go running.

Maria knew better than most that this institution was an all-consuming ritual for people involved and not for everyone. She was painfully aware of this fact, those judgments, and how all of this is interpreted by some people and how it made her feel. For now, she wanted to stay safely ensconced in her very own little fantasy bubble for a few more minutes without probing any further, or interpreting what exactly Hunter really thought about all of this, or her.

Her cell phone rang. Oh well, perfect timing, she thought as she fished the phone out of the pocket of her jacket, glanced at it, and answered. "Hi, Mom." she said.

"Maria!" she screamed. "You did it. We saw the whole thing on TV."

"Yup, Mom. We did it," Maria said as she glanced over at Hunter who had collapsed onto a chair.

"Well, they finally discharged your father.

We're home. Dinner's in an hour."

Maria couldn't help but smile. Of course. Like the rest of this tradition, dinner too would not be interrupted for anything. Nonna Mary had set that precedent years ago and that ball would never be dropped by Antonetta. Maria was sure that she'd been cooking since Christmas preparing the post-parade feast. Her efforts would not be wasted.

"Are you coming?" she asked.

"Of course, Mom, as soon as we get everything organized and put away in the clubhouse."

"Bring your friends," she added.

"I will. We'll be there soon," she said and grinned as she watched Hunter sink further in the chair, groaning as he moved.

The first thing that she saw as they walked through the front door of her parents' house was her father sitting in his recliner with his foot and ankle firmly ensconced in a boot cast, propped up with several fluffy pillows, sipping a drink. She felt herself gasp as she crossed the room, kissed his cheek, and said, "Hi, Daddy. How's the ankle?"

"Eh, I'll be fine in a couple days. Really. Ri, thank you, honey, you all did an amazing job."

He winked at her as Uncle Bruno handed him the trophy and said, "Fourth place, Tommy. Fourth place. We did okay. These kids were amazing. A-mazing! We missed you of course, but they did good. Real good."

"Excellent," her father said as he looked at

Hunter and then back at Maria, "Thank you."

"Oh my god, Dad, this is Hunter," she said.

Hunter shook her father's hand and said, "Hunter Reed, Sir. Nice to meet you. So sorry about the ankle. Hope it's not serious."

Her father seemed duly impressed. "Eh, it'll be fine," he said to Hunter, then added, "Very nice to meet you, Hunter. Welcome. Are you hungry? Get something to eat. Ri, fix him a plate. You guys must be starving." Tommy gestured to the table with a nod, orchestrating the room in the way Maria was so familiar with.

"Yeah. We're a little hungry," she said as she looked over at Hunter.

"Starved," Hunter said. "Thank you, Mr. Vigliano."

"Thank *you*. Go on now, eat."

She guided Hunter into the dining room toward his friends and her cousins.

"That's one great kid you got there, Tommy. You're a lucky man," she heard Uncle Bruno say as they inched away into the mob.

Maria's father nodded and surveyed the crowded room, "Yup. I am one lucky man. Iggy. Bruno. Go. You too, go eat."

Iggy and Bruno nodded and moved toward the dining room table as Maria heard her father say again, "Don't I know it. One lucky man."

Soon the house was jammed wall-to-wall with people. Aunts, uncles, cousins, her sisters, the Brigade, and assorted neighbors filled all corners of the space. As Maria and Hunter moved across the room, they were greeted with hugs, handshakes, and smacks on the back. Maria was about to call out to Bambi when she saw Joey whisper something to her and watched them move away, deep in conversation. Maria smiled and watched her usually brusque and to-the-point cousin flirt and look a little coy as Joey guided her away from the center of the pandemonium of the small dining room to a quiet corner.

A perfumed whiff of fresh sweet basil and tomato breezed by them as a platoon of people streamed in from the kitchen carrying large platters heaping with food, plunking them one after the other on the dining room table. The endless stream of masterpieces appeared from the depths of Antonetta's kitchen: pans of lasagna, steaming ravioli swimming in red gravy, and loads of penne in a blushed pink vodka sauce. Spicy aromas of sausage and peppers oozed into the room as large steaming pans entered followed by huge bowls of plump, steaming meatballs. Trays of hoagies, roast pork, and roast beef sandwiches and bowls of salads appeared next. Finally, an enormous antipasto tray was placed on the buffet by two men. Maria wasn't sure when she had prepared it, but there it was—all of it, as expected, another tradition kept up just as it had been done before, year after year. This was a feast that even Nonna Mary would have been proud of, even if she would have offered a tweak or two in the details.

The line of hungry people formed at the edge of the buffet table.

Maria giggled out loud when she saw that Lyndon was waiting in the line, a paper plate in hand. Lyndon turned and saw Maria watching him, shrugged and mouthed, "I'm starving." Maria winked and watched her mother maneuver him into place at the head of the line, with a terse "Excuse me. Pardon me. Coming through, first-timer here," as she elbowed Iggy out of the way, with a quick, "Move back, Iggy. He's my guest of honor."

"Okay, okay, Toni. Easy there, cousin, easy," Iggy laughed and added, "And what am I? Huh? Chopped liver, babe? Huh?" Off of Antonetta's look, he said, "Okay, don't answer that, hon." Antonetta playfully swatted Iggy's arm, maneuvered him directly behind Lyndon, kissed his cheek, and marched back into her kitchen.

Uncle Bruno busied himself uncorking bottles of wine and pouring glass after glass, distributing them to waiting hands. Beers and sodas were passed down the line from coolers in the kitchen. Maria watched all of the orchestrated and controlled chaos as food was heaped onto crowded plates. Ohhhhs and ahhhs swished through the crowd noise. The room filled with laughter and chatter as the hungry crowd ate, laughed, and ate some more.

Hunter, Joey, Elmo, and Frankie were surrounded by an assortment of her family. She watched as Connie and Lucy fussed over Elmo and Frankie, handing out utensils, putting hunks of bread on their plates and pointing at platters and describing them in great detail. "Oh, try the pastas first. Then move on to the sandwiches," Connie said.

"The sausage and peppers are to die for," Ava added as Antonetta watched and smiled from the kitchen doorway.

"Hey, Hunter, you've got to teach us those moves!" a neighbor yelled from across the room and then mimicked Hunter's struts and laughed.

"No problem," Hunter answered good-naturedly as he swooshed his feet back and forth, waving his arms and faking a strut. Maria glanced around the room and watched more than a few heads bob up and down in approval as people clapped their hands in support and gratitude.

Ava filled a plate with an assortment of pastas and headed over to a passed-out Goose who was splayed across one of the sofas. Ava gently nudged him. He didn't respond. She shook his shoulder again. Goose slowly woke, rubbed his eyes, and looked around, more a little confused. He spotted Hunter first, then Joey and Frankie. Slowly, very slowly, it looked like synapses were firing again.

"Dudes. That was some party," he said to Hunter and Joey. "Most memorable," he said as his eyes roamed the room and locked with Ava's. "Baby, where have you been all my life?" As Goose spotted the plate of food, he sat up straight and said, "Man, I am so hungry."

"Well then, honey, you are in the right place," Ava said as she sat next to him, planted a long, sloppy kiss on Goose's mouth, positioned a napkin over his rumpled tuxedo jacket and fed him forkfuls of pasta.

"Oh. My. God. That's good," he said between bites of food. "So good. More. More."

Ava giggled as she fed him.

Maria watched as Joey and Bambi huddled in a corner. He whispered something in her ear. She looked bashfully at her feet as he leaned in and kissed her. Maria was surprised when she saw her cousin blush.

She watched and listened as Aunt Sylvia interviewed Lyndon. Maria was speechless when she heard her say, "Okay, tell me again how much product you use every day," as she touched the tips of his bleached blond spikes. "C'mon? You're serious? That's all?" she said as Lyndon shrugged and nodded.

"I do a little touch-up at midday. Just a little," he admitted.

"Once? One touch-up? That's all? Really?" Aunt Sylvia asked. Maria giggled as Lyndon nodded. "Hey, Toni, get this," she said as she dragged Lyndon toward Antonetta.

Hunter and Maria piled food onto plates, exchanging looks and smiles as they moved along the buffet table. Maria motioned to a couple of empty seats near the end of the table and sat. It suddenly hit her that she was really tired, shocked at just how worn-out and sore her muscles felt now that she was finally still. She looked up at Hunter who was now wearing his tuxedo pants, his dirty shirt, and his spray-painted shoes, all ruined by her, and thought if this guy never speaks to her again after today, she really wouldn't blame him.

Hunter started to sit down next to her, but winced and jumped up, reaching his hand into his pants pocket and pulling something out. He glancing at it, grinned wide, and handed it to Maria.

She looked at the object in her hand. It took a moment for her to realize that it was her broken and missing stiletto lost hours ago at the ball. "You found it? I can't believe it," she said as she remembered rushing down the steps on her way out of the party. She laughed, thinking that midnight, the ball, and breaking that shoe felt like a lifetime ago.

Maria fished in the pocket of her hoodie and pulled out the cuff link that she had pulled off of Hunter's sleeve during her frantic escape and had tucked away for luck before the parade. She opened her hand and presented the glittering horseshoe.

Hunter raised an eyebrow, smiled, and chuckled as he sat.

Maria unrolled his shirt sleeve and put the cuff link back in place. Hunter fished the other cuff link out of his pocket and handed it to her. She unrolled the other sleeve and put the other one back in place too. She took in his destroyed shirt and covered her mouth, trying really hard not to laugh, and said, "I am so, so sorry," as she tried to brush off the ink and dirt. "Seriously. Sorry."

"You should be," he said as he pushed the chair a little closer to her and nudged her playfully. They ate, stealing glances at each other every once in a while. It all felt so normal even though she was quite sure that at any moment he was going to disappear right before her eyes. He...this...just couldn't be real. "So, tell me again, what is this?" he asked.

"Braciole," she said. "It's a thin sliced beef with stuffing. It has a little prosciutto in it and pine nuts." He looked puzzled. "It's good. Just try it."

"Mmmm," was all he said as he took a big bite.

Maria tentatively leaned her head on his shoulder and was relieved to actually feel something there. She closed her eyes as he kissed the top of her head, took a few deep breaths, heard clinking, and opened her eyes to see her father, leaning on one crutch, but standing, hoisting a glass of red wine in the air. He tapped the knife against the glass again. Everyone in the room paused and turned their attention toward him. He motioned for a toast, lifting his glass up high.

Maria watched as the room lifted a drink on his cue.

Her father looked at her and said, "To Maria, my amazing daughter who pulled everything together at the very last minute. I know how challenging today was for you. I know how hard it is to just take over without notice and pull *all* of that off. You jumped in, *and* you did it, feet first. I love you. I thank you."

Maria felt her face flush, not used to her father's verbal praise.

She watched her father look at Hunter and then one by one, the rest of the gang, "To Hunter and the rest of you, all of you, who found yourself with my daughter and my nieces last night and then pitched in to help all of us." He moved the glass in their direction. "What you did was no small thing. You did me proud, each and every one of you. And, from the bottom of my heart..." Maria watched as her very proud and usually unemotional father teared up, paused, and finally said, "I thank you. *We* thank you, all of you. Salud!"

More than a few *Hear, hears* were shouted. Around the room, glasses were clinked and everyone drank. Antonetta wiped a tear. Aunt Sylvia moved next to her and slipped an arm around her shoulder. Together, as if on cue, they surveyed the room and the table, moving into action to quickly refill platters and bowls as they appeared empty or almost empty.

Maria watched her mother nudge Lyndon back to the table for seconds, "Go. Eat." He held up his hands to protest, not realizing that with Antonetta it was a wasted effort. Maria waited, and there it was. Her mother tilted her head and gave him *the* look. Her look. They all knew it. Maria hadn't had a chance to warn Lyndon that Antonetta in person was not worth fighting. She knew for a fact that she wouldn't take no for an answer. He glanced at Maria, shrugged, and scooped more pasta onto his plate as her mother patted him on the back and said, "There you go. Diet starts tomorrow."

Uncle Bruno cheerfully opened more wine and refilled glasses.

Maria watched her father hop over to her mother's side, slip an arm around her waist, and kiss her cheek. She glanced at him and then she shot Maria a look and winked.

Maria covered her face with her hands, laughed,

and again turned back to Hunter and tried to instruct him on the finer aspects of mopping up gravy with big hunks of crispy Italian bread. "Watch. Now slowly circle—" She demonstrated moving the bread around the plate scooping up sauce.

Hunter mimicked her moves feigning ignorance.

She giggled at his awkward attempt, surprised and caught off guard at what she was feeling. *Could this actually be me feeling happy, really happy?*

Maria caught her mother grinning as Hunter dropped a hunk of bread and red gravy, splattering his already trashed tuxedo shirt with tomato sauce. She looked at the shirt, then up at him and couldn't help herself, this time, she lost it, giggling until she was near tears. Hunter cracked up. Maria grabbed a napkin and tried hard to mop up the gravy, making the already ruined shirt worse.

Hunter took her hand and stopped her. "It's okay, Ri," he said.

Maria was really taken by surprise that he had just referred to her as Ri and even more surprised that she didn't mind that he called her by this name. She was only called Ri by family and old friends. Maria was also more than just a little stunned when he reached for her face with his other hand and gently turned her towards him. Out of the corner of her eye, she saw the horseshoe cufflink glitter as he leaned in and kissed her.

As Maria opened her eyes, she saw her grinning mother watching from the corner of the room and giving her the thumbs-up. She tried her best to ignore her and looked back at Hunter. "Hey," he said as he leaned in and kissed her again. This time it was a real take-your-breath-away kiss. Maria's head was spinning a little as she gave in fully to whatever it was that she was feeling. She imagined that she was hearing bells until it dawned on her that the sound was actually her phone.

She fished the phone out of her hoodie pocket and glanced at it. Her moment of blissful happiness interrupted and gone, was replaced by horror. Maria couldn't believe her eyes when she saw that the screen read, Cee-Cee Berg.

"What? Great," she blurted.

Maria's mind raced with anger. *Perfect timing, Cee-Cee. Really? Damn it. It's a holiday. Doesn't this woman have any sense of boundaries? What could she possibly want now? Does she really need to know if I've picked a color that will make her pop, tonight... now?* Her momentary happiness suddenly flooded with annoyance as questions shot through her head.

Maria was about to answer the call. Her thumb hovered over the "Decline" or "Accept" tabs as she hesitated and looked across the room at Bambi and Ava who had stunned looks on their faces. Their smiles were now replaced with frowns and bunched up foreheads pointed in her direction. Maria thumbed "Decline," let the call go to voice mail, and said, "Hey, Bam. Do something with this, would 'ya?" as she tossed her the phone.

Bambi caught it one-handed and defiantly

marched the few steps into the kitchen. Maria watched her open the freezer and put the phone on top of frozen food and close the door as Antonetta watched and grinned.

As the party continued, Maria's father made the rounds, greeting everyone by name and shaking hands until her mother took control and shooed him back to his recliner, ordering, "Enough. You're standing up too much." She propped his foot and took away his wine. "The doctor said one glass. You've had enough of this too," she demanded and turned her attention back to the table to continue filling, refilling and clearing and straightening. This was her domain. This was her show. This was her time to be in control.

Aunt Sylvia elbowed Antonetta and then whispered something into her ear. Maria watched her mother's eyes open wide as the women exchanged looks. Shock and dismay seemed to cover Antonetta's face as she grabbed Connie and Lucy and marched everyone into the kitchen only to return minutes later with desserts. People sprung into motion, moving and making room on the tables for the trays heaping with cannoli, cookies, cakes, and sweets.

Aunt Sylvia proudly entered carrying her brownie cheesecake. She beamed, glanced at Hunter, and cut a big slice and handed it to him. Hunter put up his hand trying to turn down the dessert, "I can't eat another bite."

Maria nudged him and whispered, "Don't fight it. It's not going to work."

"Thank you," he said to her aunt as she handed

him the plate.

"Just a taste, Aunt Syl," Maria said, illustrating with her fingers a small slice.

Her aunt cut a big hunk of the cake, smiled, said, "Eat," as she handed her the plate.

"Thank you, Aunt Syl," Maria said to her and then, turned to Hunter and offered, "It's just better if you go with it. They'll never let you win."

Her mother handed Lyndon a plate full of desserts. He looked at Maria and mouthed "Help me." Maria shrugged and laughed as the crowd moved in on the dessert spread.

Chapter 29

The New Year was almost a full day old. The mood in the room had shifted. Noise, energy, and activity appeared to slow down, subdued people already mentally preparing for the back-to-reality of January, accepting that the holidays were now officially over.

Groups of people shuffled out of her parents' house as Maria and Hunter were trying to make their way to the door, saying their goodbyes. Maria kissed her dad's cheek and hugged him and said, "Get off of the ankle, Daddy."

"I will. Thank you, baby," he said as he nodded at Hunter and shook his hand.

Antonetta squeezed Maria tight and opened her mouth. "I will call you when I am back in my apartment, okay?" Maria said, not giving her a chance to speak. Antonetta nodded and smiled until her attention was diverted by someone brushing by her. Maria watched her mother stop the handsome guy that had made the mistake of trying to move out of the house without a word. It took her a moment to realize it was their new UPS driver, Sonny.

Antonetta grabbed Sonny by the hand and

dragged him over to Lyndon and proceeded to introduce them. Lyndon checked out the guy, and then shot Maria a look over his shoulder, fanned himself, and mouthed, *Hot.*

Maria hoped that her mother's newest project wasn't going to overwhelm the usually in-charge Lyndon who was holding a stack of her mother's full-to-the-brim leftover containers and trying to make an exit. He had caved in to Antonetta's determination, accepting that there was no fighting her in person as she had gleefully wrapped up several roast pork sandwiches after asking, "Did you have the pork? You've got to eat some pork on New Year's. It's good luck," she had told him. Lyndon didn't say a word when she filled additional containers with meatballs and sausages, and dozens of cookies. He turned to Maria and mouthed "Help," motioned wait and shouted over the crowd, "Wait one second. We have to talk. Ri—"

"Tomorrow. In the office. Okay?" Maria yelled over the crowd.

"But, but. Wait. It's important. I have to tell you—" Lyndon bobbed and weaved and tried to hop above the wall of people. "Holly's back—" Lyndon yelled across the room.

Maria tilted her head, not understanding. She shrugged as she waved goodbye to both her mother and Lyndon and turned toward Hunter. They walked down the steps hand in hand towards the group waiting near Joey's car. Hunter tossed Maria's bags in the trunk.

Ava and Goose had their arms around each

other, holding on tight. "Call me," Ava said between kisses, not giving up easily. She gripped the lapels of Goose's jacket tightly, and asked, "Promise?"

"I promise."

"Are you even going to remember?" she asked.

"I'll remember, babe. I'm never going to forget you. Ever. I promise you that," Goose said.

"You better not," Ava said as Goose kissed her again.

Joey and Bambi quickly entered phone numbers in each other's phones. Joey whispered something in her ear, kissed her cheek, and got into the car. Bambi pried Ava's hands off of Goose's jacket and pulled her away from him as the rest of the group squeezed into Joey's car.

"Happy New Year, Ri," Ava yelled and waved and then added. "Call me, Goose."

Maria waved to her cousins as they drove away.

Traffic was very light in Center City as Joey guided the car quickly down JFK Boulevard toward the train station. It seemed like she had arrived on this corner weeks ago, when in reality it was only yesterday. It didn't seem possible that she had only been back home for not quite twenty-four hours. So much had happened in the course of one day it was hard for her to process every emotion and remember each detail of every crazy incident that she had experienced over those hours, or comprehend that it was only a day-long trip. It felt so much longer.

They circled Thirtieth Street Station once, slid easily into the passenger drop-off lanes, and slowed to a stop. Joey popped out of the driver's side, opened the passenger side door, and waved his arm gallantly to Hunter and then retrieved their bags from the trunk.

Hunter's golden dress shoes hit the sidewalk first as he exited the car groaning as he stood up tall. He reached his hand back inside of the car to help Maria out. As they climbed out of the car, quite a few heads turned in their direction. Maria was sure that the looks were not complimentary glances, as they both stepped onto the curb looking unkempt and disheveled. She was still dressed in her Brawlers sweatpants, hoodies and sneakers, a far cry from the way she exited the church van at the ballroom. Hunter's destroyed tuxedo and spray-painted shoes looked more than a little ridiculous and very beat up.

"We must look like a hot mess," she said. The word "we" struck her as very odd as it spit-balled through her thoughts, making her careen through a plethora of emotions both good and bad, filling her with both happiness and doubt, and everything in between. Her emotions hit her all at once as she realized that she was nervous, really a wreck, and not ready to say goodbye yet. But it was time for her to head back to New York and her life and time for Hunter to go back to Washington and whatever his life was there.

Hunter walked her toward the doors, stopped, pulled her close and held her for a minute or two. She looked up at him and waited for him to say something. When he didn't speak, she felt a fresh surge of panic run through her from head to toe. She couldn't find words. "Uh, I...," she stammered, looked at her feet, and then up at him, and finally said, "Soooooo. That happened."

Hunter looked at her, nodded, and said, "Yup. That happened. That definitely happened." He paused for what seemed an awfully long, very, very awkward pause and then said, "Amtrak. New York. Washington. It's a direct line." He motioned a line with one finger. "A straight line."

"Uh-huh," she nodded and said, suddenly unsure. "And, Philly's right in the middle, I guess." She wasn't sure why she said that. She wasn't at all sure what to say. They had only spent a day together. There was so much she wanted to say, but was so afraid to say the wrong thing. She had so many questions and they were completely out of time.

"Yeah, right in the middle," he said and looked at his ruined shoes. Maria cringed and waited until he continued, "Maria, I, uh, I'd really, really like to see you again. Next weekend? Or, maybe the one after, uh, if you're busy? What do you think? You're probably really busy," he stammered.

Maria flinched a little when he said Maria, already analyzing the fact he hadn't called her Ri this time. She wondered if something could have changed during the ride to the train.

It's over before it started. "Perfect," she said trying to cover her sudden overwhelming insecurity, "Either, or, will work. Your call."

Hunter pulled out his phone. "Okay. Great. So, I'll text you. Okay?"

Maria smiled and dug in her bag, shoving her black dress, boots, and other junk from side-to-side frantically looking for her phone. Hunter watched as she became more and more animated as she searched. After what seemed like forever, she shrugged. Sensing hesitation on her part, he quickly added, "Or, not. Or, call? I'll call. I can call."

Maria felt her face flush, now in full-on panic mode, she sputtered, "Where is my phone? Oh. My. God. My phone. Oh crap. My phone. I'm never, ever without my phone. I must have left it at my parents'. Oh no. Cee-Cee," she said as she suddenly remembered Cee-Cee's call. "Bambi put it in the freezer. I must have left it there. I wasn't thinking about it when we left. My head. We were rushing," she was babbling and Hunter wasn't following any of her word salad.

"Who's Cee-Cee?" He said trying to make light of the confusion. "Why is she in the freezer?"

When she didn't explain, he paused and then said, "Yeah, rushing. We do a lot of that, you and me," he said.

"Yes, we do. Rush. A lot." Maria tried to breathe and think through the over-tired static buzzing in her head.

"We should try to stop that," he said. She looked up at his earnest face as he continued, "Rushing. We should stop all of the rushing. You. And, me."

Maria nodded and said, "Number? What's my number?" She was completely blanking. *Now? Really?* She took a deep breath, "Okay. Two. One. Five... Oh my god." she smacked her forehead with her palm,

"Oh. Two. Uh…"

Hunter laughed.

"Stop. I'm blanking. My brain is fried. It's not funny."

"It is funny," he said.

It's been a really, really long day."

"Yes. It *has* been a really, really, long day. In a good way, I think," Hunter said as he took out a pen, grabbed her hand, and wrote on her palm. Maria could only stare at the numbers as he added, "At least, I hope it was. So, call me. Okay? When you get that phone back."

Maria heard a horn honk. Hunter glanced over at the car.

Joey waved at them and said, "We'll do this again, Maria, soon. Maybe, without the whole parade thing next time, a little less chaos. It was fun though. A lot of fun."

Goose hung out of the back window and slapped the side of the car, "Yo, Hunter. Me, Frankie, and Elmo are gonna miss our flights. Dude, kiss her already. C'mon. Let's go. What are you waiting for?"

Hunter motioned one minute towards the car and said, "The guys. I'm sorry. I should go. And, you're going to miss that train of yours. It's the last one tonight, right?"

Maria nodded and said, "Yeah, it's okay. Go on. You'll have a little more time to spend with them. I kind of wound up monopolizing your entire night and pretty much ruined your reunion." She looked at his tuxedo, brushed something off of the lapels, shook her head, and said, "And, I really ruined your poor tuxedo. Last night probably wasn't exactly the party you guys were planning."

"Yeah. Well, the tuxedo..." Maria looked horrified. Hunter paused and then said, "Hey, kidding. It's just a suit. The shoes, well, the shoes, however..."

Maria laughed, "Yeah, oh my god, the shoes. I am so, so sorry about the shoes."

"And, for the record, I'm totally fine being monopolized by you. It's okay. Really, okay. The guys, we don't normally *plan* things out exactly, anyway. We've perfected our go-with-the- flow, see how things turn out when we're together, kind of reunion. I'm thinking that this one turned out just right," he said.

He leaned in again and kissed her.

"Call me," he said as the horn honked again and he stepped away. She watched him slowly get back into Joey's car and could only stand there and wave as they drove away.

Millions of questions shot through her head. There were so many things she wanted to know. She wondered if she'd ever get the chance. She was the queen of *what ifs*. This particular situation was going to torture her until she saw him again, *if*, she saw him again. She turned toward the train station just as another car skidded up, horn blaring on and off frantically.

Maria spun to see Uncle Bruno's car with the driver's window sliding open.

"Ri. Your phone. You left it at your mother's,"

he said as he tossed it to her.

"Yeah, great. Thanks. Perfect timing, Uncle Bruno. You're the best," she said as she bobbled, then caught the phone and sighed.

Great timing. That couldn't have happened five minutes earlier? This was how her life went most of the time. It was what she expected. Disappointment. She had perfected disappointment. No expectations, she thought. It's easier.

She tried to convince herself that she really should try to commit to positive thinking this year. Maybe that would help her direction and results. Maybe she could turn this around somehow, she hoped. If for no other reason, she was exhausted from the constant commotion and the inevitable letdowns.

Maria took comfort in the fact that at least she had Hunter's number even if she was already worrying about the fact that the ball was now firmly and uncomfortably in her court and she would have to call or text him first. Her mind raced as she glanced at the number scrawled onto the palm of her hand and calculated the acceptable amount of time to wait before she sent a text. *Should I call? He said to call. Did he say to call? Great. Decisions. Uncertainty. Just great.*

It already felt like they had shared a lifetime of ups and downs in one day. One day. That realization stung. Despite the fact that it felt like a month-long relationship, it really was only twenty-four hours. Even if it wasn't a first date, she rationalized, it was somehow a first night—their first night. *Should that mean more? Should it mean anything?*

Confusion was making her head ache. Or, maybe it was the exhaustion. Either way, she decided she'd wait until the morning and ask Lyndon when he got back to the office. He was the keeper of all of the rules of relationships, and was current on all dating etiquette, texting, and appropriate waiting periods.

Maria saw her mother lean over across her brother and heard her yell, "Call me when you get back to the city, Ri."

"Okay, Mom," she said.

"Happy New Year, kiddo. Make it a good one," Uncle Bruno said as he smiled and waved, closed the window, and drove away.

She looked at her clammy and damp hand. The numbers already looked a little blurry and smeared. She immediately felt a dark sense of desperation and more than a little anxiety not wanting to chance losing the only real evidence that these past few hours had happened. She quickly put Hunter's number in her phone and hit save. She turned, entered the train station, feeling miserable and very, very alone.

Maria glanced quickly up at the schedule board and rushed down the steps to the tracks. "All aboard," bellowed through the air just as she jumped onto the train. She was more than a little bit conflicted that she had not missed the last train and stayed until morning so that she could have the opportunity to re-hash the day with Ava and Bambi to figure out what exactly had happened to all of them. She knew that rushing back to the city first thing in the morning would have been awful, but she couldn't help herself. She wanted to review the night with her cousins before zipping back to her other reality.

She moved slowly through cars until she found an uncrowded area away from as many people as possible and took a seat. She settled in as the train moved forward, closing her eyes, attempting to relax. Hunter was heading back to his life and she was on the way back to hers. She was having a very hard time accepting that the evening, and potentially the relationship, was over.

Maria was just starting to doze off when she heard her phone chime. "Oh, come on, Mom," she muttered, moaned and thought, I just left ten minutes ago. She was willing herself to ignore the phone when it chimed again. "Please do not be Cee-Cee," she said out loud. Across the aisle, a man glanced in her direction and shot her a very judgmental and annoyed look. She dug out the phone and looked at the screen. Hunter—2 messages.

She grinned and tapped the phone. Her text messages lit up. She bit her lip as she read:

Got your number from Joey who got it from Bam. Guess I'm in your phone now. So... when you get your phone back...call me.

And the next text read:

Hey...Get-together in NYC in the next couple of weeks? D.C. if you want. Okay? Talk later.

Maria was smiling ear-to-ear when the conductor walked up and stuck his hand out for her ticket and cheerfully said, "Happy New Year, Miss."

His eyes sparkled as he winked.

"Happy New Year to you too," she said back, meaning it this time.

Well past overtired, her head was buzzing a strange high-pitched buzz again. She wasn't at all sure she knew what was real and what wasn't. Her fleeting contentment was now being edged out and commingled with doubt and dread as she read and reread Hunter's text messages trying to glean meaning and emotion in his words. She hated communicating like this. Searching for subtext drove her crazy.

As the train sped further away from Philadelphia, part of her hoped that she hadn't imagined the emotions of the whole experience. She felt a sense of melancholy creep in and consume her. She reread his texts. The hell with rules, or checking with Lyndon, she decided to text Hunter back and typed:

Hey. Glad someone had a phone. Got mine back right after you left. NYC is fine. D.C. too.

She settled back into her seat and thought, *hoped*, that maybe it was going to be a happy new year after all. At least at this minute, she was trying to feel optimistic. She had taken charge and taken a chance. From here on, whatever happened, happened. Maybe her mother was right. Something good *could* happen at any moment.

Her phone rang. She glanced at the screen, saw it was Hunter, and scrambled to answer and heard...

"Hey..."

"Hey," she said back, grateful to hear his voice again.

"You okay?" he asked.

"I'm fine. Tired, really tired, but fine. You?"

"Same. Tired. So tired. And, I have muscles hurting that I didn't know could hurt," he said and laughed. "Soooo, next weekend, or the following, if that's better for you, how about we do this again? Well, not the whole parade thing. I mean let's get together again. I'd really like to see you..."

Maria grinned from ear to ear, not caring a bit when the guy across from her grunted, stood and stamped his feet, and moved seats. She turned to the window and snuggled in. "Philly's fine," she said, agreeing that meeting in the middle would be a perfect solution. She thought the compromise was a good idea. It would be a do-over of sorts and no pressure to be on each other's turf yet. She'd have to make sure to give her mother a few parameters to keep her from being too intrusive. They chatted until the train passed Elizabeth, New Jersey. As they neared Newark, she and Hunter had finished planning a first real date for the following weekend.

When they had finally said their goodbyes and she hung up, Maria thought about her mother's insistence that the family always record their resolutions and try to do the unexpected as each New Year rolled around.

Maria catalogued her intentions: *Number one: Break the rules. Number two: Take chances. Number three: Have fun. Number four: Expect good things to happen.*

Maybe, just maybe it was time for something good to happen in my love life for a change. She wondered if this would be the year that she could try to expect only good things. She decided right there and then the new year was going to be a great year.

She was sure of it.

A sneak peek at the sequel...
A Second Chance
(Available soon.)

Chapter 1

"Life is never a straight line, Maria. Remember that. It zigs. It zags. You get bounced around. You hit walls. Sometimes you hit bottom. Always, always remember that when that happens, and it will happen...you pick yourself up, dust yourself off, and then...you adjust."

Maria was startled awake by an annoying, loud rippling bell chime. She felt around for her cell phone, grabbed it and answered with a groggy, "Hello."

Lyndon blurted a loud incomprehensible glob of words that slid together into what seemed like one mashed up sound. Maria blinked, rolled over and put the phone on speaker as Lyndon word vomited in her ear.

"Lyndon, slow down, please."

She could only decipher two words... "Holly's back."

"Huh? What?" she managed in between yawns. "Who?"

"Ri, Holly... Holly. Is. Back." Maria's stunned and confused silence was followed by, "I'll explain it all when you get here. I tried to warn you yesterday. At dinner. At your parents. Oh, and by the way, why in the world were you keeping Sonny a secret?"

"Who?"

"Sonny. It doesn't matter. Oh my god. We'll deal with that later. Just get here, like as fast as possible, sweetie. Back to reality. Tick tock," he ordered as he hung up.

Yesterday? She closed her eyes and rolled over, trying to piece together yesterday. She fell back into a warm and cozy memory of the previous day's events.

Yesterday.

New Year's Day.

Home.

The parade.

Hunter.

Ohhhh, Hunter. She sighed and looked at her phone and scrolled through her text messages to make sure she hadn't dreamt it all. She grinned a wide grin, and jumped out of bed tossing clothes across the room as she searched for something presentable to wear. She glanced at her bed head in the mirror and decided that given the urgent sound in Lyndon's voice she wouldn't waste time on flat ironing her hair. She rushed through her morning routine and dashed out of the apartment as fast as she could.

Lyndon's words rolled around and around in her brain as she made her way across the city to the office. Holly's back? *What did that mean exactly?* Holly? Holly who had leveled up. Holly who had left and whose position she had been given, that Holly? The Holly that should have been in Sun Valley, or Paris, or somewhere amazing. That Holly? Why would she be back in New York now? Why in the world would she be in the office? And what could it possibly have to do with her? Holly had an Instagram-perfect life thousands of miles away with her amazing rich handsome husband. When Lyndon had shared Holly's IG page with her, Maria learned that she posted incessantly about her fabulous life. What could she possibly be doing in Rotelle, Herbert, Tobias, and Associates now?

Maria's promotion and bigger office was amazing and something she had received at what seemed to most like warp speed. Maria worried then that it had all happened too fast. When Lyndon shared the "Holly's infamous origin story"—the Holly that she was tasked to replace—Maria was stunned. She had insisted that she had a plan that was all her own. Maria had vowed she wasn't following in Holly's path; she was only going to be occupying her old office.

Between cocktails that night, two years ago, Lyndon had confided that Holly *Day* was a woman whose reputation and libido blazed through R.H.T. and Associates as if her conquests were bullets on her resume. After Holly tore through R.H.T., New York, she moved on to the corporate honchos. Hers was not an originally crafted story by any means. It all seemed somewhat vintage to Maria. But it was Holly's story and according to legend, she owned it. She was the flipside of the #MeToo conversation most women were having these days. Holly was unabashedly proud of her determination, convictions, and successes. No consternation for her. She traded up, both her job and her life and as Lyndon had explained, without regrets or looking back.

In the halls of R.H.T., Holly was notorious in her own way even though her career path was self-determined before she ever drove her fifteen-year-old Honda Civic cross country to New York. R.H.T. was simply the place she launched the plan. Her *fictionalized* retelling of the story of a successful farm girl who journeys from Nanny to the sparkler of Madison Avenue and marries the head of a multi-platformed communications dynasty in less than four years was simply her inspired way to use her skill set and create her own unique platform. Morning television and a committee of publicists propped up Holly's backstory and unbelievable trajectory. The gig and the book landed her the lifestyle. The large diamond ring on her finger and the guy she had maneuvered somewhere on Lexington Avenue in the back seat of a Town Car would eventually be collateral damage when she uncoupled her eight-figure starter marriage.

When Holly's book hit The *New York Times* Bestseller list *and* stayed at Amazon's number one spot simultaneously for the better part of two years, she had completed her life's work at twenty-six. The sweetest part of this story was that Holly wasn't expected to write another word. She was now in residence in one of four places at any given time: The Hamptons, Cannes, Los Angeles, or Sun Valley—always Sun Valley for the holidays with her current husband.

Maria insisted then that her career would not be a pit stop to another life. She was adamant that she had a plan all her own. Maria had vowed she wasn't following in Holly's path; she was only going to be occupying her old office. She had things to accomplish and even if she didn't always feel like Hal's rising star, she was determined to succeed. Blazing my own trails —she had added then, not sure Lyndon was even listening.

Maria's warm and hopeful holiday hangover had dissipated after Lyndon's frantic wakeup-call had interrupted her sleep and brought her crashing back to reality. She couldn't focus on Hunter, or their previous twenty-four-hour adventure and the excitement she'd uncharacteristically let overtake her usually sensible and measured brain. She had been so busy allowing herself to be consumed by the day's events and the wonderful and weird sequence that led to her crossing paths with this amazing guy that she had ignored Lyndon's need to have a discussion before leaving her parents' house.

What could be so important? Her brain went into frantic worry overload and flitted back and forth between worse case scenarios. She was fired. The agency had lost all of her accounts. She had okayed the wrong final concepts on something, anything, or... everything. What could be happening that he was so insistent that she get to the office ASAP? He never cared when she clocked in. This was completely out of character for him. She felt her throat tighten and her stomach clench as the anxiety crept through her entire body. "Come on, come on," she said out loud as if her words could make the train speed up.

After what seemed like days, she arrived at her stop, raced up the subway steps, crossed the corner to her office building, and jumped into the first available elevator.

Maria exited the elevators, marched into R.H.T's lobby, and crossed toward Lyndon's desk. He motioned one minute as he finished a call, hung up, and looked at her wide-eyed and panicked. She glanced at several boxes that were sitting in front of his desk and felt something like a punch to the gut when she looked down and recognized her sketchbook teetering on the top of one. Her panic increased and her face flushed red as she realized that they were all of her personal belongings in the overflowing boxes.

"Am I fired?" she blurted as she felt tears begin to well.

Lyndon shook his head no as he pointed to the cubicle behind his desk.

He whispered, "No. No. No. You've been relocated, that's all."

Maria swiped at her eyes, "What the—" and heard...

"Darling! It's been soooooo long. I'm so happy to hear your voice again," come from inside her office before the door clicked shut. Maria strained to hear more of the conversation, but the words were muffled. She was puzzled. *Who could the voice belong to?*

"Who is that?" she stammered as she stared at the closed door and then noticed her name plate was off of the wall and had been shoved into one of the boxes too. She turned to Lyndon. "What is going on?

Lyndon put a finger to his lips and shushed her. He stood, rounded the desk to her side, and whispered, "Holly." He grabbed a box off of the floor, motioned with his head for Maria to do the same. He hurried to the first cubicle in the open corral with Maria following, deposited boxes on the floor, and said, "It's Holly. Holly Day."

Maria scrunched her face, squinted at him confused, and shook her head, "Who?"

He said, "Holly," again as he placed the box on the desk, turned to her and said, "Hol-ly. I'm sure it's temporary, sweetie. It's probably just a lovers' quarrel, that's all. She's done this before, a couple of times. She doesn't stay. Believe me. I'm positive that she'll be gone before Valentine's Day."

"Valentine's Day?"

About The Author

Carol Sabik-Jaffe

is a multi-hyphenate Writer-Artist. She has been known to draw, paint, and as an Art Director, design things. Now, she designs with words and pictures as a writer, screenwriter, and an occasional Blogger. Several of her screenplays have won awards and she is ever hopeful that her work will get produced one day!

Her formative years were spent in Colts Neck, NJ. She now lives in the Philadelphia suburbs with her husband and a crazy rescue dog named, Enzo. She is a proud Mom of two creative and successful adults.

She is fond of romantic comedies and characters that are a little less than perfect. She is usually at work on numerous projects in various states of development or tossing a ball for Enzo (but, that's another story).

Find her at www.carolsabikjaffe.com
or on social media: Twitter, Instagram, and Facebook.

Made in the USA
Middletown, DE
20 November 2020

24547185R00179